NEW YORK REVIEW BOOKS
CLASSICS

# THE SIMPLE PAST

DRISS CHRAÏBI (1926–2007) was born to a merchant family in French Morocco. He attended a French high school in Casablanca, followed by university in Paris, where he earned a degree in chemical engineering. Deciding to become a writer, he worked as a night watchman and laborer until the publication of his first novel, *Le Passé simple* (1954), which was a success in France and caused a scandal in Morocco, where it was banned until 1977. He published his next novel, *Les Boucs* (*The Butts*), in 1955—the year he married Catherine Birckel, with whom he would have five children before they divorced. In 1959, Chraïbi joined Radio France as a journalist, and in the 1970s he taught Maghrebi literature in Quebec. In 1978, he remarried, to Sheena McCallion, with whom he also had five children. Chraïbi wrote some twenty novels and collections of short fiction, including six mysteries featuring the Moroccan Inspector Ali, as well as two volumes of autobiography. He was awarded the Prix de l'Afrique Méditerranéenne in 1973 and the Franco-Arab Friendship Award in 1981. He died in southeastern France and was buried in Casablanca.

HUGH A. HARTER (1922–2011) received a BA in French and a PhD in Spanish at Ohio State University, and an MA, also in Spanish, at Mexico City College, the University of the Americas. He has translated from both the French and Spanish, including two other books by Driss Chraïbi, *The Butts* and *Mother Comes of Age*. Harter was the director of the International Institute in Madrid from 1984 through 1987.

ADAM SHATZ is a contributing editor at the *London Review of Books* and a contributing writer to *The New York Times*

*Magazine, The New York Review of Books*, and *The New Yorker*, among other publications. He has been a visiting professor at Bard College and New York University and a fellow at the Dorothy and Lewis B. Cullman Center for Writers and Scholars.

# THE SIMPLE PAST

DRISS CHRAÏBI

*Translated from the French by*
HUGH A. HARTER

*Introduction by*
ADAM SHATZ

NEW YORK REVIEW BOOKS

*New York*

THIS IS A NEW YORK REVIEW BOOK
PUBLISHED BY THE NEW YORK REVIEW OF BOOKS
435 Hudson Street, New York, NY 10014
www.nyrb.com

Originally published in the French language as *Le Passé simple*

Library of Congress Cataloging-in-Publication Data
Names: Chraïbi, Driss, 1926–2007, author. | Shatz, Adam, writer of
  introduction. | Harter, Hugh A., translator.
Title: The simple past / by Driss Chraïbi ; introduction by Adam Shatz ;
  translated by Hugh A. Harter.
Other titles: Passé simple. English
Description: New York : New York Review Books, [2019] | Series: New York
  Review Books classics | In English, translated from the French.
Identifiers: LCCN 2019011258 | ISBN 9781681373607 (alk. paper)
Subjects: LCSH: Berbers—Morocco—Fiction. | Women—Morocco—Fiction.
  Morocco—Social conditions—20th century—Fiction. | Morocco—Politics
  and government—Fiction. | Culture conflict—Fiction.
Classification: LCC PQ3989.C5 P313 2019 | DDC 843/.914—dc23
LC record available at https://lccn.loc.gov/2019011258

ISBN 978-1-68137-360-7

Printed in the United States of America on acid-free paper.
10 9 8 7 6 5 4 3 2 1

# CONTENTS

# INTRODUCTION

W H E N Driss Chraïbi's *The Simple Past* (*Le Passé simple*) was published in 1954, it was as if an explosion had gone off in the small, old-fashioned mansion of North African literature. Everything that had been written about the Maghreb seemed to lie in ruins—not just exoticizing Western novels and travelers' accounts but also the few novels in French by North African writers. Even *The Pillar of Salt* (1953), Albert Memmi's remarkable bildungsroman about a Jewish boy growing up in Tunisia, looked quaint by comparison. Published two years before the end of France's protectorate in Morocco, *The Simple Past* was a journey to the end of the colonial night, written with an intransigence and fury that Louis-Ferdinand Céline might have admired.

Chraïbi's title was suggestive on several registers. The *passé simple* is a French verb tense used almost exclusively in formal writing, referring to actions that have been definitively completed, residing entirely in the past. In Chraïbi's novel, the idea of a past entirely cut off from the present is held up to merciless critique. For Driss Ferdi, the young Moroccan who is the hero and narrator of the book, the past is an unbearable weight and an inescapable burden; it is a force of oppression and sometimes of evil. Locked in an agonizing struggle to free himself from the past, Driss drifts inexorably towards confrontation with his tyrannical father, Hajji Fatmi Ferdi, the so-called seigneur, or Lord, who styles himself as a representative of a tradition uncorrupted by French colonialism. In fact, the Lord has signed a pact of cooperation with the colonial authorities (shadowy figures in the novel): in return for good behavior he has been given free reign over his own little kingdom, the Ferdi family, a dictatorship based entirely on his whims. By the end of the novel, two members of the family have been crushed by his rule, and the Lord himself, a once-prosperous tea merchant, has lost his fortune and been exposed as a liar, philanderer, and hypocrite. The "simple past" does not exist, except as a cruel dream—or as a flimsy rationale for a humiliated man's arbitrary power. Chraïbi was no supporter of French rule, but he was already preparing for another, postcolonial battle: the struggle against the traditionalist old guard. His depiction of the Lord drew blood.

Yet for all the scandalous content of Chraïbi's novel—pedophilia, casual anti-Semitism, collective masturbation and sex in brothels, patriarchal brutality, and, not least, the unmasking of the many hypocrisies concealed by religious piety—what shocked readers most was the violence of its *style*. *The Simple Past* is told entirely from Driss's perspective, in frank, vivid, often coarse language and jarring, Faulknerian shifts in focus and temporality. Allergic to picturesque praise of the homeland, Chraïbi instead evokes the "pungency of horse manure" and the "perfume of the poor" that—mixed with the more pleasing "sweet smells of hot bread and honey cakes"—give Fez its dense and peculiar fragrance. "I don't like this city," Driss tells us. "It is my past, and I don't like my past ... it grasps me and makes an entity of me, quanta, brick among bricks, lizard, dust." At a funeral, he sees a group of religious scholars and thinks: "The *talebs* are still howling their Koran. They are always in the cemeteries, permanently ... they *sleep their lives away* in recesses of doors, on cornices, the length of ditches and only awaken to go to howl over a tomb. Later on they'll go back to their lethargy, hardly interrupted."*

The unexpected exuberance of this bleak and fiery novel comes precisely from Chraïbi's commitment to sacrilege, his scorn for what he calls "A good novel of the old type: Morocco, land of the future, of sun, couscous, wogs ... the souks, the shantytowns, pashas, facto-

---

*The Algerian novelists Rachid Boudjedra and Kamel Daoud would echo Chraïbi's fearless mockery of religion in their debut novels, *Repudiation* (1969) and *The Meursault Investigation* (2013), respectively, both of which can be read as children of *The Simple Past*.

ries, dates. . . . An old monkey is going to mix all of that up, between two cocktails, between two farts, between two yawns, *is going to make a novel out of it*: a comitragic love story with local color." The profane candor, urgency, and impatience of Driss Ferdi had never been heard before in North African fiction. Like Céline's Ferdinand Bardamu, J. D. Salinger's Holden Caulfield, Raphael Schlemilovitch in Patrick Modiano's *La Place de l'étoile*, or indeed Philip Roth's Alexander Portnoy, he is a young *écorché vif* hurtling towards an unknown future, spitting on (and desperately trying to spit out) the world of his father.

Chraïbi belonged to the Generation of '52, a group of rebellious North African writers who came of age in the last days of French rule, which included Memmi and the Algerian novelist Kateb Yacine, whose novel *Nedjma*, inspired by his country's independence struggle, appeared in 1956. Like Memmi and Yacine, Chraïbi was a classic man in between, an "almost Europeanized" native in a colonized society who had been shaped both by his religious community and by a French education that had estranged him from his community and family—the "lion's mouth," in Yacine's words. The son of a middle-class tea merchant, like his protagonist in *The Simple Past*, Chraïbi was born in 1926 in El Jadida, a small city south of Casablanca on the Atlantic coast. He studied for three years at a Koranic school, then attended the Lycée Lyautey in Casablanca, where his family had moved. After receiving his baccalaureate in 1946, he went to Paris to study chemical engineering and neuropsychiatry, before abandoning formal study. (The titles of the five sections of *The Simple Past*—"Basic Elements," "Transition Period," "The Reagent," "The Catalyzer," "Elements of Synthesis"—are indicative of his scientific formation.) He wandered around Canada, Italy, Germany, and Greece, and spent two years in Israel under a Jewish pseudonym while teaching himself to write fiction. After the publication of *The Simple Past*, he married a French woman, with whom he had five children. They eventually divorced, but apart from a yearlong stay in Morocco, he lived in France and insisted that he was a "writer of French expression, period," not a Moroccan or Francophone writer.

Nevertheless, in his fiction Chraïbi never left behind the land that had formed him. Secretive about the details of his life, he drew upon them in his fiction, practicing a kind of "autofiction" avant la lettre. Impervious to the folkloric nostalgia that a prolonged exile often creates, he preferred the bitter taste of truth and applied it unsparingly to the experience he knew most intimately: the "cultural schizophrenia" experienced by Western-educated former colonial subjects, which the Iranian philosopher Daryush Shayegan has called "*le regard mutilé*," or mutilated gaze. In *The Simple Past*, Driss has been torn from his roots without being welcomed into French society:

> You were the issue of the Orient, and through your painful past, your imaginings, your education, you are going to triumph over the Orient. You have never believed in Allah. You know how to dissect the legends, you think in French, you are a reader of Voltaire and an admirer of Kant. Only the Occidental world for which you are destined seems to you to be sewn with stupidities and ugliness you are fleeing from. Moreover, you feel that it is a hostile world.

A cruel story of youth, *The Simple Past* calls to mind Paul Nizan's famous remark in his memoir *Aden, Arabie*: "I was twenty. I will let no one say it is the best time of life." When *The Simple Past* opens, Driss, who is nineteen, is haunted by the sense that his future has already been confiscated by his Lord, and ashamed of his own complicity in the theft. "The Lord is waiting for me. His law is indisputable. My life is ruled by it.... What is stupefying is that I keep on listening to him. I even appreciate him.... This man in the tarboosh is sure of himself: a fly will not take flight unless he gives it permission. He knows that every word that falls from his mouth will be engraved on my mind."

In the character of the Lord, who ruthlessly polices every detail of his family's life, Chraïbi created one of the most terrifying fathers in modern literature. The Lord ridicules Driss for his fair complexion, his European clothes, and his assimilation of French culture ("To look at you, who would take you for an Arab?"), even though he has sent him to a lycée so that he can acquire the intellectual "arms" of the "enemy": "We are from the century of the Caliphs, you will belong to the twentieth century." As it turns out, those "arms" can't be acquired without internalizing some of the enemies' ideas—without coming to resemble them in some fashion. In one scene, Driss is at school staring at

> a blackboard on which a piece of chalk had just elegantly written out the subject of the essay on France: "Liberty, Equality, Fraternity." The boots of the monitor sound a coming and going that reminds me of the pendulum of the clock of the Lord. Noisier, no doubt, but just as regular and clearly defined.... Liberty, Equality, Fraternity. I am thirsty for words, hungry for incantations.

A French classmate, however, sets him straight on the limits of his dreams: "Because if by chance you become our equals, I ask you: with regard to whom and to what will we then be civilized?" To go to the lycée is to have one's hopes for freedom simultaneously raised and thwarted.

This experience, this frustrated hunger, would lead the French-educated youths of the Maghreb to demand independence. But the first target of protest, in *The Simple Past*, is closer to home, as the Lord is only too well aware. Not only is he jealous of his son's education; he suspects (not wrongly) that it is turning him against his authority. "He knows that the Occident towards which he has propelled me is outside his sphere. Therefore he hates it. And out of fear that there be in me an enthusiasm for this new world, he flails, shatters, cuts off, and dissects everything I learn." Why, then, does he run the risk of sending his son to a lycée? A father's "dearest wish," he says, is for his children "to be better than he in every way." The Lord wants, in spite of himself, the best for his son, even if it means he will lose him. That his authority is undone by his "dearest wish" does not quite redeem him, but it certainly makes him less of a cartoonish villain. It is also a tribute to the complexity of Chraïbi's vision that the Lord ultimately comes to seem a prisoner of his own regime, as we learn that he is no less susceptible than his son to the temptations of the West. His traditionalism does not represent the resilience of the "simple past" but rather the convulsions of a traditional society that has undergone modernization and colonization at the same time.

Driss is not the only victim of the Lord's rule. His brothers are also captives, while his adoring mother has been turned into a beast of burden: "one of my terrestrial contingencies . . . obedient, submissive, honest," in the Lord's description. Yet Driss, his mother's favorite son, confesses that he too "judged her to be weak and awkward, eating, drinking, sleeping, excreting, having intercourse. Respecting the menus established by the Lord, the Lord's tea, five times a day, or two times a day, and according to the wishes of the Lord." He tells her as much, and so she is doubly victimized, first by her callous husband, then by the son who despises her weakness, perhaps because it reminds him of his own in the face of his father. "My religion was rebellion, even against my mother whose glands I knew were dried up and whose monstrous tenderness I recognized." Although *The Simple Past* is not an explicitly allegorical novel, it is tempting to see, in the figure of the mother, a metaphor for the colonized motherland, whose unconditional love is spurned by both the traditionalist father and his angry son.*

*The Simple Past* takes place during the last days of Ramadan. What should be a time of spiritual reflection and familial festivity heads, inexorably, towards a violent encounter between father and son. Everything seems to be pointing towards parricide, but the future is no simpler than the past. It is one thing to rebel against your father, another to kill him—particularly if to do so is, in a sense, to kill yourself. As the Lord reminds Driss, "we are not enemies, and even less so, strangers." Driss grimly concludes that his father is "a capable

---

*The critic Hédi Abdel-Jaouad, in an essay on mothers and sons in Chraïbi's work, has suggested that "the Maghrebian text in French—predominantly the story of an Oedipus searching for a Laius to kill—can in fact be seen as the vindication and glorification of motherhood."

chess player.... With him one has to be subtle, nothing but subtle, more subtle than he. Islam. People live here that way, from subtleties—and you can't escape otherwise, except by mental suicide." Liberation may depend on achieving emancipation from the Lord, but a frontal battle isn't possible. "I am a Moroccan, and in a way, Morocco belongs to me," Driss declares, but there does not seem to be enough room for both him and the Lord, and in the last pages of the novel, he boards a flight to France, vowing to return. Three years after the publication of *The Simple Past*, Chraïbi's father died. He did not attend the funeral and rejected his inheritance. But he immediately set to work on a sequel, *Succession ouverte* (1962), in which Driss Ferdi returns from France for his father's funeral and experiences the epiphany that the Lord "had to die so that I could suddenly realize that I was a living being."

Laila Lalami, a Moroccan American novelist who grew up in Rabat, has praised Chraïbi as "the first writer I read as a child who created Moroccan characters that were believable." But they were perhaps all too believable, and certainly too troubling, when the novel was published in 1954. Some Moroccan readers claimed that Chraïbi's portrait of Moroccan traditional society was consumed by self-hatred, even a betrayal of the independence struggle. The novel was banned in Morocco until 1977. In a 1962 interview, Chraïbi remarked, "Had there been only the Protectorate and colonialism, everything would have been simple. Then my past, our past, would have been simple. No, Monsieur Sartre, hell isn't others. It's also in ourselves." The original edition of the novel included an epigraph, dedicated to François Mauriac: "At that time there was hope and revolt." In the 1977 edition, Chraïbi amended the epigraph with a question, addressed to King Hassan II, then presiding over a reign of terror against left-wing dissidents, and to "the other brave leaders of the Arab world": "Is there nothing more than revolt?" The same question, alas, could be asked of today's Arab leaders.

—ADAM SHATZ

# THE SIMPLE PAST

*To François Mauriac*

1954. At that time there was hope and revolt. D.C.
To Hassan II and the other brave leaders of the Arab world.
Is there nothing more than revolt?
1977. D.C.

And the black minister said to me:

"We also have translated the Bible. We found there that God created men as members of the black race. One day Black Cain killed Black Abel. God appeared to Cain and said to him: 'What have you done with your brother?' And Cain was so frightened that he turned white. And ever since then Cain's descendants have been white."

—ALBERT-RAYMOND ROCHE
(Remarks chosen by the author)

# 1. BASIC ELEMENTS

*Silence is an opinion.*

AT THE hour when a descendant of Ishmael can no longer distinguish a black thread from a white one ...

The cannon of El Hank thundered twice. In the ensuing concert of muezzins, we got up, Berrada, Roche, and I. We lit up our first cigarette of the day, the first also for Roche, the Christian. And suddenly the gong of the drama reverberated in me.

Much later I remembered that moment charged with a sudden presentiment that spread through me, threw me into a panic, and set me apart with perhaps the same violence as the *Slender Cord*. What am I saying? I still recall our silhouettes etched into the raw green of the fake palm trees, the sirocco blowing level with the ground, and the Annamite trousers of Roche that fluttered like a pair of flags. Speaking of the beggars whose cries reached as far as us, Berrada said, "They aren't fasting. Listen to them, Monsieur Roche. Their voices are too strong to be tired by any kind of abstinence."

"Complain!" said Roche. "What are you complaining about? Eh? Kraut Head ..."

The "Kraut Head" is me. I hardly blink. My nerves have calmed down. I stammer a laughing excuse, a circumlocution instead of a real goodbye, and leave Murdoch Park. The Lord is waiting for me. His law is indisputable. My life is ruled by it. Roche is an adultery for me, two hours a day and three days a week, for a year now. In the interval I am at a standstill. I call a standstill everything that is definite, like this field that I am traversing and that house toward which

I am walking. I swear to you that once I'd gone through the garden gate with no more than the recollection of the Lord seated cross-legged like a tailor on his pious square of felt, I became once more a simple pedestrian on the Straight Path, the path of the Chosen of God over which those He has damned never shall pass.

The muezzins fell silent. The twenty-fourth evening of Ramadan swallowed me up. I follow a line of carts that are pulled by old men with bare feet. At every door there is a beggar who knocks like a fatality and beseeches, entreats a morsel of bread, a piece of sugar or some cigarette paper. I know that monotonous chant, so conscientiously feigned that it becomes a reality, one in which every saint of North Africa from Saint Abd El Kader to Saint Lyautey, the most recent saint to date, been howled about. There are also beggars in front of the stores and Moorish cafés—Huns and bloodsuckers, covered with sores, diarrhetic speech, multicolored tatters, runny eyes that are preyed on by flies, the same flies that swarm on the produce left in the open air which a palm-leaf duster tries in vain to chase away.

Those starving creatures and I are alike: we are the end result, they of thirteen centuries of Islam, I of the Lord, the embodiment of Islam. And we are dissimilar for the same reason. A wolf is more to be feared than a pack of cubs.

A beggar grabs my hand, kisses it twice, and holds on with all his strength, with all his misery. I give him no alms. I have nothing on me to give. The Lord does not provide pocket money. He isn't stingy. He just feels I have no need of any, and that's it. I pull my hand away, and the beggar calls down every calamity in the heavens on my head. I don't even shrug my shoulders. I am not afraid of heaven. It is peopled by rare gases and human ratiocinations. Roche told me that.

For this particular impertinence, I'm guaranteed ten thousand years of Gehenna. The Lord told me so. Not five thousand. Not a hundred thousand. Ten thousand! The pronouncements of the Lord are weighed with exacting impartiality. In any case, he who greets a Jew will have his hand cut off, and any woman who looks at a man other than her husband will have her eyes torn out.

Sixteen hours of fasting per day, drought, harvests set afire, plagues of locusts, failure, grievances, copious sweating, ardors, I also know the clamor of that sluggish mob that I am a part of and cut my path, laboriously, methodically, worried about not being late (the Lord does not like to wait) and scornful of niceties because my clothes are European, and I have become more and more Europeanized.

Two boys, half stretched out on the sidewalk, play a game of *bidding*. The stakes are between the competitors, their switch-blade knives under their buttocks. They are the future gallows birds, the bouncers in the whorehouses who will be shipped out by the law courts to crush rock for the roads of the Protectorate to the greater glory of the road workers and engineers of the Department of Bridges and Highways. For the moment, nobody lays a hand on them. That last remark pleases me. It's from Roche. In my adolescent brain stuffed full of paternal abstractions, several mordant quotations are stored away for any and all purposes. I am doing nothing to transform them into a virus. The Lord says: "The rash man acts rashly out of rashness and will harvest nothing of any worth from the rashness of his acts."

During four years the Koranic schools taught me law, dogma, the limits of dogma, and *hadiths*, with cudgel blows to the head and on the soles of my feet—administered with such mastery that even till the Judgment Day I never will forget them.

I walk faster. If I am late, the Lord won't lose his temper because his nerves are as unbending as his laws. Listen to him: "Whether it's a rabbi or a Yid that dies, it's one Jew less. Next thing two are born. Therefore why lose one's temper?"

I saw him lose it once, however, while we were living in the town of Mazagan: he was very calm.

Was it the charm of that rustic village at evening? Nothing has a hold on me anymore, not even the emotion of habitual things. What is known is known, just as what is dead is dead, thus declareth the Lord. The level crossing over the single track of the so-called railway station mockingly known as "Gare Mers-Sultan," had to be traversed despite the bellowing of the one-armed guard (a train was coming), and I had to yell at that passive faggot (the active one was Roche), "The Lord! Don't you know the Lord, you dog-son-of-a-dog?"

Bending double, he let me by. He'd heard about the Lord. Then I meandered through the butcher stalls heavy with mutton, the homeless sprawled on the pavement, the piles of stinking garbage, the crowd around the snake charmer, passed a lost or abandoned child, watched sales on the black market and in the open air, mashed a rotten tomato, avoided a shin-bone stuck out all of a sudden with a foot as sure as a mule's hoof, fast, always faster! (the response is automatic, pardon me: consciously) just like yesterday, like the day before, for seven years, every single day except Sunday and holidays, four times a day, from house to school and back unchangingly—nothing changes—to the rue d' Angora, to the house of cast concrete, in front of me, the presence of the Lord seated facing statuesquely straight ahead and looking straight ahead, so little like a statue that he is dogma, and so little like dogma that once you are in front of him all other life except for life with him, even the bustle of the street perceived through the open window, everything, is annihilated.

His first words were the following: "Our soup resembles our traditions. It is an appetizer, a main dish and a dessert. That is, if appetizer and dessert constitute anything more than inventions of the Christians. But God is just: Christians have a talent for inventing the superfluous. However, we give you permission to consider the aforementioned soup as the Christians would. You are studying their language and their civilization, but a Christian 'would not let his appetizer get cold.' Son, sit here on our left. We shall formulate your appetite."

I am not to respond. Gestures first. Rituals. The Lord affirms that before reflection comes the act.

At the door of the room, six pairs of shoes are lined up. As I put mine in place, I notice something: Camel is not home yet. I wasn't wrong a while ago. My ears had heard good and hard.

I pull up my trouser legs. I take off my necktie and hang it on a nail. Only then do I take my place on the *seddari*.

"We comprehend your being dressed like a European," decreed the Lord one day. "In a jellaba and a chechia you would look like a camel at the North Pole at your French lycée. But once you come back here, do not wound our eyes. No necktie, no long trousers, pull them up like knickers the way the Turks wear them. And, of course, shoes outside. The room where your father sits is neither a corridor nor a stable."

How did I get the right to wear these garments rated as alien imitations? My report book! "Honor roll," first prize or honorable mention in Latin, Greek, German, French elocution and other venerable course material. If I suffered, stayed up nights, sometimes sobbed with fatigue, it was neither from zeal nor from taste. Nor was it pride in being chosen from among some half-dozen male children for the "new world." Rather for the following: a necktie, long trousers, socks. From then on I was nothing but a studious pupil. The wheel had been a long time turning. It was still turning. And my Report Book is still full of praise. Before that . . .

Even as a small child, I had a passion for justice. Either an easy chair or the ground! Just imagine a Negro who turns white from one day to the next but whose nose, either by luck's omission or by spite, remains black. I was wearing a vest and a pair of trousers. On my feet were shoes. A shirt. A belt around my waist. A handkerchief in my pocket. I was proud. Like a little European! As soon as I was with my comrades I felt grotesque, and I was grotesque.

"Those short-legged pants! Are you going fishing?"

Dirty little brats who made me suffer! And my shirt! Clean. Not a hole in it. Not a tear, but not ironed after washing.

"You sleep in it?" came the brats' ironic question.

The Lord had expressed judgment: "That's a shirt? Does it have a collar? Any buttons? Then what more do you need?"

He doesn't understand. He wears the Moroccan shirt, without a collar, with the opener and fastener on the shoulder. He wears *babouches*. He has no socks.

"You don't need any either, son. Your shoes cover your whole foot, but we have our heels free."

And the necktie. All my school friends had one. I wanted a

necktie as bad as a dying man wants a woman. So, yes, I stole. No one saw me; no one ever will know. I exacted a tribute from the Lord's wallet. I bought both a tie and socks. I didn't wear them at home. I'm not that dumb. Only outside. With the tenderness of a wife who caresses her lover or of an Arab ex-sharpshooter who caresses his war medal. As for my shirt, I made way for the Lord's judgment:

"The sheep has no feathers and the bird has no fleece. Thus is it with the son of Adam: he cannot have everything. Otherwise, son, contemplate the Christian Trinity, the hermaphrodite and Chaos."

That went on till the day I got the first part of my diploma. Suits, shirts, socks were all offered to me. And even gloves, fancy handkerchiefs, and a wallet for my identification card. All of that. Nothing but that. Everything utilitarian.

These fluxes of bile, of bitter chewing gum, I chew in the silence that followed my installation to the left of the Lord. For silence is there, and the longer it lasts the stronger it grows. Precisely, may it not last! It must not last. Camel still has not come home. Lord, do you need anything else? A quarter of an hour after the sacrosanct cannon shot, your eldest son still is not home. With that alone, I think, you have more than you need to call down curses on the rest of your offspring and to repudiate your wife. One day you taught me the *hadith* of ablutions: Amen, Lord amen! Camel is not at your right side, and the silence weighs heavy. I can't do a thing. Then: God has cursed the Jews: we are your Jews, Lord: open your mouth and curse us!

"Son, after the day cometh the night, then the sun, then once again the shadows. And tomorrow will in no way remove the monotony of our existence of thankless labors. God be praised notwithstanding!"

That is the prelude. What next will flow forth? A fable? No, something else. His voice is resigned and the last sentence is far from being a glorification of God. The fables of the Lord never start that way. And it would have been revolutionary if that particular evening there were any kind of change in the rituals.

I intone: "Praise be to God!"

That much is necessary. If the Lord pronounces the word God, you should recite a formula from the Koran. And if it's about a saint, say: "God bless and praise him." That is also sufficient. I am consequently excused from any further commentary. It is for the Lord to continue, and he does:

"But the clouds cover the sun, the moon spreads silver across the sky, and in the evening we take our relaxation with you. What did you learn today?"

Nothing. I didn't go to class. I walked around all afternoon on the beach at Aïn Diab. But why doesn't he say anything about Camel? Since I don't like to lie, I try a shortcut.

"Not much. We more or less did some reviewing. Exams are coming up. In two weeks we make the big leap."

"Our heart will be with you ... But still?"

That's how it is every evening, Ramadan or no Ramadan. The gestures, the fable, the hash of the school day passed through the sieve. And after that? No, not the soup. After that ...

Tonight I am accursed. I have fasted for sixteen hours. I am talking about Ramadan: neither drink nor eat nor smoke nor copulate. That's tough. I know it so well that I arrange things so I fast only one day in two. Of course the Lord thinks I'm a good Muslim. But woe to the Jews, today I fasted. I did some quick calculations. I don't have a watch (superfluous), and the big clock is upstairs in the Lord's bedroom. But I have an idea of the hour: it's about nine o'clock. Camel, I know where you are, leave the buddies, the whores, and the alcohol. Six stomachs pierced through with hunger await you. I don't count the Lord. If the idea got into his head, we would fast day and night, like a fakir. To set a record? For Islam! And yet ...

"Well," I say, "there's something that bothers me. The gods of mythology amuse me. I can't take them seriously."

I said that as if I had said: "Sir, I need to go pee" (and as a matter of fact I felt the need). I felt like talking.

"Why not?"

He smiles. I have just proffered him the first link in the chain. The evening is about to begin.

"We are willing to believe in pagan gods and demigods," he went on, "because positive beliefs have not yet been attained, even in our century. With even better reason, myths prevailed in the thinking of those poor idiot Greeks and Romans. If you reestablish the facts and if we make a point of it, we would sooner believe what the legend ought to be, that those gods strutted about in the heaven called Olympus well before the creation of the world. Through holes in the sky, they sent their bodily and other wastes out into space over a period of millennia. Finally, the day came that those wastes formed a more or less spherical block which the Olympians baptized Earth. There were fermentations from which beings were born: vegetal, animal, men. We do descend from the Gods."

What is stupefying is that I keep on listening to him. I even appreciate him. I forget about Camel and my hunger. This man in the tarboosh is sure of himself: a fly will not take flight unless he gives it permission. He knows that every word that falls from his mouth will be engraved on my mind. On his mask-like face, there is not a shudder. I removed this mask and read: he is illiterate and consequently proud of maintaining any kind of conversation in whatever subject matter. I would willingly compare him to those little old men who know everything and who have experienced everything: children, grandchildren, diplomas, fortune, reverses of fortune, mistresses, fornication, chancres... if not for the hatred because of that illiteracy. He knows that the Occident towards which he has propelled me is outside his sphere. Therefore he hates it. And out of fear that there be in me an enthusiasm for this new world, he flails, shatters, cuts off, and dissects everything I learn. Cheapens it.

I have not looked at him twice. His eyes are burning. I lower my head. He is reading me too.

"We are not telling you this twaddle for you to make parables of it," he went on. "We are not Christ, and we do not have a preposterous spirit..."

Great heavens, no! Reading the Koran has never made me smile.

"...but we are certain that you must see things in a healthy way. Our role as a father is the role of a guide. Learn everything you can and as well as you can so that all you have learned will serve you as a useful weapon, first of all for your examinations and secondly for your comprehension of the Occidental world. We have need of a generation of young people capable of finding their way between our Oriental lethargy and the Occident's insomnia, capable of assimilating today's sciences and of teaching it to future generations. Don't ever let yourself be tempted by what you have learned, by these mirages that until now you have never heard about and that could seem to you sufficient to be considered dogmas. Don't forget that all of today's civilization is based on postulates. We foresee in you an explosion near at hand because you are endowed with a lightning-like temperament and excessive pride. We hope with all our heart that that explosion will be the cause of a transformation that can make a modern, and above all, happy man of you, and only that."

Fine! Perfect! Thank you for your good wishes, but I've had enough of it. Write on water, and hang up the corpse. I'm hungry.

"When there is a shipwreck at sea, most of the passengers lose their head. Those are the only moments when human nature is revealed with all its cruelties and cowardices, and sometimes with its courage. People throw themselves into the water, they kill each other, they empty their belly one last time because death is near, and they cling violently to their final moments of life. Only a rare few grab hold of a plank of wood and hang onto it . . ."

His words drop out like the beads of a chaplet, dry, certain and each one inferring the other. I say to myself: just like a pebble. Pick up a hammer and hit it and the pebble breaks. Hit the fragments and you get particles. Hit again and keep on hitting until you have molecules, atoms, and fissions. Man, are you going to recite me the whole manuscript of Ibn Rachid until Camel comes home? He calls that excessive interest, but my stomach has churned up its emptiness to such a degree that I'm not hungry anymore. Old philosopher frozen into stone, look at these hands respectfully crossed on my squarely set knees: they are capable of hurling a switchblade knife.

". . . dominating their fear and the unleashed elements in the hope and the tenseness that that plank will bring them to shore. That shore is symbolic, son. It represents a goal. The sea is the world where man rarely is capable of controlling circumstances. Therefore remember that . . . Beg pardon?"

He launched that reprimand so suddenly that I jumped. What had I done? Closed my eyes or shaken my head without realizing it.

"Nothing."

"'Nothing?' Then why are your hands trembling?"

"My hands?"

I look at them. They have probably betrayed my inner hyperexcitement. Watch your hands, warns the saying, they are your weapon and your executioner.

"You can look at them. You may be prudent, but you aren't watchful. Have you something to say?"

I am lucid. Everything that went on before has been no more than a passage of arms. The chain will soon have two links.

"I asked a question, son."

"To which, father, I believe there is no answer."

"When the village has a feast, it is because a Jew has died . . . The French say that there's no smoke without a fire, isn't that right? In your soul and in your conscience, what's the matter with you?"

"Hungry."

"You're hungry?"

"Yes."

"Truly hungry?"

"Yes."

"Couldn't you say so sooner? It's quite natural to be hungry. Hunger is no sin and nothing to be ashamed of. Such being the case, you can await our convenience . . . Yes, you, last in the line. Come here!"

Lord in heaven, until now they had not existed. The shoes lined up by the door belong to them—and the empty bellies. There are five of them, all lined up along the wall. They are seated by age, forming an almost perfect trapeze. The eldest is named Abd El Krim, seventeen years old. The youngest is nine: Hamid. They don't scratch, don't sneeze, don't cough, don't belch, don't fart. They are thin and edgy. They keep their hands flat on their thighs and breath at a moderate rhythm, without a sound. Their eyes are dull and their complexion colorless. These are my brothers.

When the Lord pointed at one of them, five Adam's apples gave a leap. Hamid detached himself from the others and went to kneel before our father.

He is frail and gentle. He is nine years old but looks a good two years younger. He looked up at me and then lowered his eyes. That lasted only a fraction of a second, but I should have caught his glance: SOS, a whipped dog, the despair of the ghetto, the destitute, Icarus's dream, so intensely that I think my mother would have been better off to have practiced uterine pressure at the moment she gave birth to that kid.

"Your hand."

If he held it out, what punishment would be wreaked upon it? And why? He had fasted like everyone else, had not lingered with the kids of the neighborhood, had flushed the toilet after taking care of his needs, and had made up his bed. He did bite his nails, but did it in secret, and he had been beaten up by Naguib for a cigarette butt, but he has no desire to complain, and he has reproached no one, not even the Lord.

"Name of the Lord! Am I a monster or what? Your hand!"

It's a tiny little hand, pale, delicate, and refined, without an ounce of flesh on it.

"Hold it out and spread your fingers . . ."

It's nothing more than a louse, a white louse with a black spot in the center of its back. The lord caught it somewhere under his jellaba.

The clock struck. At first I wasn't conscious of it: the sounds penetrated the thickness of the ceiling, and I clearly counted nine strokes, nine o'clock. Then I realized that I was listening to the clock strike. That I *was able* to listen to it. Could there be a flaw in the Lord's omniscience? That surprised me. When there is a loud noise followed by a sudden silence, that silence is startling.

That freed me. I took note of the yellow color of the lights, the white temples of my father, the grimy edge of his tarboosh, a mathematical exercise inscribed on the newly whitewashed wall. And, by what mental divergence I do not know—perhaps the flaw had extended itself—I *saw* my mother in the kitchen amidst her tagines and her tole braziers. She blew on the soup because it was too hot and put it back on the fire when it got cold, blew on it again, reheated it . . . She bit on a lace handkerchief and sobbed tearlessly, without a sound, as women do who have sobbed for forty years. From time to time she made obeisance with her forehead touching the black and white squares of the kitchen floor: Greek saints and Russian saints, I have invoked our saints but they have not heard my prayers. They are devoted to my lord and master . . . Greek saints and Russian saints, typhus did not kill me, dysentery did not kill me, I have given birth to seven children, and I am still on my feet . . . Greek saints and Russian saints . . .

I was thinking: that clock rings like a curse. People here don't live their lives, they just exist, and time isn't worth spit.

"Don't touch my babouches."

Hamid lifted up a sandal and mashed the louse. Then he went back to take his place in the trapeze, his same posture, his same docility. It was then that I decided I'd be anathema.

"You told me to wait. To wait for what?"

He looked at me. One day a man told me that my father's eyes were full of goodness and honor. I ask you to be objective: that man had been sweeping up the Lord's store for twenty years.

He only looked at me for a second. Then he turned away, and nothing more. I compared: a signature, a stamp mark.

"Wait for what?" I repeated.

He did not deign to reply. Another day another man said to me: when I run into your father, I say hello to him and go on my way. I ask you to be objective: that man tried in vain to get the job of sweeping up the Lord's store.

"To wait for Camel or who or what? If you want me to go . . ."

"Listen!"

My palate was dry, and my eyes were burning. Those five shadows against the wall, the silent sobbing in the kitchen, this law that exacted the obedience of dogs . . . of dogs? Don't be silly! Dogs are banished from the Arab world. Precisely because there are human dogs, me, the trapeze, the keeper of hot soup slithering before the Lord—and at a distance at that. A dog is ready to piss. If the Lord commands: "Don't piss!" the dog will piss all the same. When the dog is named Hamid, he won't piss.

"I am listening."

"You are listening? You say that with a tone of authority. You are listening? The gentleman consents to lend an ear to our twaddle. You are listening? Very well. Listen to this."

He looked straight at me. He liked theatrical surprises.

The lighting came from a globe of frosted glass, and the mathematical operation was a multiplication plus casting out the nines. I was struck by two certainties: in the kitchen there was no light except the reddening of the brazier—and only against the wall could there be the figure of the man at whom I was trying not to look.

"When you get ready to mail an envelope, where do you stick the stamp?"

Even if he neither could read nor write, he calculated very well. And when he spoke, no one could be more sarcastic than he.

"You have just attacked us. You ask for explanations. We are ready to give them to you. At least have the courage to look me in the face."

I did. The nose was straight, the mouth and the eyebrows strictly horizontal. I discovered with surprise the peculiar mixture of colors: the white temples, the pepper-and-salt moustache, the beard of black that was almost blue.

"Straight in the face!"

I saw his eyes. I ended up seeing nothing but those immense black eyes. Camel? Effect, unexpected, detail. There was something far more serious. Great heavens! Could . . .

"Perfect. The father and son who look at each other. Nothing could be more touching. And now tell us—you know that we are ignorant and we ask nothing more than to learn—please enlighten us (in French, if you don't mind): is the better sandwich made of ham or of pâté?"

I have not stopped staring at the black eyes. A question bore into my brain: who was the s.o.b. who . . . And all of a sudden I felt a cramp in my stomach: fear.

"In every slice of ham there is some fat. We do not like fat. Consequently you cannot recommend the ham sandwich. What about the pâté? There is fat in it too. What about sausage? Sausage is closer to our kebabs, and I understand that there are some varieties made especially for Muslims. What about wine?"

The clock struck the quarter hour. I granted it a bit of spittle.

"Red wine is common to a lot of people—'roll over and stuff it up your ass'—and the consumption of white wine sets the pace for Saint Guy's dance. But fortunately we have aged wines, champagnes, special vintages. What château do you recommend for us?"

He gruffly seized me by the wrist and pulled me.

"And our gentleman can't wait?" (He was not shouting. His voice was always the same, biting.) "Do you take us for Hitler or for Pasha Glaoui? And to think that you were our pride and joy! We wore old babouches so that you could have a new pair of shoes, and we voided our guts of surplus, even what was necessary, so that you would be the awaited one. And what have you accomplished, you whose wrist we are holding and could break like a wisp of straw? You go into the European part of town with ease. You have a fair complexion, blond hair, and blue eyes. The prophet has not marked the forehead of his chosen ones. Why would he have done so? He did not foresee that his people would count chameleons among them. To look at you, who would take you for an Arab? That is one of your vanities. As if you can be proud of urinating red and shitting blue! Two sides of the coin, head, tail. On the headside: the Station Boulevard, the *Place de France*, our gentleman is a Bolshevik. He eats pork, he drinks wine, he laughs and jokes, talks, and has a fine time. Fasting? Not for our gentleman. That's fine for the old folks, the North African Arab, and the *fatmas*. Why should he bother? By pure chance, he was born into the world of the flea-ridden. On the tailside: he very carefully rinses his mouth, cleans his teeth, and comes to sit at our table like someone half starved. Where did you get this gift for deception? However little strength of heart you may have, our duty is to take you by the neck like this (he loosed my wrist and grabbed me by the neck), and to haul you outside. Whipped till you're bleeding, lynched, incinerated, that's the punishment reserved for the blasphemers like you. And our gentleman has complaints beyond that? Our gentleman just cannot wait? Dog!"

He pulled me toward him, then thrust me away. Between the two movements, I saw only the gold incisors. The clock struck the half-hour. The spittle slid down my face.

At the very moment death strikes, a child is born. Who ever said that the truest drama is one that makes us laugh? The beggar who began his chant beneath the window had a stentorian voice.

"Four times you've been to Mecca, once I've been, Hajji Fatmi Ferdi. Do you hear me?"

"Hajji Fatma Ferdi, you are of an old line, and my name is Ahmed ben Ahmed. You have a thousand hectares of land, furniture, animals, you are powerful and honored, while me, I sleep in the stables of Moussa, the pasha's procurer."

"Hajji Fatmi Ferdi. Do you hear me?"

"By the Prophets, by Saint Driss the first, Saint Issa, Saint Ussef, and Saint Yacoub, toss a piece of bread to him, or a little coin, or a chicken leg."

"Hajji Fatmi Ferdi, do you hear me?"

"May the Prophet protect you, may Saint Driss the First keep you as fit as a fiddle, may Saint Driss double your harvest . . ."

Nothing is more exasperating than a Moroccan beggar. That one was exasperated. Neither threats, nor insults, nor blows bothered him. He came bellowing his serenade every night without fail. The Lord listened for a moment as if to appraise, then made me a sign with his chin. I went to get a piece of bread, and threw it out the window.

"Prosperity to the lordly gentleman," shouted the beggar. "Long life to the fine gentleman. Happiness to the gentleman, in the name of the Prophet, Saint Driss the first, Saint Driss . . . Shit! More barley bread!"

He went off muttering, "Jew son-of-a-Jew, son of a bastard, offal, miser, son of dogs, father of monkeys, barley bread while you eat bread of tender wheat . . . Fine! I'll come back until you decide to give me something else besides this bread that your wife bakes just for me.

I'll come back tomorrow and the day after that and all the days to come. I'll give you no rest, by the Prophet, by Saint Driss..."

There was no change that night. The Lord made a sign to me. I got to my feet.

"Go wash your face!"

Then he added: "Don't talk with your mother."

My brothers were like stone. Not one of them had budged.

"Hajji Fatmi Ferdi. You are hajji four times. I am hajji once. D'you hear me?"

That spittle was added to all the earlier spittle, to the blows with his fist, the kicks, the slaps, the stamping on my feet. The list was already a long one, and the scales are off-balance, Lord. I was not born a criminal.

I found my mother stooped down blowing on the brazier.

I turned on the light.

She got to her feet and came to press herself against me.

"Driss, my son, whom I love among all of my sons, by this belly from which you came, by the nine months that this belly held you, by this breast that fed you, Driss, my son, find me a sure and rapid death. Driss, my son, he came in like a whirlwind. He went into every room and found that cleaning wasn't done right, that there was dust under the beds, lice in the mattress, the walls too hot, the tile floor too cold, and the air impure. He cursed my ancestors and threatened to divorce me."

"You aren't the only one. He just spit in my face. Look."

She stopped crying. Her eyelids were purple.

"To you... to you..."

"Of course! Being a student doesn't make me immune. Did you think he wouldn't dare touch me? But tell me, is it because Camel..."

"Of course not. He came home at four, and he didn't know if Camel..."

I plunged my hand into a bucket of water and splashed my face. Twice.

Then I turned out the light.

"Give me a little piece of bread."

"Stay a little longer, Driss, my son. Can't you do something? By this belly…"

He attacked as soon as I crossed the threshold.

"What is that?"

"It's for the beggar."

"What beggar?"

"I thought…"

"What? Take that bread back. No, put it down here."

I put it on the prayer rug, on his right where Camel should have been sitting. I crossed my legs underneath myself.

"Hajji Fatmi Ferdi, throw me a piece of barley bread, a little coin or a chicken leg. Do you hear me? Do you hear me?"

That beggar is an iota. He would complain for a long time, insulting, pleading, cursing, perhaps until dawn—and then he would go away. Everyone that my father had subjected to his abrasiveness had burst like a goatskin.

Everyone except me. Ordinarily I was happy to be passive. This particular night, I was ready to fight. We waited.

For better or for worse, as I recall, my first recollection is of waiting. I was four years old. Now I am nineteen. If my calculations are correct, that means almost five thousand times that I have waited. I think it is fair to count the three years while the Lord was in Mecca, supposedly to meditate at the Black Stone. The rules had been set down, and in his absence, we kept watch and awaited him in a frightful silence.

The first time of waiting was one winter's dawn in a dark house named Dar El Gandhouri in the town of Mazagan.

A candle dimly lights the little room where two children and a woman sit.

"Go wash your face."

Camel gets up, rubs his sticky eyes with his fists and pulls the covers over his shoulders.

"He washed it, Mama," says Driss, in a bold-faced lie. "I saw him. He even brushed his teeth."

The woman starts to unwind her prayer beads. When she finishes a hundred of them, she pauses and silence falls. But the candle continues to accentuate the mouthings of her lips. Then slowly, bead by bead, the rosary uncoils to a soft sound of clicking.

The room smells of a sleep suddenly interrupted by the ancient pealing of a heavy bell, a bell whose pendulum's scruffy yellow outline is barely visible in the half-light. We ignore the ticktock. We have been hearing the same thing for so long that we forget it.

The white bowl full of black olives on the low table has violet reflections. Near it, a plate of terra-cotta gives off the lingering rancidness of four-year-old butter.

"Camel! How many times have I told you to leave that matting alone?"

Camel has been pulling strands of the matting for several minutes. His eyes closed, his hand comes out from under the cover, and the strand tickles his brother's nostrils. Camel's hand disappears as if by magic. Silence falls on the woman who has gone back to her rosary and on the two children, the one muffled up to the ears and with his eyes closed, the other with eyes open and sniffling.

Suddenly the scene changes. In place of the candle, there is a carbon lamp. It gives a stark light to the wide-awake heads of the children who sit quietly with their mother around a table. A kettle steams on some white coals near the door.

Outside in the courtyard, you can hear someone snort and slosh his hands about in a pail of water. The sink gulps down the water tossed into it in full-force belches. In the room, there is a musty odor. Silence falls again, colliding with the whine of a fly and a cracking of knuckles. A man walking on bare wet feet, arms outstretched and with a white cap on his head, comes into the room. He is tall and thin, and his full-face beard gives him a saintly air because at the very moment he appears, the muezzins of Mazagan call the faithful to dawn prayer.

The woman is standing with a towel in her hand. The man wipes his face, his hands, and his feet. And the prayer begins. On a square piece of greenish felt, the father directs the prayer. The woman is in back of him with the children elbow to elbow. The four silhouettes bend, kneel down, and prostrate themselves in rhythm. Then, seated cross-legged, the left hand flat on the left knee, the right index finger moving to "put out the eye of Satan-the-cursed-one," father, mother, and children, eyes turned toward heaven, maintain an expression of blankness.

The fly buzzes again, and the kettle simmers on the cinders. Everyone has taken his place around the white wood table spotted with grease. The unit in the lamp draws in the water with a sucking noise. Driss and Camel cut a piece of barley bread. Every mouthful is smeared with butter and followed by an olive. In front of them, the pits pile up on the table. No one says a word.

The father breaks a cube of sugar with the bottom of a glass, crushes a fistful of green tea in the palm of his hand and picks the leaves off a bouquet of mint. The steam from the water poured from the copper kettle into the nickel teapot that he holds at arm's length blots out the figure of the woman crouched in front of him. The brazier is between two trays, one for the glasses and the teapot, and the other holding three leather containers filled with sugar, tea, and mint. The teapot fills the glasses from on high without a drop being spilled. The man tastes the infusion and clacks his tongue as a sign of satisfaction.

Nothing has changed since then. The beard of the Lord is still black, and we jump out of bed for the dawn prayer, in winter as in summer at the same hour like well-regulated puppets. The family has grown to five members, but so what? They suckled for one year and cried for two—the exact amount of time set for earliest childhood—and immediately afterwards grew up in fear and learned to be silent. Like tonight, every night they are five shadows against the wall. I have been groomed to be everything that the Lord has not. That is why I am at his left and for my own good have been gratified with spittle. Then, there is Camel, unthinking, irresponsible and, in the presence of the master, the most perfect of puppets; and my mother, tender and submissive, five feet high and eighty-eight pounds, whose destiny it is to be ignorant of any act that would fulfill her. She has been that way for forty years of existence, and not a hair of difference.

For her and, if she opposes it, for me, and, if at the last moment even I take pity, for art, for nothing, I shall act ... one day or the other ... this very evening perhaps, who knows?

And what does that jackal of a beggar complaining there beneath the window want? He is a stranger to our life, a stranger to our drama. The Lord does not really hear him. Not an iota, less than an iota. Does he think he's the only one bemoaning his fate at this hour? In every city in Morocco, in every village, in every douar, on the doorstep, underneath a window, two million like him are embittered by revolt and crime and madness—and, instead of acting, they remain humble, mean, lamentable, begging for a little bone, gnawed clean, sucked bare to the marrow, but one that a beggar's tongue can still lick.

My life dates from that first time of waiting. Quite recently I read a work on Freud's theories, about complexes and inhibitions ... and as I closed the book I thought: "Fine! So we give these poor little words a chance."

Day found me still seated at the same table in front of the olive pits. My mother called me. I opened my eyes. I was alone in the room.

She gave me a container of soup to take to my brother Camel who had gone to *m' sid* before dawn. I recall that I saw a telegraph pole lying along the sidewalk that had been knocked down by the wind squall the night before. It is a precise and rather strange memory.

When my brother finished his breakfast, I wanted to stay with him. That's how my schooling began. It lasted four years. Everything I learned in that interval would easily fit onto a postage stamp.

For my official enrollment, my father came to drink tea and to barter the rates of my schooling with the schoolmaster. Camel, who has a good memory for certain typical scenes, assures me that the conversation began with promises based on next year's harvest and ended up in good Oriental arguing and due form, including quotations from the disciples of the Prophet and protestations of mutual friendship. At the end of the meeting, my father gave the professor a twenty-five *centime* coin and thundered at the entrance to the shop, "Camel and Driss are now your children. Let them learn the holy religion. If not, kill them and let me know about it: I'll come bury them."

Camel was five and a half, and I, four.

I remember that as soon as my father left, the master sent out for some doughnuts. He gave me one. I ate it in silence. When it came time to go for lunch, one could see a large pool of urine where I had been sitting. I had been so afraid that even at the age of thirteen I still wet the bed.

It was my turn to learn the dawn awakenings, the silent sufferings and repressions, the pain of the soles of the feet, the rages that were quickly snuffed out. I learned to get along as all the others had.

The students in this type of school are the most studious and the most miserable in the world. They get up at the muezzin's first call and don't have time either to wash or to eat. Before the sun is up, they must wash one of the sides of their study board with their numb little fingers, which they then coat with a kind of grayish clay and which they stand against the wall to dry in the sun. It is a hard polished board with a hole pierced in one corner through which there is a string. For writing, there is a piece of reed that has been shaped with care and dipped into an ink made with dried sheep dung and which could be easily detached. The students have neither notebooks nor books. They have their board and their memories. As the lessons are learned, the boards are washed in the school's watering trough. It is no less expected of the students and everyone else that the lessons will become indelibly engraved on their memories.

The school in question is quite simply a shop that is generally dark and has an earthen floor covered with mats. Children from four to twelve years, and sometimes adolescents, sit cross-legged on the floor all day long, holding their board on their knee, speaking in nasal accents, reciting in a drone, and squeezing their fists with every mistake of memory. This hubbub is colored by suffering, hunger, silent tears, and resignation.

The earthen floor is humid and the kid's rumps get cold, but you can't say anything, only learn. Cockroaches, bugs, and lice crawl through the rotting floor mattings. Spiders, hanging on a thread from the ceiling, almost invisible in the half-light, descend straight down and tickle the shaven, scabby heads. These kids are afraid. Most of them wear no pants under their jellaba. They scratch themselves and get skin problems. Their mothers take care of them with old wives' remedies. They finally go to a dispensary when there's nothing else to try, no more magic herbs or talismans. That's without counting on the contamination of the younger boys by the older ones as these schools almost always serve as tacit courses in applied pederasty, with or without the tutelage of the honorable master of the school.

While the board is drying, the students take turns in reciting the lesson that they have learned the night before and reviewed before washing it off the surface. If the lesson has been learned, they fill up the virgin face of their board with the dictation of the professor. Some of the youngest do not know how to write. The teacher then has recourse to a clever trick. He traces the lesson in pencil, then there is nothing left to do but to go over the letters in ink.

If the lesson has not been learned, one of two things: either the teacher is in a good humor and the student escapes with a crack on the head with a pole (one or two, no more) or else he is in a bad humor. In the latter case, he calls on the eldest of the children, a sort of helper, who lifts up the feet of the *lazy one*. According to the bile level of the honorable professor, the blows to the feet number between ten and a hundred. It is true that the little ones have a right to no more than ten, but the bigger boys can stand more.

All rules have exceptions. Consequently, boys with the heads of angels escape all punishment, sometimes also the rich, but in the matter of compensation, there are both hard heads and scapegoats. Otherwise, there would be no need for shackles and *falaqas*. As for me, an ordinary student, I am sincerely grateful to my teachers for having so well leveled off and firmed up the soles of my feet. I can walk for miles without difficulty. All the students who have passed through these schools are extraordinary walkers. The Moroccan couriers are an example.

The professor is a *fiqh*, which is to say an individual who has learned the Koran by heart—or almost—and who has rented a small shop. People turn their children over to him. He has his food assured and the shop to sleep in. Indulgent parents invite him to eat with them sometimes or send him special dishes and cakes. When evening comes, the students hang their board on a nail, kiss the hand of their teacher, put on their babouches and leave. The teacher unrolls his mattress, has his dinner, says his evening prayer, smokes his *kiff*, and blows out his candle. A tranquil, fulfilling life.

One afternoon, I played hooky without being aware of it. I wandered through the streets, whistling at the birds and following the flight of the clouds. Finally I got lost. An old lady found me, gave me a kiss and a two-sous coin. I put the money in a matchbox I had picked up somewhere.

At evening, I saw a well-known silhouette striding toward me. It was no other than my worthy and respected father. The settlement of accounts between him and me took place, at my expense, in three acts:

ACT I: We went to reassure the schoolmaster. In order to fully profit from such an occasion to demonstrate the devotion that each fiercely expressed for the other (according to the bilateral verbal agreements sworn to the day of my matriculation) my father turned me up in the air, and the master lashed the soles of my feet a good hundred times. We picked up Camel on the way home, and all three went to the house.

ACT II: Back at home, after various explanations, salaams, and bows, and the tears of relief of my mother, the earlier scene began again, but with a minor variation. It was my mother, so happy to see me safe, who held up my legs, and my father who took his turn at the rod. A good half hour.

ACT III: My feet bloody, I threw myself into my mother's open and consoling arms. My father admits of no weakness, and consequently remonstrated with all of us before going slamming the doors out of the house. We stood there, Camel, my mother, and I, lamenting like a group of crying Jews.

EPILOGUE: Later on, I remember, I smiled and poked around in my pocket for the matchbox, opened it and showed what it held. All the same I had earned my day's wages. Mother puts the coin carefully into her sash and embraces me.

I don't know if I had been dreaming or simply dozed off. First of all I felt guilty for feeling sorry for myself over my past—even if it was my own—then I came back to myself and everything struck me at once, like shrill high-pitched notes: the beggar was not bellowing anymore, the clock struck eleven, and the Lord was on his feet, looking at Camel who was taking off his slippers. Clearly, Camel was drunk.

Immediately after that, I foresaw the consequences, and I knew my feelings were at fever pitch. The back of the Lord's neck was red. Puffs of cool air blew through the window, and my brother's face, as I could see it from my corner, looked strange. I suppressed everything but that face, analyzing, defining, calculating, trying to see what would happen. Quickly, in a brief instant. Was it the effects of alcohol or the results of that feeble moment of intuition? Two arches of eyebrows, two cheekbones, a nasal appendage, a jawbone and some shaded zones, that head had something brutal about it.

One of Roche's saying came to mind:

"The habit makes the monk. Persuade yourself for a quarter of an hour that you have a toothache, and half an hour later, you will really have a toothache."

Maybe that was what it was: since the Murdoch Park episode, everything had taken a dramatic turn, and everything ought to seem so to me. But Camel lifted his head and I was sure it was the head of a rebel. I saw that the back of the Lord's neck had turned purple. My spine oozed cold. I plunged my fist into my pocket and closed it over my switch-blade knife.

I smiled. That knife had cut everything: the uncut pages of my books, the throats of roosters of Aïd Seghir (thirty-two in all), the throats of sheep from Aïd El Kebir (ten in all) and, once, at Hamid's birth, my mother's belly. After this last exploit, it had been thrown into some boxes in the barn where I discovered it, cleaned it and sharpened it, so carefully that it had taken on the look of a leather worker's knife. Then I put it in my pocket, certain that it would serve again, other sheep to be slaughtered, another caesarian to be done, and one day among the days created by God, with a little dexterity and a little cold-bloodedness, to hurl it toward the Lord, somewhere in the Lord's body, toward the nape of the neck, for example, where it would penetrate up to the hilt, like a needle.

"Woman!"

His hands cracked like a whip. The nape of his neck was returning to normal. The knife was sticking halfway out of my pocket. I quickly stuffed it back in. "The man whose face you don't want to see in the street will turn his ass to you in the Turkish bath," say the Bedouins. I was disappointed, but resigned.

My mother was present as though she had stepped out of a trapdoor, with her ample garments, her head the dimension of an open hand, and her hair hanging heavily down to her hips.

"Master ..." she began.

She subscribed to all the catastrophes that were to come. What was she other than a woman whose thighs the Lord could padlock and over whom he had the rights of life and death? She had lived all her life in houses with doors barricaded and windows barred. Only the sky could be seen from the terraces, and the minarets, symbols. One female among the creatures of Allah that the Koran had penned up: "Fuck them and refuck them; through the vagina, as it is the most useful; then pay no attention to them until the next orgasm." Yes, my mother was like that, weak, submissive, passive. She had given birth seven times at regular intervals of two years, with one son who was a drunk and the other, myself, who judged her.

He did not even look at her, and I understood that Camel had been pardoned, at least provisionally.

"Has everyone done their ablutions."

It was a ritual question. Tonight it came two hours late, that is all. Yes indeed, my brothers have not so much as farted, my mother is in a perpetual state of grace ... oh yes! Camel has been drinking and I am disloyal, but so what? Faith is safe and Allah omnipotent and merciful.

We formed ourselves into an isosceles triangle, and the prayer began. The head duck, of course, was the Lord. We knelt down, prostrated ourselves, he on his prayer rug, and we on the cold mosaic floor. He declaimed one verse after the other, choosing the longest ones, the most rhythmic and the most monotonous. We chanted "Allah is great" each time we knelt and "Glory to the All-High" each time we prostrated ourselves. I listened to that grave voice devoid of any quiver of pleasure. It was the voice of a man who speaks with God as his equal.

We...of course! even I, we moved our lips and conscientiously carried out our mimicry and mentally recited what the Lord was saying out loud. But our true prayers were:

Camel: Bousbir from Bousbir! What a long drawn-out dressing-down he'll be dealing out to me. I should have stayed in Bousbir!

My mother:...devoted to my Lord and master...Saints of the Greeks and the Russians, a little accident, a fall down the stairs, an undiscovered microbe or a German bomb, no matter what, I want to die...Saints of the Greeks and of the Russians...

My other brothers: Nothing.

Me: what could be wrong with him?

And above it all, like the trumpeting of the Archangel, the racket of the beggar who has suddenly returned to the assault:

"Do you hear me, do you hear me?..."

We knelt down one last time, gouged out the eye of Satan and said "Amen," and the Lord got to his feet, grabbed Camel by the body and hurled him against the wall.

"This for the wine you did honor to."

He literally picked him up and threw him against the wall again.

"And this for the idea of rebelliousness that you just had."

Then he turned around and faced me.

"The knife!"

I was still kneeling. I got up.

"What knife?"

He thrust his hand into my pocket.

"This one."

Holding it between his thumb and index finger, he made a brief gesture. The blade sprang forth white, thin, and long. A real leather worker's knife.

"Here."

I took it.

"I'm going to turn my back and count up to ten. At ten, you will throw it."

He smiled.

"Toward the nape of the neck, for example, you were measuring it a little while ago."

His smile disappeared.

"Unless," he added, "you can't wait till I get to ten."

He turned around and began counting. The half hour after eleven sounded. The beggar chanted his litany of curses.

"...two...three..."

I looked at the knife, looked at Camel, looked at my mother. Camel had fallen to the floor beside the barley bread, at the same place he took every evening. He did not make a move and looked at me without seeing me. His account had been settled. All the rest, the vast rest, made little difference to him. He was bleeding from the nose, the lips, and a cut from over the eyebrows.

My mother didn't move either. Her head remained obstinately bent over. Her lips mumbled like the lips of a preacher, but it was probably the saints of the Greeks and the Russians that she was evoking, since everything was already written, even the murder of her husband.

Five pairs of eyes followed my gestures: one gesture and five stomachs would settle down, five existences would blossom in the sun.

"...six...seven..."

I looked at the knife. What had Roche said?

"From the time of the caliphs, you Arabs have not stopped digesting and sleeping. What you need is a good little war."

There in the palm of my hand was an action that could fulfill us all. I closed the knife.

"...nine..."

"Stop!"

My mother stood up in front of me. I handed her the now inoffensive knife. Her mouth twisted: recognizance or disgust? There wasn't even time for the dust to settle, the knife was already in the Lord's hands.

"Fine, woman."

That was his only commentary. The round table was set up, the copper gleamed, steam streamed out of the kettle, and we found ourselves seated, with a glass of tea in our hand, tasting the infusion as if nothing had taken place, trying our best to swallow the burning-hot liquid. Tea is an aperitif that should be savored rather than drunk. We had to wait a little bit, a poor little turn of the dial on the clock, perhaps two . . . or three, when the Lord would retire to his apartments, and we would rush to the faucets and water jars.

This tea was *gunpowder*. The Lord taught us about it saying:

"From the province of Tsoung Tse, harvest of 1940, brand A.E.T.C.O., American reserve. A little strong, a little cloudy, but excellent for the Shluh tribe in Sousse. One hundred twenty francs the kilo, no more."

We tasted other examples: Mee Lee, Sow Mee, fine, demi-fine . . . ten, twelve, I can't remember anymore, desperately shaking my head if he did not like a certain brand, asking for more if it had pleased the Lord.

When I took a look at that horde ready to drink all the tea in China, or boiling oil or the water of the sea or anything else just so at the end of it they would have their lentils (I was comparing them to shipwrecks, prisoners, tamed dogs, solitary women, and *tutti quanti*), I said to myself . . . of course, for twenty-six years the Lord has been a tea merchant, a wholesaler in teas, importer of teas, expert in teas, vice-president of the conglomerate of experts, importers, wholesalers and merchants (teas) and a lengthy tasting was an ordinary occurrence . . . I said to myself: "One spitting episode, one son assaulted, the scene of the knife, three dramas that have no further nominal value: this man is essentially strong, combining the two factors that make for a strong man: time and forgetfulness."

That is the way I had always perceived him. From that came the respect and admiration that I had never ceased to feel for him, the whole of my long hatred of him.

I said to myself again: "He is our god, side by side with us, but what in the devil does he want of us?"

Here I began to laugh. My mask was rigid. Once upon a time a story was told to me, one that could be a response.

A rich man meets a poor one.

"Tell me what you wish," he said, "and you will have it right away."

The poor man was starving, a skeleton, without shelter, and dressed in rags.

"I want a ring," he said.

The glasses were bordered with gold, the fine sand of Zenatas daily cleansed the serving pieces, the odors of mint, sage, and ambergris spurted from the teapot when it was uncapped, the mattress that my behind left in billows was stuffed with wool, a quintal of untreated wool, the ceiling was high and far away, almost a sky, and, two stories above that ceiling, a square-shaped room was bursting with sacks, boxes, jars filled with everything from honey to olive oil, from white beans to green tomatoes, durum wheat, rice, charcoal, tinned meat, melted butter, dates . . . everything necessary to make the foundations of a *fassi* household. There were two or three small boxes of tea, naturally. A door closed off this storage space. It had neither lock nor chains, just a simple latch. The Lord had declared: "Woman, use but do not abuse. As for you children, no need to tell you that you have no business in the storage room."

Yes indeed, there was no need. Only one had broken the rule: me, one single time, the day that I found the knife.

But there had never been any need for anything. Just like the barley bread that was destined for the beggar a while ago, I could easily have taken a mouthful, or better still, have eaten it all up and then asked for another piece from my mother. The Lord would have noticed nothing. He is not miserly, I repeat. But would the idea have come to me that I had not followed up on it? Why? "In the midst of abundance, we are dying," said the Prophet Isaiah. For an inveterate smoker who for financial reasons has been deprived of tobacco for a long time, what does a cigarette butt represent, I ask you? If it were granted to me to satisfy my hunger, I would empty the storage room.

And if, at the same time, the Lord had said to me: "There is something in you that we do not understand and that frightens us. You are no longer a part of our world. Speak, explain your wishes. We grant you that," I would reply: "Liberty" and I would refuse the wish.

Between this curved ceiling and that multicolored mosaic, eight beings wait for another being to open his mouth. The nocturnal life of the city could be heard outside over and above the cries of the beggar. I could imagine the marketplaces, the *dellals*, the circle surrounding the public storytellers, the games of lotto on the sidewalk, the furtive matings in the crowd, the sales on the black market, the pickpocketing, the banks of guitarists, the Istiqlal rostrum, a whole world of orgies and violence. I could see the people that surged toward the Bousbir, a veritable closed city where some three thousand migrant workers of every blood and color worked in assembly line (their most productive month was the holy month, Ramadan); the little old men who scurried along, knees trembling, with a patriarchal turban, a prayer rug, a heavy strand of prayer beads, in search of a little boy lost in the crowd. I could imagine those people who have no law and no lodging, going from one group to another, from one confidence to another, a nationalist to be denounced, a wallet to be filched, an illegal bit of business to be arranged amicably.

The prescribed silences and noises, those determined by the teapot and the utensils for making tea dominated between the mosaic and the ceiling. The open window was a wall. We were the Ferdi family, descendants of the Prophet, the race of Lords, and eight of us depended on one alone. I was lucid: that man with the face of an ascetic had something to say to us.

When would he make up his mind? Later on, a bit later on, as our exhaustion was not yet complete, because what he had to tell us must be astounding.

When Jehovah's wrath was visited on the Hebrews, they must have been stunned: they had expected their total destruction. Hajji Fatmi Ferdi, I have read the Zabor, with all due respect. And until the moment that you allow your incisors to unclench, I escape you, through my imagination which is vast, as you yourself have recognized.

Consequently I began to compress my imagination and extracted an old story that I recounted to myself. Pardon me, Lord, if I do not tell it to you: it is of a kind that a lord of your saintly qualities ought not hear. Pardon me too for knowing it. You have only taught me serious things, but in business matters, I challenge you: go on wearing us out as you do for that beggar, until dawn if such is your wish, and until dawn I'll tell myself a whole string of stories, all of them as sacrilegious as the one about Old Man Abbou. Look: I don't like tea, and I've already drunk a liter of it.

*Once there was a merchant who sold grilled grasshoppers. His name was Abbou (which means The Joke). He was old as a dried out crust of bread, and he pushed his little wagon loaded with grasshoppers and a steelyard, crying out with all his strength: "Saaaaaaalted and appetizing."*

*It's mostly the children who eat the grasshoppers. One evening Abbou gave a handful to a little Berber boy of fourteen years who struck him by his beauty. Subsequently the child passed between the legs of Old Man Abbou, a notorious pederast. One day Old Man Joke told the boy:*

*"We know that I screw you every evening prayer, but you eat more grasshoppers than your behind and those gazelle's eyes are worth. And so, my son, since you have no parents and you wander the streets doing nothing, you're going to push my cart and cry: 'Salted and appetizing.' I'll pay you for your work from time to time. At sixty-five years of age, I'm getting old and I'm losing my voice. You push, you cry out, and I sell."*

*The kid pushed the cart and yelled: "Saaaaaaalted and appetizing." The man sold more grasshoppers than before and doubled the number of evening prayers, but the boy grew more and more demanding, so that finally Abbou spoke to him in the following manner:*

*"Listen, my son, you are becoming impossible. I have been more than a father to you. I picked you up and saved you from the street and from bad company. Thanks to Allah, you will be a fine merchant when I die,*

*because I intend to will you my cart and my grasshoppers. There you have it, but all young people are ungrateful. Last week you asked me for fifty francs to go to the movies. I love you as a son and I gave you the fifty francs. Yesterday it was to go to the barber. You show your teeth and demand one hundred francs supposedly for a scalp massage. I gave you twenty and advised you to go to the ambulatory barber down by the station under the tent. I can see that your hair is the way it was yesterday, and you're asking fifty francs to go to the bordello. Aren't you ashamed to talk like that to a man like me who could be your grandfather?"*

*And since the kid kept on demanding, Old Man Abbou got mad:*

*"Listen, son, I don't need you to sell my grasshoppers. You can go where you want. When you go by here and I need to put my carrot in your inkwell, I'll call for you and give you your due with a little extra."*

*And Abbou, with a magnanimous gesture, fired his little associate who had not taken twenty steps away when a hairy hand fell on his shoulder. It was the watermelon merchant who had been watching the whole thing. He was called Ould Rih, which means "Son of the Wind," an enormous big guy with a red face and everything in proportion...*

The Lord clapped his hands.

"Listen."

It was like a magic wand: eight pairs of eyes, eight pairs of ears. Had I won?

"We are going to inform you of certain serious events on which all of our futures depend. You as well as the children, wife, are going to listen to me carefully. Then we will listen to your suggestions respectively and we will make a decision."

"This is what it is all about. Listen carefully. We shall not repeat."

Silence, the odors of mint and sage, the beggar...

"Rarely do we talk with you about our affairs. For you, we are the head, the leader of the family who provides for your needs. You ask no details, and in that you are right. At least you know that we sell tea. Tonight we are all equals and are in the same predicament. To be brief, we are informing you that we have been one of twelve importers of tea to Morocco for some years. But the war has changed everything, and the Moroccan Service of Provisions by official decree has taken our place and named the sole importer who sells us the tea at whatever price he decides to fix. For example, a Mee Lee SAFT forty-two costs us two hundred fifty francs the kilogram. The Twelve receive thirty to forty tons per month which, after taking their profits, they divide up among the wholesalers who in their turn, resell to the middlemen, and so on down to the consumer. Now remember these two points: the wholesaler or middleman have all the time they want to purchase such and such a quantity according to their available monies, or not to buy any at all. On the one hand, we Twelve are legally obliged to take thirty to forty tons at the set price, while on the other hand, the same Mee Lee we were talking about just now is finally sold to the consumer for three hundred seventy francs the kilogram. Did you understand all that?"

Vaguely, but eight heads nodded in agreement all the same. As for me, I made a rapid calculation in my mind, and the results frightened me. I didn't know our father was so rich.

"Now, the Americans landed here some months ago. They dumped tons of tea on every market in the Empire, and paid no attention to the distribution services or to the local official regulations. It's tea they seized on Japanese ships or took from the Axis powers. The result? It made you smile, almost laugh: the Mee Lee SAFT forty-two, to go in the same vein, is being sold for three hundred seventy francs on the official market and one hundred thirty francs on the black market. Funny, isn't it?"

Perhaps. Even preposterous, but it didn't interest me.

*Ould Rih said to the boy:*

*"Don't you worry, my little friend. You'll be right at home here. I'm young and the Joker here is old. He sells grasshoppers and I sell watermelon. Here, take a taste: it's sweeter than honey and as velvety as your charming behind, I am sure. I buy them in Marrakech, and speaking of that, I need to do some buying. We'll both go to Marrakech tomorrow."*

*In a rage, Old Man Abbou, who heard it all, covered up his grasshoppers in his jellaba and went home. He said to his wife:*

*"Listen old woman! You can't sell grasshoppers anymore. I have about twenty pounds left. You can eat them, you and the children. You can give some to my son Moha who is married, but don't give any to his wife who is thin and has no behind. Give some to my daughter M'barka too, but when her husband the sergeant is not around. I don't want him to eat the grasshoppers of a decent man, because he runs after kids, what a shame! I'm taking the bus to Marrakech tomorrow morning at the first call of the muezzin. Go find me the sock I hid my thousand franc bill in."*

The Lord pointed toward the wall with his finger:

"I totted things up a little while ago and look! Four months of stock, thirty-four tons per month . . . It's a catastrophe."

He took the tarboosh off his head, sniffed at it, and capped his knee with it. His bald spot was a delicate shade of rose.

"My land, my villa in Mazagan, my liquid assets, this house that shelters you, even those glasses you are holding in your hand, every bit of it will be swallowed up. And the black market prices are going down every day, one hundred fifty francs last week, one hundred thirty today, one hundred tomorrow, and if Allah wills, down to fifty; only He remains eternal, the end of the world is not for tomorrow. Go on, say something now! You have all the facts. It's up to you to resolve the crisis, because you should know the following: we have worked, we have created happiness for all of you, amassed a fortune for our old age and to take care of all of you in your lifetime. You have accepted everything calmly. Tomorrow we won't have a copper penny. Speak up. You first, wife, with respect for your age and the responsibilities you assume in this dwelling, but speak clearly."

"Oh me, Lord I'm just a poor woman (her eyelids had no lashes), what do you expect a poor woman to do except pray to our saints . . ."

"No saints."

"It seems to me . . ."

"We distinctly declared."

"Well! It seems to me that . . ."

"That's enough. We'll remember your suggestions, although 'the hand of the midwife and yours bring forth a one-eyed child.' Your turn, Abd El Krim."

"If the tea…"

I knew I would be the last one questioned, and since my answer was already prepared, I went on with my story. The Lord would not miss my sleep-filled eyes, my absent air and my indifference, and that would please me greatly. Throughout the evening what had he been but a knife in the wound?

*In Marrakech he was persuasive and generous. He had found the object of his journey and brought him back to Casablanca in spite of the fists of The Son of the Wind. And now he too was selling watermelon, and even dates and melons, nuts and figs. He had—Allah be praised— his tent set up in the very center of the marketplace. The child remained comfortably with him, pilfering from him and growing up in a short time.*

*That was the way it was until some charitable souls well-informed by that pirate Son of the Wind went to tell Abbou's wife all about what was going on. Old Man Abbou gritted his teeth:*

*"Listen old woman. You eat? You sleep? You drink? So what horse fever do you need? Aren't you settled down at your age? You have two grandchildren. I think the jinn have cooked your brains and you need to go see Si H'mad Wahhouch who will give you a piece of leopard testicle to break the spell that's bewitching you. You don't want me to nose around in that old skin of yours between your legs, do you? Watch out for the sixty watt bulb! Otherwise I'll have to tie you up to a ladder and give you another one of those Sudanese thrashings. So fill up the teapot and stop looking at me with those pistol shots in your eyes.*

*Madame Abbou said nothing, but the next day at dawn she went to watch her husband's tent. The boy came out around noon.*

*"Hey you, boy, come over here a minute…"*

*And when the boy…*

He was waiting. He wasn't looking at me. He was waiting. *And when the child got close…* I have never experienced anything like that silence that suddenly fell like a dead body in the midst of the banquet hall, a palpable silence, thick and living with a life that was extraterrestrial. *And when the child got close, the hoarse voice of Madame Abbou attracted a crowd…*

He was counting on that silence to drown our materiality, our lives, our equations, everything that is humanly assimilated, to create a poem of consonants harassingly monotonous, with the same soporific rhythms of the Koran, of simple but extremely precise terms ... *got close, the hoarse voice of Madame Abbou attracted a crowd of passers-by:*

*"Aha! So you're the girl with balls? You're coming with me to the judge, to the khalifa ... "*

The demi-somnolence, the precipitous secretion of my glands, the sadistic pleasure of prolonging the instant, the threat and the danger (his word was: usury), the consciousness that this sentiment was ill-founded and useless, consciousness by association of ideas with the refined Hindu art, so cruelly refined—and why not?—the late Mohammed, prophet, warrior, legislator, and also, directly or indirectly, by transcendence of something else (I don't want to know which), the determinant of this waiting and of our guts (2.2 yds. per person) massaging the sublimation of Islam. At full speed I noted: the filthy language of Monsieur Driss Ferdi when he is in an emotional state— and something I had forgotten but remedied right away: "Allah bless and honor him!" as I had just thought of the Prophet.

What do they need? Lentils? And after that? Gang of whirling dervishes, didn't you understand? He said: "The end of the world is not for tomorrow." Mother, brothers, you'll be on watch again tomorrow night and all the nights to come, just listen to that beggar, listen to him: "... for the better! I'll be back, I'll be back tomorrow and the day after and all the days in the future ..."

What do you need? To quote only one person, I'll quote you, Mother. Mother, he is right, no saints, that's all they are, saints, but for the living, for human beings, a man for you, an adulterer ... no! Don't say: "Oh, my ear, you have heard nothing," you understood very well: a lover. A lover to possess and satisfy you! You see I have discovered your secret, but I cannot give you consolation, I am only your son ... No! that sentence is not ambiguous. It is very clear, so don't be afraid, you understood very well.

Yes? Reproach is in your eyes as you say: "Driss, my son, whom I love, etc ... etc ... Let it go, give in, bend one more time. You want to defend me and wave me like a flag. You are wrong. I'm not worth it, see, my breasts are flabby and my skin is bloated, you are rigid, too rigid, the palms of my hands have shriveled up like an old fig and I can't smile anymore. Maybe once upon a time, but now? I feel no more desire, not even in spurts, either in my soul or in my consciousness. Give in, Driss my son, give in again. This time will be the last, and I will bless you..."

And so. I turned my eyes away. Raymond Roche talks drivel. A good little war? Desirable, acceptable, and as soon as it's over, the Arabs will go back to sleep, surely in an even deeper sleep than before. In the midst of a deluge, of what use is an umbrella? Better: "If idiot children are the result of your tainted sperm, treat them like idiots." Upstairs in the Lord's room, there are venerable parchments. I have consulted them all. They all affirm: "The son of Adam So-and-So tells us that one So-and-So had heard it said that one So-and-So heard someone tell So-and-So that he remembered that one So-and-So..." etc... etc... Here a dogma followed by its usage: not to comprehend, not to judge, to believe, that is all that is asked of you. Amen!

I gave in, at the same moment as, rudely: "And you?"

"I have been thinking. I haven't missed a word of the conversation. I have no suggestion to make to you, Father, except for a reminder."

I was smiling. So was he.

"I am listening."

"Three years ago, you gathered us all together as you did tonight, and informed us of a grave situation similar to the one you have just told us about... Shall I go on?"

"Of course!"

"I remember everything, especially the names of the freighters, the Durban Maru sunk off the coast of Madagascar and the Tricolor torpedoed by a German submarine just off Dakar. There were both carrying tea, some hundred tons I believe, all at your risk... shall I really?"

"Go on? Of course."

Our smiles did not leave our lips. Mine was forced, useless, stubborn; his was a laughter.

"How you avoided ruin is something I still wonder about. The F.T.C. demanded full payment for the merchandise for which you had only arranged a security guarantee, since Lloyd's refused insuring using international statutes in wartime as a pretext. The lawyer you gave the case to was a Jew and like a Jew was demanding fabulous fees. You thanked him and then waited like a Tuareg waiting for the rain. One day you told us that you had won the suit, and not only that, but that you also had the right to restitution for the percentage you'd lost from the F.T.C."

"You're forgetting the damages and interest, but go on."

"Afterwards you explained your maneuver to me. I only remember several points like the one about the annulation of the commercial treaties between France and Great Britain before Marshall Pétain came to power, and the fact that an English law still in effect only allows one deadline in a trial of an economic nature. Pardon me if I repeat to you I didn't understand very well."

"Of no importance. Go on."

"But I did recall this: all of our belongings had been seized, your buildings had been sealed and you had practically nothing left except the gold bracelets that Mother had given you with a tender gesture; you took them, and then you shook your head and said, with your eyes half closed: 'We're going to try to do something.' And what did you do? Six months later, we had this house, two trucks and your property in Aïn Diab . . . plus fifty to sixty million."

"Inexact: forty-eight."

"And the suit was underway."

"Right. But the moral of this long winded story, if you please?" His smile had become triumphant. I wiped mine away.

"The moral?"

That was why he was smiling and why he had interrogated me last. Why I had had my foresight in Murdoch Park. He had foreseen what I was going to say, and I knew what the result of my words would be. A new ruin in sight? Come on!

"The moral? You will win out again."

"Why, son?"

He pronounced these words softly, almost like a groan. I didn't answer. Several seconds went by and he cried out, "Why? For who and for what? For you the turncoat and intended patricide? For Camel the drunk? Or for the shifty others trembling over there? For that woman whose only capability is giving birth and saying yes lord? Of course we can turn things around. We have leather for skin and can bite through steel bars with our teeth, but who for? For all you waiting for me to die? What for? To come home to this house, to see this woman on her knees, she has finished her time and can only be down on her knees. If we have worked, is it for our son who premeditated our death with a knife big enough to cut down a tree? In the bathroom upstairs, one of the walls is used like a towel, a urine wiper. There are traces of every penis, from Camel to Hamid...And you, you who we thought were going to be our glory, who are you? Go for the knife, go for Ramadan, but your dream? It's to leave us and to forget all of us, quickly and completely, as soon as you're on your way...to hate us, to hate everything that's Muslim, everything that's Arab. Don't you know what happened to your old professor Abdejlil from the Guessous school? He is in Paris. He's become a Catholic and even a priest...Try to do better than that! And may Allah assist you! Maybe you'll be the Pope...or perhaps temporal matters interest you too much? A pair of boots, an officer's cap and a riding crop and you can stripe the backs of the NorthAfs, right?"

"No, father."

Who asked you? Or did you only speak to show me that you can still talk? So you have the last word? Do you know what the law permits?"

He paused. I didn't know.

"To kick you all out."

There was another pause. Silence is an opinion.

"Women can be purchased and children engendered. And if need be, we can pass new laws...But your punishment will be to stay here, every one of you and to go on with your turpitudes, your hatreds, your widowhoods, and your rages...you above all, Driss."

His smile had disappeared.

"Is there any need to sum up? You can do it yourselves. And we thank you for your sagacious suggestions, and particularly yours, Driss."

"Father . . ."

"Conversation terminated!"

He turned toward my mother.

"What have you prepared for us tonight, wife?"

"Soup and lentils, Lord. I thought I was doing the right thing, I tried everything, roasts, chicken, dishes go bad, the children are less and less hungry . . ."

"Fine. Serve us."

She disappeared. I got to my feet.

"If you will permit me . . ."

"Nothing is less certain . . ."

"If you will permit me, Father . . ."

He looked stupefied.

"Father?"

I was surprised by the question.

"Yes, Father."

"Well?"

"With your permission, I'm going upstairs to bed. I'm not at all hungry."

"On one condition, son."

Once more, the vicious cycle.

"I accept."

"Answer me this: is it because you've waited so long that you're no longer hungry? Or is it because you've decided not to fast after tomorrow?"

I barely reflected before answering frankly.

"Both, Father."

"All right. Go along."

He reminded me that I was in the patio.

"Take this barley bread."

I obeyed. The tagine of lentils steamed agreeably on the table.

"You may need it."

He added: "Or give it to the beggar."

He handed me the knife.

And his last sentence was: "Or wait until we've turned around again, who knows? Good night."

I opened the window wide. My room was sunk in shadow. I didn't want any light.

To breathe? To breathe what? The so-called pure air from outside, a nocturnal chill, the leavings of kitchens, a mixture of urines, of dew, of horse manure and of fresh cement, the refuse of markets, the putrid breath of the poor and here and there, like a fist blow in this semi-sleep, the barking of the beggar. But also, this house in front of me, this block of houses, this neighborhood, where other patriarchs identical to the Lord filled and slowly emptied the teapots. I carefully closed the shutters and was in the fundamental darkness.

The Thin Line, the Thin Line, I call out to you like a sleepless child would call a maternal lullaby.

I breathed in bread, animal, strong instincts, the hay of sentiments and words, my stomach contracted by twenty hours of fasting. "Whatever you do, whatever you are, you will be a puppet. Sometimes we intentionally forget you, and you take advantage of it to construct bridges, wings, chimerical dreams: then we stretch out a hand, give you a good shaking, and there you are a puppet again."

He had thoroughly frisked me tonight. Then he gave me the alms, the barley bread. I imagined his half-smile. "You'll find yourself in your room, you'll be decided and stubborn, and you will satisfy your stomach." I threw the bread somewhere into the shadows. I could still fast. Dawn would come soon, and the weight of a new dawn is considerable.

I stretched out *de cubitus* on my bed. Thin Line, Thin Line...

*The khalifa was a man of common sense. He looked at Old Man Abbou, at the wife, and then at the boy. His verdict...*

And if, precisely, that very evening, this new matter of the tea, had the Lord already resolved it?

*His verdict was a very simple one:*

*"You are both up in years. Go on your way in peace. I don't want to hear anything more about your monstrosities. As for the kid, I'll take care of him."*

But then why all of that stage setting, that inquisition, the final act left up in the air? A little play of the Lord?

*He surely did take very good care of him, better than either Old Man Joker or the Son of the Wind ever had done.*

And it is through the Thin Line that I escape. It fell into this room like a flash. Lord, look at your puppet.

Behind my eyes so desperately closed in my tension to go to sleep, it first is like a spider's web, such a slender thread and so impalpable that it is unreal. This thread is a letter, a number, or a broken line. It does not move, but I see it growing, oh so very slowly, so softly, so imperceptibly at the beginning. And, as it becomes more precise, as it grows, letter, broken line, or number are transformed into matter and move, swing back and forth, dance faster and faster. The Thin Line becomes as thick as a finger, bigger than an arm and takes on the look of the valve of a motor, the propeller of a plane, the trajectory of a rocket, becomes as enormous as a mountain, but keeping its shape of a number, a letter, or a broken line. And as the speed and the size of the Line attains its climax, its materiality now visible and palpable acquires a kind of sound, muffled at first and then clearer and clearer, then like the whistling of a bullet, as precise, as strong, as violent, as thundering as the noise of an auto's wheel on a tar road, on a paved highway, on a rocky road, to end up a gigantic clamor of a train going at full speed. And all of that is behind my eyes so desperately closed in my tension to go to sleep, inside my eyes congested with fear, in my brain completed deafened by this din, overwhelmed by this weight, chopped to pieces by this speed

Then the gamut of sounds descends a tone, then one more. And still another. The speed diminishes, the mountain becomes a block, the block a beam, the beam an arm, the arm a finger, and, once again, the broken line, letter, or number, behind my eyes so desperately closed in my tension to go to sleep, is no more than a Thin Line without sonority or movement, like the thread of a spider's web, a thread that is so thin, so impalpable that it seems unreal.

Then suddenly the Thin Line disappears and I find myself in my darkened room. The beggar calls on Saint Abd El Kader as witness to his hunger.

I turn on the light, open the window, pick up the bread and let it fall into the street. I close the window immediately.

"They have eyes, but they do not see. They have ears, but they do not hear." Gods of the Greeks and Russians, why am I not like them?

# 2. TRANSITION PERIOD

*Mehr Licht!*

THE DRIVER of the three-ton bus of the "line from Casablanca to Fez and vice versa, all loading, all speed, all prices" (I quote from their announcements) told me his name was Julius Caesar. Seeing my astonishment, he gave me the following explanation: "So? Just because I'm an Arab, does that mean I have to use some prefabricated name like Ali ben Couscous?"

I smiled. He showed me his Identity Card.

"Look here!"

There it was. Name: Caesar. Surname: Julius. Son of Mohamed ben Mohamed and of Yamna bent X. Born presumably in 1912 in the village of Aglagal, region of Demsira, tribe of Taskemt, legal control of Imi-N-tanoute, province of Marrakech, Morocco. Profession: bus driver. Nationality: citizen of the U.S.A.

"How did you get this?"

"The commander of the Circle, of course. He is one of those seasoned Colonials we should have in wholesale lots. Morocco for him is a land of adventure and mystery just as it was described by Pierre Loti and the Tharauds. He communes with the sun, lives on dates, roast lamb, and wears a turban—does a little poopoo, a little peepee, some outfits, stamp collecting, Tartarin de Tarascon and Robinson Crusoe, to such a point that the song-inventers from Beni Mellal to Jemaa el Fna make fun of him. Ha! They's used to watch guards. As far as I'm concerned, I knew that his principal goal was an Arab woman. I turned my sister over to him, and he gave me this Identity Card."

And as I went on staring at him: "And you, what's your name?"

"Driss Ferdi."

"The son of Hajji Fatmi?"

"Of Hajji Fatmi Ferdi."

"Shit!"

He spit on the windshield and pointed to my mother who was covered from head to toe except for her eyes and the tips of her fingers.

"Is that your sister, your wife, or your grandmother?"

"It's my mother."

He repeated "shit" and went over to tap a pair of meditative Shluhs on the shoulder—who then mounted onto the roof of the bus amid a pile of casks and a canoe. We took their seats, mother and I. Julius Caesar stepped over a heap of chickens tied claw to claw and turned around to look at his voyagers.

"Coreligionists, listen to me. Among you there may be cowards, pregnant women, cardiac cases, people subject to vomiting and diarrhea. Let them get off while there is still time and go to put themselves in the trusty hands of a French company of 'La Valena' that guarantee the safety of its passengers with a written receipt... Well?"

Not a soul moved.

"Perfect!" said Julius Caesar. "That ends the talk, so let this Chevrolet snort away like Old Man Adam. Because..."

He put on his cap.

"... either I'll get this machine to farting or it will kill us all."

And he took hold of the steering wheel.

"Ready?"

"Ready," cried the mechanic.

He slammed the door, and the bus took off in a cloud of smoke. My mother murmured through her veil of tulle, but I could not make out which saint she was dedicating her soul to. She closed her eyes and did not open them again.

Julius Caesar drove well. From the very first hundred yards, he scraped the sidewalk, scattered a crowd of Franciscans, ran over a Pekinese. Half lying down on his seat, he held the steering wheel between his thumb and index finger, with a sort of disdain, as he would have held a cigarette. Now and then he turned around to give me a smile. He possessed a citizenship that gave him the right to sweep everything before him, traditions, chains, in plain language. The road stretched before us, as dizzying as a river in flood, and he made a business of looking the sun straight in the face. His smile evoked in me the primitive philosophy of Ali Souda, one of my numerous cousins. Ali Souda was a shoemaker. He made a pair of babouches. Sold them. Closed his ship. Then three or four days of leisure, three or four days of rest, then he went back to work. Someone asked him: "Why don't you make two, six, twelve pairs of babouches? Then you could rest longer." He didn't answer as he did not understand. Ali Souda mastered work. For him, the first stage, if it was necessary, was equally sufficient.

Comparatively, I began to think about the Party of Allah. It was composed of imams and of merchants. Its purpose was to kick the French into the sea. The Prophet had told So-and-So who repeated to So-and-So . . . who engraved this precept on a sheep's shoulder blade. Irreparably, irrevocably, a fixed idea—like the animated cartoons of Walt Disney where the bear wants absolutely to smash Mickey's head. The first stage. After that, the deluge—or maybe even not.

Julius Caesar accelerated, turned, honked. Buildings, eucalyptus, pavement, everything sped by, hardly glimpsed. Across from me a Berber was reading a newspaper. The bus rattled on. My mother felt for my hand. I gave it to her. She held it tightly in her thin hands, as little as a bird's, a presence and a comfort to her. As a young woman, she had been cloistered. As a wife, the Lord had first put her under lock and key. Then she had become pregnant, seven times, one after the other. An open door had no further sense for her. Her last trip had been the one of her marriage.

Under her white haik, she had dressed in ceremonial clothes, tea-rose colored kaftan, a badia embroidered with silk and silver, a massive gold belt, babouches sewn with thread of gold and silver, and each of her wrists encircled with a dozen bracelets. She was going to Fez, but she had not put any perfume on: she was the Lord's wife.

In Fez she would knock her head against the tombstone of her late father, the saintly marabout. The Lord had explained her desire to do so. A few moments before the dawn prayer.

Even though her eyes were closed and her breast was rigid, I knew that she was upset. No other term would have fit so well as that of upset. This bus was taking her at full speed toward the city of her ancestors, the city she had left so long ago. So long ago that she had become resigned to cry no more, to beg no more to be permitted to go back just once before her death. For her it was like that Mecca that was the dream of a million believers. She was far from that house of cast cement, square, high, and white. And Julius Caesar's foot stamped on the pedal.

Joy? She could have shaken with joy, to the point of urinating. This air was another air, her fellow travelers existed, in front of her, behind her, beside her. How many houses had burst out of the earth since her last trip! And noises, lives, shudders, unknown things and people. She closed her eyes. Well! The Lord's hand suddenly would stretch out, and everything would be back where it was.

Julius Caesar was a demon, and this machine was infernal. Bats are nocturnal. But she accepted the following: an accident. The Koran is explicit: "He who perishes on a pilgrimage will be admitted automatically into the realms of heaven."

I said "amen" out loud, and Julius Caesar slammed on the brakes. We were in front of a roadblock for Transport Duties. The French sergeant who opened the door was half-asleep. An interpreter helped him. They were wearing bandoliers, one with a regulation pistol, the other a satchel. Behind them were some goumiers, Moroccans recruited by the French, armed with submachine guns, men called Zaërs that the Lord used on his farm for work for beasts of burden, men I've seen wipe themselves with a stone rather than paper.

I lowered the *Securit* window and filled my lungs with the dry hot air. A chorus of locusts deafened me. I stuck my head out and saw a Jeep, motorcycles lying side by side, motors still going, and a sentry box surmounted by the French tricolor.

"How many chickens," asked the interpreter.

"Twenty," said Julius Caesar.

He had taken off his cap and dusted it against the steering wheel. His eyes were malicious, with a touch of concern and a suggestion of menace.

"Too many," said the interpreter with a tone of reproach, "far too many. Taxes or an arrangement?"

"We'll see."

"Fine. How many passengers?"

"Sixty. Forty-two seated, the rest standing, plus the two Shluhs up there on the roof… and me."

"Too many," repeated the other, "a lot too many. Taxes or an arrangement?"

"We'll see," said Julius Caesar.

"Fine. And the casks?"

He rubbed his hands. Softly and methodically. He had once gotten a diploma, then he was named interpreter for the Transport Duties section. He had his place in the sun.

"Seven," replied Julius Caesar.

"And what's in them?"

"Powder."

The interpreter gave a start.

"For the Nationalists in Sebou," added Julius Caesar quietly.

And he handed his Identity Card to the sergeant, who examined it with care. Nothing could affect him in this blessed countryside.

"Go through," he said.

Julius Caesar put his cap back on, put the car into gear, shifted and hummed the *Marseillaise*. The Imperial Route opened before him. He wasn't born master, he became one. He mocked laws, goumiers, firearms. No one without a sister or daughter to sell could call him a procurer. He accelerated. Once he had been a jackal among jackals looking for a carcass. He had become a wolf, that's all, a wolf in the midst of a fat flock of lambs. What was morality?

The sun was wreathed with a white halo. The asphalt shone like a mirror, bordered with giant mulberry trees and the pitiless stretches of barley fields, with a single house, with a barrier, just reddish-brown congealed. Fearing I'd be impulsive, I looked away and began to look at my neighbor who was still reading his newspaper. He was young, his eyes riveted and his lips moving. There was something strange about it: unless he was a fakir, he could not be reading that newspaper.

I said to him, "Say there, brother, what's the news?"

He looked at me and gave a little cough, then he turned his attention back to his reading and moved his lips even faster.

"Same as every day, brother," he answered me. "You know how to read, do you?"

"No," I replied prudently.

"Too bad. You're dressed like a European . . . You know, things are going bad in England. Uncle Haj went to London accompanied by the Mufti of Jerusalem, Amin Husseïni. He and Hitler are like brothers. Well, they went to London to convert Churchill to the holy religion of Mohamed. That's as good a way as any to end this war. Then, it seems that when they return they's going to seriously look into the affairs of the Glaoui."

He communicated this information to me in some kind of extraordinary jargon. I listened to him politely and then stood up. All in all, he *could* read that newspaper. Julius Caesar smiled at me in the rearview mirror, I affectionately squeezed his shoulder.

"Tell me, if the son of Hajji Ferdi had need of you one day, would you help him?"

He almost missed a curve.

"Of course!" he said.

He added, "You can find me in the Bousbir one evening out of two."

He honked the horn a long time, even though the road was empty.

When I got back to my seat, I thanked the Berber and turned his newspaper right side up: he was *reading* it upside down. He made a ball of it and stuck it in his pocket looking very serious.

———

We were in Fez. From the Ftouh Gate to the section of the Adouls, there was two hours' walk. I turned my mother over to a muleteer who had no passenger. He lifted her up onto a donkey that was low in the legs and with a couple of kicks got the caravan on the way. I was delighted. I was alone. The sun was like a cloth around my head.

I don't like this city. It is my past, and I don't like my past. I have grown and evolved. Fez is dried up. That's all. All the same, I know that as I move into it, it grasps me and makes an entity of me, quanta, brick among bricks, lizard, dust—without my having to be conscious of it. Is it not the city of Lords?

A house, no matter what boutique, the corner of an alley, is a brutal spewing forth towards matter. It is not because Fez is timeworn or because the appurtenances of the machine age are barely percep-tible here, but because this city gives off, if I dare say so, an odor of sanctity that pervades the buildings, the mentality of the people and the atmosphere, a sanctity that has nothing to do with that of mon-asteries or pilgrimage spots, but made out of respect, of a passivity that one could have for a two-thousand year old hermitage. I know how it awakens, how it passes its days, how it falls asleep. It has an odor, a color, a tone all of its own. Even those who exile themselves from it keep these characteristics. Wasn't the Lord born here?

Moroccan cities know the monotonous change of beggars, above all at nightfall. At Fez, the beggars mill around. Their lamentations, however, are not the positive and demanding ones that they are in Casablanca. Those who ask for a piece of bread or a bowl of soup do so vaguely, and the names of the Lord or of the saint of the town add a note of gentleness and sadness to their song. The dawn chant is low toned: their throats, like the houses, are half-asleep. Courtesy is equally a characteristic of the poor, because at that early hour the only people who are up are those who go to work in the gardens of the suburbs, the children who are getting dressed to go to the Koranic school, and the servants. Artisans and owners of small businesses get up around nine to ten o'clock, the well-to-do of the middle classes, around noon.

The muezzins of numerous mosques don't succeed in drowning out the modulated calls of Moulay Idriss and of the Theological

University of Qarawiyyin. The cocks on the balconies crow, the ringdoves coo, the beggars weep softly, the donkeys hammer the stone torn from the earth, the fountains murmur and, here and there, at almost every street corner, ovens glow red in the black streets. At this hour, the city smells of earth sprinkled with the pungency of horse manure.

Soon the perfume of the poor will dominate, an odor of used clothes, old graying walls, and aging reeds covering the public squares. It will be mixed, depending on the neighborhood, with the sweet smells of hot bread and honey cakes, the sweat of crowds, the moldy odors of babouches and of the grocers' shops. But that perfume will dominate everywhere, whether it be in the Deggaguine where the little hammers and drills chisel copper or silver trays; in the Chrabliyine where beaters flatten leathers and where goat skins stretched out on the ground under the feet of passersby stink; in the Harrarine where the spinning wheels turn out multicolored silks; at the Ftouh Gate where businessmen wet their fingers as they count their money among the odors of olives and oils; at Bou Jeloud where the mints perfume the teapots in the Moorish cafes; in the homes where housewives knead bread and chase flies; in the mosques where the mats and the rugs have protected so many pious rear ends from humidity; in the shops of notaries where the powdered lime dries the scrawlings and illegible signatures; in the homes of passersby, charlatans, unemployed, sickly folk, porters, the potbellied, donkeys, public criers, the sellers of kif, and the fountains, everywhere.

The commercial streets and the public squares are alive with people. The crowds move slowly. The fever of the century has only stimulated the figures and audacities in heads; feet get in a hurry only in exceptional circumstances.

It is noon. The crowds have left me reeling, and I'm tired, famished, insomniac. "Hurry up," he goads me, "Your uncle is waiting for you, your mother's waiting for you, and here you are wandering about for a good hour. Ever since Julius Caesar unloaded you you've been wandering about. What zero are you headed for, what bile, what nausea? You call that exteriorizing, parenthesis, poem. Damned idiot, are you coming along with me?" I'll beat his brains out. What else is it but the voice of the Lord?

I imagine a camera focused a few centimeters from the ground: it would film a tranquil and almost silent swarm of snakes. Perhaps it's a couple of bare feet with stony heels in worn babouches: their owner is probably a grocer or a muleteer; stockings of heavy colored wool and babouches with thick rubber soles: perhaps belonging to a faqih to whom one gives a little tip or a plate of couscous for going to recite a couple of versicles over the tomb of the Dellaline or a tobacco merchant; the legs of a man sheathed in white silk and feet delicately lodged in babouches of quality, pale yellow or white, babouches that we call "of the doctor," revealing a notary, a businessman, an imam, an artist or a man at leisure; but there are also shoes, sandals, naïls and bare feet, the latter belonging to boys working at the ovens or to school dunces.

It is the hour, under the softened sunlight at its zenith, when some heads stand out over others, the hour when the mosques empty out after the noon-day prayer and the faithful go into the streets, then to their homes, where the nonbelievers and the malingerers have preceded them or will follow them. The shops, the public squares, the intersections, the markets, the streets, the alleyways, the dead-end streets, everywhere that the crowds have been, retain, from these hours of work, from these shoes, from these armpits and these heads, an odor as aged as the sands of the Sahara drinking in the setting sun. This perfume will rise from the shadows and from the sun-touched corners of walls, rooftops, the cupulas of saints' tombs and minarets, then, mixed with the encrustation of the facades and the sleepy interiors, it would be the same one that the pigeons flying from roof to roof would smell, if I could catch them and smell them, in that interval of time made for the siesta, beneficial for the needy as well as the businessmen, the former fatigued and trying to forget the next day in their sleep, the latter, snuggling down into a pile of cushions and asking, while their three or four wives dance and sing bare-footed, breasts bare, rump chastely covered, what new idiots he would have to pluck to put together the million necessary to have for himself the charms of the little thirteen-year-old expressly guaranteed a virgin. Hiha! Dreams predominate.

I was walking in the city. I was roving about, listening for clicks. Like a dog's life, I pushed the burden of civilization ahead of me, a burden I had not asked for, but of which I was proud. And I felt myself a stranger in this city from which I came. I threaded through streets and alleyways, ideas and visions. I accused every passerby, every stone. He was the one who would not dare throw a stone at me. It was the stone that he would not dare throw against me.

I did not belong to those people who would empty a container of gasoline on a tribe of Jews, as once happened, the awakening of medieval epics, and watch them be burned alive like living torches. Nor was I one of those who licked the dates from Medina and cultivated the cult of fossils. My father's name was Roche, my brothers were called Berrada, Lucien, and Tchitcho. My religion was rebellion, even against my mother whose glands I knew were dried up and whose monstrous tenderness I recognized.

I had shaken hands with Julius Caesar at Bab Ftouh a little before noon. He had turned his bus completely around, and I had penetrated into the mazes of Fez, six hours of walking, six hours of pseudo-freedom. Sometimes intentionally we forget you as we hold out our hand, etc... "Go," said the Lord, "go to Fez (the path to Damascus) you will accompany your mother. Her father is a holy man, a marabout. You..."

I walked until evening. An electric light went on. It vaguely lights up the little streets where I meander. The fountains and trickling of underground water make a lapping sound. The doors of the city have closed. Cats leap out of the dark, meow, and fly off like projectiles. Humidity has taken back its empire, the walls sweat, the doors drip, and the earth steams. A horse in a stable that serves as a haven for indigents snorts. I am sad, as if I had just taken a walk through a cemetery.

I bend double on the threshold of a doorway because I am very tall and the door is low. The corridor is dark, and mold from the walls and running water blossoms near a small enclosure: the toilet. I go through another door, and feel the sky and the dawn from on high. A small man with the head of an ascetic bows before me.

"Dark Christian, you wish? I have paid my taxes, I have no lice or fleas to declare, I don't get into politics, and everybody who lives in this house has been vaccinated many times against every illness in creation. Consequently…"

I help him straighten up.

"Don't you know me? I'm Driss."

He seems surprised and stretches out his hand to be kissed.

"It's quite possible," he said. "Since the treaty of the Protectorate was signed, anything is possible here below. Allah be praised!"

He turns towards a door some nine feet high. Majestically the panels of the door slam shut.

"We were worried about you. Come in, nephew, come in."


There are three of us seated around a table that holds a tagine and a hot loaf of bread. The faqih folds his hands in prayer and recites, "Praise be to Allah, King of the Universe, very Compassionate, very Merciful."

He is big, enormous. He has white teeth and a red face. My uncle's thumb makes a line of holes in the warm bread. That is the Moroccan way of cutting the bread. The holes steam. The guest goes on at a quicker pace.

"It is You we worship, and it is before You that we prostrate ourselves. Guide in the Path of Righteousness, the pathway of Your chosen ones and through which the damned by You can never pass."

Everyone says "Amen."

We take the lid off the tagine and put the lid under the table. Fingers plunge into the sauce, the chicken is broken up into bits, chewed, the bones crack, all in a few seconds. I satisfy myself by eating some bread dipped in the sauce and some olives that I dredge from the bottom of the plate.

"You're not eating anything, my child," says the saintly man. "Here take this: all children like this."

There is a danger looking into his eyes. I take what he offers me: the rooster's testicles.

I know him by name and by reputation: Si Kettani, crook. I didn't know he was a homosexual. Munching on what he had given me, I study him. Held by the skin of his neck and stooped in front of the Lord, he would take on the look of a cigarette lighter. A turn of the knurl: a flame. Which the Lord would snuff out after it was utilized. Then he would strip it down, fluid, wick, flint, and that would give an authentic coloring of rust.

I struck the cold metal. I was offensive and harsh.

"Si Kettani, excuse me..."

"Yes, my child."

He had picked up the plate with both hands and was lapping up the sauce.

"Among your prayers, you must certainly have one or two that you don't ask money for."

"But all prayers are free," he said, surprised, "for you, my child."

"Well then, reserve several for me. I need them."

He was licking his fingers. The tongue that he was using for it—I stress this intentionally—was as pointed and firm as a bull's organ.

Then he looked at me attentively.

"I am listening to you."

"In whose honor? I am only asking you to pray for me. Or do I have to pay you? I'm sorry to say I have no money."

"Please forget these words," breaks in my uncle. "I knew him when he came out of the cradle. He hasn't changed. He's nervous and antisocial."

"I can see that," says the faqih. "And I forgive him, but I still have to know what directions my prayers will take. You don't kill a dog because he's lame."

"I think I can give you the answer," says my uncle. "In a few days he's going to take his exams for his high school diploma, second part. His father sent him here to relax with us. I think he's acting like a good Muslim asking you to..."

"Very good, very good," the faqih concluded. "He can already consider himself the beneficiary of Allah's support. In fact . . . (he got up a bit from his seat and farted very loudly one time, "to your good health," said my uncle; "thank you" said the faqih, "that gas was grinding up my innards, and now it is gone, Allah be praised!") in fact . . . the diplomer . . . diplo . . . what's that called?"

"A high school diploma."

"What does that signify, a high school diploma?"

"Qualification to go to the university."

And since he still didn't seem to understand, I wickedly beat the still cold metal, desperately cold. With a thrust of my legs that table could be sent flying, with the plate he licked, that head of an ascetic, that red face . . . the discomfort that I could not throw off . . . where was the action? No matter what action? The end of the wick that would end up in an explosion? Thief. Donkey's groomer. Gravely injured. Senile. Minister or hangman. Yes, indeed! This villain with his showy strong appetites. His appetite for me. Thirty-six felons, I know nothing of that. But: "You will go to Fez. You will accompany your mother to Fez. Her father is a holy man, a marabout there. You . . ."

The Lord never stopped being polite. I was polite.

"Let's say that a diploma of this kind," I explained, "will have the same power and consideration as a faqih."

"Driss . . . Excuse him, Si Kettani."

"Let him speak. On the contrary!" said the faqih.

Every bit of benevolence had disappeared from his eyes. I looked there for a little shiver of desire. In vain. He really was a cigarette lighter.

"And," I added, "the elite of the future will all be people with a high school diploma."

"What about other people? What about us?"

I kept from smiling.

"The best I can say about it is that I don't know a damned thing."

"Driss . . ."

Then: "Excuse him, Si Kettani."

"No."

He realized that he had shouted. The result was a smile. His red beard pointed.

"No," he repeated.

And he turned towards me, all of him. Head, chest, seat, legs. He did so with the help of both hands, the left one his support on the mattress, and the right holding up his belly, like a woman with child.

"Continue, my child."

"Of course," I said.

The metal was red hot. Why this man whom I did not even know an hour before? Him rather than another? I don't like words. Why distress, stupidity, suffering, death? Take the words away and distress, stupidity, suffering, and death still exist.

"Of course," I say, "of course. I'll continue. My uncle is in agony, but I'll continue. You are my host, but so what? You are called Si Kettani, and so what? One of my classmates is the son of a general, which does not keep me from beating him in every subject in the program. Times have changed, Monsieur. Ten years ago I was here in the house of this man who is wringing his hands. Just look how he's wringing them. You know the saying: he who says hello converses and on leaving gets buggered? So, I was here. The Lord was in Mecca. Supposedly in Mecca. Because when he got back—in addition to a good kilo of dates from Medina, supposedly from Medina, and with a honorific title, supposedly honorific: *hadji*—he gratified us with the good news, namely that almost the whole of his fortune had vanished in Damascus. As a result of what miracle? You are a *hadji* yourself and no doubt can understand it. I was here. I was eight years old. I could finally begin to live, fill my lungs with air, laugh, cry, shit at ease, and until then a pure and simple dream, a furtive satisfaction, to masturbate just to commit an act that was not a dogma. Error! I was awakened at the crack of dawn, taken to a Koranic school, taken out of it in the dark of night, beaten again, first at school, then at my uncle's house, on the back of the neck, on the bottom of my feet, on my back, on my fingers, in the name of the Koran, for constipation, for lack of appetite, for a pain, for throwing up, a number of hands to be kissed, my aunt's in the morning, my uncle's both morning and evening, the hands of the faqih, of the *mokkadems*, of the *talebs* and hajjis that marked out my day. I got a slap on the head, for the glory of Allah! In the evening I kissed my mother's feet. For the glory of the Lord! Then I curled up on a pile of old cloth, dirty cloth, and that was my bed. I have killed, you know, I have killed great numbers of lice, and so I have that many crimes on my conscience. Like you and like me, lice are creatures of Allah, isn't that so Si Kettani? One day my uncle took me to bathe in the sulfur waters of Moulay Yacoub: scabies. Another day, a barber with a white goatee tied my arms behind my back, seated me on the sill of a window, and spread my legs: circumcision. The Lord came back carrying dates from Medina and his new title, and everything was consummated. This afternoon I was walking around Fez, recalling all of that, armed with my hateful past, ready to start whacking the first faqih who dared look me in the face. And, worse than a converted Jew, every stone, every shadow, every drop of manure in Fez made my nerves sing with emotion. So there..."

My legs lost their tension. The table flew against the wall.

"...that is why I speak to you, Si Kettani."

I refolded my legs under me.

"Secondly, you are a hajji, as is the Lord. Rich, as is the Lord, and powerful, sure of yourself, honorable and honored. As is he. I hate you."

They looked at me, Kettani stroking his red beard. My uncle slapping his hands. "Crazy equals Christian," he murmured, "He's become a Christian. Christian equals crazy, he is crazy..." I suddenly felt an infinite weariness.

"I hate you. Not you intrinsically, but at this moment I imagine that you are the Lord. And I am not even reciting a Koranic formula. That's it. I'll prop up the wall, it's about to fall down. If you only knew how drunk I am. I'm standing up to you, Lord, and I tell you: I hate you. You are ruined. I have no money. I'll become a thief, so I can give you alms. You, always, everywhere, you sound me out to my very marrow. And pity! I want a little shit of my own. Remember this morning. Get up. Get ready. You will accompany your mother to Fez.

She will pray to her father the marabout. He can save us. Be prepared, and you went off to sleep."

"Christian equals crazy..." The bony head had the swing of a pendulum. The other one: thick, immobile, waiting. They say that dogs perceive a strong emotion such as fear. I distinctly felt a diarrhea of violence.

"Here is a woman ... (I noticed the lowness of my voice, the fatigue of my bones, my hardened eyelids) a woman who has waited for forty years and who suddenly is to be satisfied. I went down. She was scouring a teapot carefully and tenderly. I don't know if you have ever cared for a sick child. I have. I took care of one, my little brother, Hamid. Well, you can believe me that it was with the same affection, the same tenderness, something with a sense of resignation, of shipwreck. Mother, we are going to leave. She put down the teapot, softly, tenderly. Yes, I want to. We waited, dressed, ready, impatient, patient, one hour, two hours. The sun rose. He was sleeping. We waited."

I was no longer in control of my ideas, that much I was aware of. I looked for the place where the table had landed and saw an oil lamp that an idiot butterfly was circling.

"He-had-not-given-us-any-money. It wasn't an oversight, a negligence. Intentional. Plow and sow, one day it will rain. Lord, you are a truly a lord. You were sleeping. We were waiting. Nonetheless, when you awakened, I can imagine your fury. We were far away, with your money."

I grabbed Si Kettani's hand and pressed it. It was fat, soft, and moist.

"But you aren't the Lord. His hand is thin, long, and hard, and that is why I rambled on. Yes, uncle, I am crazy, you are right. You can understand me. And so good night. I'm going to my mother."

I wanted to get up. The faqih's hand held me back.

"Among my servants," he said, "I have one whose exclusive function is to accompany me at 11:40 every morning to the place called the toilet so that he can clean my ass cleanly and quickly. Sit down, my child."

I obeyed.

"Another," he went on, "has the duty of crouching at my feet smiling: I blow the smoke of my cigarette into his face whenever I decide to have a smoke, because I don't smoke very often."

He talked on, gurgling as if his mouth were full of water, striking the syllables and hitting against the consonants. I saw his face: veinlets at the temples, the grimace, the zygomatic bones, everything relaxed. Only his word was hard. Speak so that I can see you! said a disciple of Antisthenes.

A brief instant, a bright interval, and then my fatigue weighed on me like a fog.

"I know," I said. "I know. Your references are litanies ever since twelve million Moroccans have murmured them. Why are you repeating them to me now? To impress me? I'm going to tell you a story. My older brother is named Camel. Several years ago he had a car-repair shop. Someone came in with a motor that wouldn't work. When the owner came back, Camel told him: 'It was sure time. The Delco was all screwed up, the contact points were done for, the spark plugs were no good, liners, valves, pistons were all done for. I had to take the whole motor apart, clean off the grease and solder it ... Now it's working, word of honor! Ten thousand francs, please.' The man paid without turning a hair. The truth of the matter, I assure you, was only that the jet in the carburetor was stopped up."

He stretched out his arm, perhaps to take over the conversation again, perhaps also to give me a whack. I grabbed it in midair.

"Will you ..."

"No," I cried. "No use. What do you want to tell me? That you are a homosexual? I know that. Or how you became the imam of the Cherifian schools? Everybody knows all of that. One morning you wrapped yourself in an almost white sheet and went from door to door, from one street corner to another, from one mosque to another, shouting that you had seen the Prophet discuss the world situation with Franklin Delano Roosevelt in a dream. You were given a *zaouïa* where you suddenly retired and a substantial pension that you accepted with the disdain of the vanities of this world. Then you had other dreams that were quickly blessed by specific donations, notably the office of jurisconsultant and a Cadillac. The Residence named you counsellor general of Makhzen, and everybody in Fez society wanted you as a guest. You are at my uncle's house tonight—I don't know why—and you have done honor to his chicken with your thirty-two teeth, twelve of them in gold. As for the ill humor I have subjected you to for over an hour now, I beg of you to consider it a confidence: sometimes one confides in an enemy; you aren't my enemy. Even less: a stranger. So?"

"Who is this young man?"

The oil lamp was of wrought iron. Someone had painted half of it, probably to use up the rest of a can of paint. The butterfly had disappeared.

"I don't recognize him anymore," said my uncle hastily, "I don't recognize him..."

He bleated like a wife accepting her husband out of duty. He had crouched down, armpits on his knees and kissed the faqih's hands intermittently, kiss, several syllables, kiss...Little devil, just look at what your good-for-nothing tongue has done. The room was decorated with pouffes, silks, rugs, wall hangings, bas-reliefs of wood, golds, and gilt, the ceiling dark with small joists from which hung chandeliers that were dark but which reflected light from every crystal, as did the green and red tiling of the walls. The tall heavy door was fitted with immense locks. I thought of Julius Caesar's American boot stepping on the accelerator.

"Don't make me repeat myself. Who is he?"

"My nephew, Master, just my nephew. Just look..."

"Imbecile! I'm asking his name."

"Driss Ferdi, the son of my wife's sister, and so..."

"Hajji Fatmi?"

"You know my brother-in-law?"

"Imbecile!"

And before my very self I had a sudden transformation. In spite of my Western education, I still lived, acted, and judged by parables, just like the public storytellers that install themselves on a street corner, furnished for any and everything with an empty stomach and their fatalism, but in whom the smallest offering, the lightest laughter, the least gesture triggers a spurt of stories, that they embellish, interrupt, or adapt to the measure of any and everyone at the risk of controversy or a skeptical silence.

The sudden crawling of this man made me think of my chemistry manuals: acids on bases, exothermy and salts, brutal reactions and consequently not very moving. "A sedentary being like you attracts violence," said Roche, "the way the most common cloth are those that represent the eternal snows in the hot countries."

I let my hand be held, my foot be held, my knee be patted. And in the accumulation of sentiments that shook me it could be discerned, first of all, a ludicrous pity: the enormous belly of Kettani, flattened out in such a way, must have made him suffer. Could it have been for that reason that he groaned like a Jewish mourner?

"...never would have come to mind that I was speaking to ..."

The accumulation became more precise, a panorama of ensemble, fragmentation, regrouping. I read somewhere that an expedition to the South Pole discovered a dog that had been left behind thirty years earlier, and that it was surprisingly well preserved, having frozen standing straight up. I am able, as I look at my uncle, and with all due respect, to establish such a connection. I went back over the conversation: what was the last word he pronounced to give his mouth such a shape?

"...of great notoriety...your honored father...to such a point that..."

The accumulation was: pride in being the son of the Lord, fatigue and fury at recognizing the leprous-sovereignty of the Lord, rejoicing in this transcendent, even prismatic proternation, and the excesses of logomachia, of senses and violences, from which came the notion of an energy that I had expended to transform it into action and which ended up glorifying the Lord. And over and beyond that, the call to euphoria, may everything whirl around and be drowned and drown me: Pity! I had not stopped being lucid for hours and hours. A moribund: the more moribund he becomes, the more his sexual appetite is whetted.

"My honored father? How you see it. As far as I'm concerned, he hasn't changed. He has nerves of steel, an authority of steel, an expression of steel. The sun that sees that steel reduced to rust will never shine: stainless, that steel. Look, Si Kettani, look: he is the person who has determined our present attitudes, independent of either you or me. Even though you are not accustomed to playing the reptile, and I don't like reptiles."

I paused for a moment and took a breath. The air was lukewarm with an odor of old leather, the contours of the chicken, and the crackling oil. Where was the perfume of the poor common to every home in Fez? Then I stuck in the other nail.

"But as far as he's concerned, him, listen to this shocker: he is ruined."

He was shocked. He got up with difficulty, and lowered his skinny buttocks like a hen about to lay an egg. I surveyed the stomach that pitched and rolled and took on the look again of a wineskin half full. I pressed my index finger against my uncle's breastbone.

"Completely ruined," I yelled.

My uncle fell to his knees.

"Shut up!"

He closed his mouth and swallowed his saliva. I leaned over a bit: such an emaciated head must have a big Adam's apple. I rubbed my hands: I was right.

"You have recovered your self-assurance," I said. "That's logical. How could things be otherwise? One jackal less, and the rest of the jackals become more ferocious."

I had not seen this basin when I came in . The patio was dark then, and the sky was already a twilight sky. It should only have been in marble, either black or white or green, in the style of Moulay Ismaël, that senile castrated old fool that History has dug up and compares with Louis XIV. But come on now! Morocco is almost modernized. It has to have titles and nobility. A wager, Roche told me. As for the water fountain, has it ever stopped up and disappeared? I don't think so. One day someone said to it: "Here is your jet, here is your water, you will pass that water back through the jet, you will struggle up a slope twelve feet and four inches in the direction of Allah, and then you will fall down and spread yourself about in this basin, and now, weave time."

It had woven time. And why not?

"So," I said again, "he is ruined. It's a story about tea that is rather complicated. I won't try to tell it to you now as I am very sleepy. A little while ago, I asked you for some free prayers from your repertoire. They are for him. One more stone, more or less, in the ocean, and the ocean won't be full because of it. Like the dead man who lies in a catafalque that has been stained with walnut oil because it's just simple pine, whom I have never seen or known. His name was pronounced this morning at the hour that a descendant of Ishmael could not distinguish . . . yeh . . . I must go to invoke him, one stone more or less in the ocean. He's a saint, number 2740 in the catalogue. I have questioned my mother. She knows nothing, she never saw him. Like some kind of blind, deaf, and dumb person, reduced, said the Lord, in his old days to the state of one of those broken toys that a child still carries under his arm. He was slowly dying in a straw covering, a former *taleb*, a former *mokkadem*, a former human being. With the help of a cord and a pulley, he was lowered twice a day, to let him do his ablutions in the morning and to give him his porridge and read him a chapter of the Koran in the evening, as was always his habit. Then, bam! The cord was pulled, the basket went back up toward the shadows and the cobwebs, and the cord was reattached to a button on the door. He was canonized, I don't know why, and has his mausoleum and his faithful. I'll go pray to him."

I beat the air with my arms. If there was another fountain in this place, it ought to be me.

"I think I've told the essentials, but the abscess is far from empty. I clean it out for good one day. Tonight I've tried, but I couldn't, excuse me. So, Si Kettani?"

"So what?"

I knew the game. You take some dry figs, then you flatten them out, pierce them, and string them on a plait of palm. The son of a douar takes the necklace and hurries off to sell it. Now, at that very moment, there is always someone who remembers it: add that fig, I have forgotten it. Days and nights go by, and by way of figs, it is finally a cartload that takes the road to the marketplace. Si Kettani had his fig to add.

"So," I said, "I know the game. You take some dried figs, then you flatten them out, pierce them, and string them on plait of palm. The son of a douar takes the necklace and hastens to go sell it. Now, at that moment, there is always someone who remembers it: add that fig, I have forgotten it. Of what does yours consist, if you please?"

He decided to smile.

"In my soul and conscience," he said, "I can only give up. You are a boy who deserves to be beaten like a donkey, or to be dearly loved."

I collapsed on the rug, as thick as a mattress, ready to go to sleep.

"Would you hesitate?"

"No," he said with a sigh, "Between you and me, the relationship is formal: to be dearly loved, my child, to be dearly loved."

You said it, old bloat.


Late in the evening, the bloat gave us a reading of the act. Nothing had prepared me for it. I awakened. Had I really gone to sleep?

I asked some questions and, by reassembly, I learned that my aunt Kenza was waiting in a neighboring room, still with her veil on and her feet on a bundle of rags. She must have been conversing with my mother, as only two Moroccan women can converse, vertiginously. Annihilating the high and intelligible voice of Si Kettani, I turned an ear, but could only hear the murmuring of the fountain. They must have contented themselves with gestures.

I understood very well. The night before, Kenza served a bowl of soup. That soup was cold. My uncle does not like cold soup. Consequently, he picked up his babouches and went to knock on the door of his neighbor the notary. Kenza was repudiated. An act in good and due form.

Neither simple nor simplistic. One screws or one farts and evil to him who judges. A natural function!

This evening, Kenza was once more the legitimate spouse of my uncle "by means of a new act, that of the annulling of the previous act and by the theological, moral, social, and human possibility, accorded and blessed to resume marital contact with the aforenamed Kenza Zwitten, who had strayed, as so often happens in this poor world, in her sacred duties, who on her part had quickly regretted this error in her ways and who promised—the husband having certified under oath, all ablutions carried out, on the blessed leather of the sixty chapters of the Holy Koran—to maintain to the very end of her days, Allah permitting, the soup judiciously hot until the arrival of her lord and master, and may Allah bless him for having had such ease and rapidity in his pardon, amen! Levied for the price of the stamp, purchase of stamped paper and the costs of registration the sum of francs: III. Affixed at the bottom of this act the date of the twenty-fifth of Ramadan the fingerprint of the applicant.

|  |  |
|---|---|
| The *adel* | The assistant *adel* |
| SI KETTANI | illegible signature |
|  | Followed by the seal of the *Cadi* |
|  | *Praise be to Allah!* |
|  | *Amen"* |

Si Kettani handed the act over to my uncle and got up. Putting on his babouches, he asked for five hundred francs. He had had to insist with the qadi, who was in bed with a fever. A servant had mislaid a grain of wheat in the qadi's bed. That grain was enough: the qadi had a fever. I hold back from invalidating: for a long time, the qadi, a famed philosopher, had confided a copy of his seal to every *adel* or every pseudo-*adel*. As for his signature, it was rigorously illegible.

But, if my uncle judged it good, he should turn over a sack of pitted olives or a remnant of Italian serge. I translate: throw me some barley bread, a coin, or a chicken leg. Of course, none of that had any importance. We shared the dishes and conversed with the mouth of a friend to a trusted ear.

My uncle got up in turn and gave him four hundred francs. I saw the gesture. Sharp.

I asked: "And the servant woman, Si Kettani?"

He looked at me for quite a while, a small mouth, downy cheeks, ringlets of hair like a Greek ephebe's, damned blockhead . . . if you weren't Ferdi's son . . .

"Three hundred lashes at daybreak, on the left breast and the right buttock, face down, in Moulay Driss Square. Then she was taken back into the qadi her master's household and placed under the orders of a slave woman of a lower rank."

He held his hand out to me. There are sweatinesses that are the expression of a quiet cruelty.

"Come to see me one of these days. I'd like to see you again. Promise?"

I barely hesitated.

"I am potent," I said.

"And so?"

"I don't like old men," I said.

He crushed my hand.

"And so?" he repeated. "For an untamed and charming young man like you, an old man like me keeps a throne in reserve. Goodbye, my child."

I shoved him rudely and closed three doors behind him.

Then I rubbed my hands together. And after these gentlemen! American novelists have taught me facility. The elephant did not break much in the china shop. He gets a piece of cake.

Once back in the patio, I lit a match.

"Not only have you become a Christian," cried my uncle, "and act like a lout, now you're smoking?"

I don't know by what singular accident of projection, but my uncle's silhouette took the form of a half-moon on the wall. "The night will be total, and the bones of the earth will groan, and the crescent will appear as an avenger above your heads, impious people" so spoke the shepherd of Koreïch. I broke the match in two before letting it drop.

"Perfect," I said. "Do you have some tobacco?"

The basin was of white marble, the water a dull blue-green, and the spray itself the color and rigor of a commandment from Allah. My stupor vanished like a mist.

My uncle trotted ahead of me barefooted. A corridor, an angle, a door whose bolt he unlocked. A diffuse light could be seen.

"You will fry yourself some eggs," said my uncle. "Only the feet of the chicken are left. Then you will watch out for things. I'm going to the mosque. There are too many sins in the day of an honest man."

His hands fitted into his babouches as in a pair of mittens. When he lowered his hands, the babouches fell with the same and unique dry bang.

"I'll be back within an hour, God willing, and I may need a bowl of soup, Kenza."

He put on his shoes and trotted off, gentle and aged. The shadows gobbled him up. "The night will be total, and those who have only half believed will melt into nothingness there," so spoke the shepherd. I went inside. Two women in tears were embracing. Kenza was a wife once more.

Her pile of rags was there. I pushed them with a couple of kicks: rags, casseroles, a mattress, a stool, a woman's belongings. The fittings were as follows: a low ceiling, two mattresses, a mat, dust, two candles, one of them on an upturned bowl and the other on the floor (I am wrong: on a newspaper, a commendable precaution), stale hot air, plaster at the base of the walls, the women's room.

"I know," I said, answering to an exclamation of astonishment, "I resemble a Christian, even if I take off these clothes. As for my character, more than Christian: a Persian carpet in an igloo. With that said, my greetings, aunt."

I went over to give her a kiss on her forehead. She stretched her hand out to me.

"Go on with your exchange of your memories and impressions, please. Don't worry about me. Mother, tell her how we were able to leave. I'm going to stretch out on this coconut matting and will soon be asleep."

It took a little while, nevertheless, the time to get some sense from their lips.

They were there, mother and aunt, talking a great deal, each in turn, gesticulating together, and their lips lied.

Every time I could, I examined the lips of women. I have a mnemonic of them, a soporific and a source of amusement, but until this evening the marital blinds hid the faces of women, and I am not interested in girls, as far as I know... my mother, *mea culpa!* My collection only consisted of lips of European women. And so...

I have seen mouths turned downwards in mindlessness, shapeless with sensuality. I have seen wrinkles of distress, of irony, and of ferocity. I have seen lips without lines, a unity, full, impersonal but revealing their secrets because they were painted rose or scarlet, from dry to oily, a line like a flower, thickened, thinned down, designed with artfulness, smeared on in haste, lips of a spinster despite a ring on her finger, lips surprisingly young in the middle of parchment, sarcastic lips, ready for anything, even to telling the truth, venal lips, disgusting with bestiality and calumny, tight-closed on an enigma or some suffering, made tense by vexation, by envy, by cancer, twisted by hepatic symptoms or in closed smile, commercial, circumstantial, low, open over white teeth, rotten, equal, unequal, on a denture, on a game of piano keys, on a mixture of gold, of lead, of platina and of ivory, or quite simply on gums without teeth. I have seen lips that were always open, breathing in place of nostrils a mixture of oxygen and nitrogen, from coquetry and cupidity, from astonishment and from passivity, from a smile or from boredom, from apathy and from hope.

Disagreeable lips, agreeable lips, lips that leave you indifferent, lips swollen with life and that incite you to bite them to punish them, provoking, insensitive to our whispers and to our bitings; innocent lips, with or without rouge, beautiful even in their irregularity, so sweet despite their lack of harmony, so charming that a kiss would soil them and on which a dream floats, and on which our caress, as smooth as their velvetness, passes. Lips of old women, of adolescents, of concierges, of saleswomen, of whores and of average wives, they all had my attention, and I know many that are unforgettable. They are the lips of European women, of French women, which is to say, Parisians. They have a right to the cream of civilization. The men's lips that place themselves on them kiss the apogee of a refined scientific industry.

Sic.

I went to sleep.

Pursued by your lips, mother and aunt, your lips that have whispered, shaken, kissed, sucked, calumnied and prayed, fervent and sealed by heat and shadow and silence, smiles, laughter, sobs, credulous and faithful, atavistic and resigned, then became wrinkled.

Someday someone will close them as they will close your eyes, typhus or extreme old age, and will act like smashing open doors.

Once you were nubile, and afterwards you have never stopped being dead.


That night I did not see the thin line. Early in the morning I called it, in vain. But when evening came . . .

I went out carrying a green rug, dressed in a jellaba and with a fez on my head.

"The twenty-seventh night is the night of revolution," my uncle had told me.

"A night of faith," added Kenza.

"The Night of Power," said my mother.

She was licking a date, the last of a couple of pounds of dates that the Lord had brought from Medina. They both asked at the same time, "Where are you going?"

"I don't know," I said, "to roam around, to stroll, to smoke and drink in a tavern. Maybe go into a mosque and in that case, pray who will. Father's business matters are still to be reckoned with, don't forget."

It was the Night of Power. An ulema of the Qarawiyyin had lit a candle of virgin wax, and forty minarets had lighted up, streaming with blue, yellow, red, and green bulbs, forty gullets had cried out the call of the faithful, the contents of shops suddenly emptied into the streets, markets and herds perfumed with sandalwood and incense, and those who did not believe believed, those who trailed behind walked, firecrackers and Bengal lights shot up, transformed into wood fires over which young girls and old women jumped, jumped the way one jumps rope, holding each other by the hand or in circles, young ones and old ones and not a one remembering that she was hungry or thirsty, cold, hot, distressed, uncomfortable, and that this young girl and that one there would grow old, toothless, worn thin, smelling of dung, of cloves, of urine, and the beggars whose numbers were enlarged by those who would join their ranks tomorrow and who dove into the crowds like a drill, porters of straw baskets made out of palm fiber, sacks of jute where normally Islamic charity ought to manifest itself in hard coins, but where only worm-eaten figs, pieces of nut, rags, the sticky bottom of casseroles, old shoes, worn clothes, come back next year, twenty of your brothers have already passed by, temporal sequences: these hands with their white tendons and violet hollows between the tendons, nervous and haggard, receive a chunk of bread and then are transformed, worthy of a dyne or of human warmth, going to take the chunk of bread to another beggar, one who has no bread and has only stumps or a legless cripple attached to a block of stone for fear he'll be overwhelmed by a fantasy to roll over like a keg or get lost like a child in this cataclysm of noises and lives; sequences also in this pair of eyes of a chlorotic hoodlum where overexcitements, lights and noises plant themselves and graft themselves, eyes that he closes as my mother did hers in the bus of Julius Caesar and asks himself if it is not a question of all the creatures of Hell that Allah, on lighting the candle of virgin wax, has let them loose so that they can fraternize with angels this Night of Power.

A philosopher had taken out his mattress and installed himself in the middle of the street. The crowds stepped over him, and he-and she-mules had to detour around him. I came to a stop.

"Move over a bit."

I stretched out beside him. He filled a Flemish pipe with green tobacco, and we had long drags on it, consecutively, in silence, islets in a sea of fury. Up above our heads, the starry night was an abyss.

Under a great doorway, a Bambara from Black Africa was counting the beads of his rosary, his temples covered with ringworm, his eyes closed in blindness. A radio was his seat, which could certainly howl at full force, like the light of a candle in full sunlight: I could only see it vibrate. At his feet a slender turtledove on a sprig of barley, so frightened that its wings were between two decisions, half-folded. The Bambara was singing. I couldn't hear him, but his lips had the flux and flow of the ocean, no doubt one of those chants to glory from those who enslaved the Bambaras. I lifted a rigid finger, lifted his eyelids. He stopped singing and went on telling his beads, staring at me fixedly with his eyes whitened by cataracts.

"Yessir," I said.

And off I went to mix with the crowd, that lifted me up, carried me, pirouetted me, that smelled of sweat, woo, crying, singing, complaining, compact, one movement, one energy, in which an American soldier, ex-soldier, ex-American, come there as a tourist and who had been undressed, unshoed, assaulted, still standing, and whose apoplectic face I saw in a Dantesque vision. He said he didn't know what it was all about, someone cried into my ear, and slipped a potato into my hand, but the American had already foundered, I don't know when, I don't know where. I succeeded in placing the tuber into the open mouth of someone who was calling Allah, whirled, swirled, compressed, already drunk, and perhaps, like a mechanical steering wheel that continues its rotation even when the current has been turned off, stupefied in a sudden emptiness, suddenly gratified, for a long, long time, as the mass slowed down, stopped, dispersed. I was in front of a red and green matting stretched out on some large paving stones. I still had my prayer rug under my arm. As earlier, the starry night and the silence were an abyss.

I moved forward, my shoes in my hand, along the matting. Some groups in the darkness gesticulated quietly. The air was cooler, almost cold. I avoided some columns, passed under some vaults and arcades, and under oscillating lanterns. I stepped on paving stones and on rugs. People passed by me, furtively, crouched down, became denser, seated in rows with their arms crossed and their heads nodding. I kept on walking as a voice came to me, a voice towards which all of these beings were stretched.

You are perhaps five thousand, perhaps ten, perhaps two, the certainty belongs only to Allah, and I can only say: perhaps. Perhaps because this Saint Driss Mosque where I speak to you and you listen to me, when it is full, I could say: we are thirty thousand. And I repeat to you, Allah alone knows what you have in your hand and what you hide behind you. Now, my brothers, think: think of the forty mosques of Fez, of all the mosques of the Empire, of those that are in other states, in every corner of the world. You know Algeria, you have heard Egypt spoken of, and most of you have not even asked yourselves where Pakistan is found. The latter, no doubt, are the wisest: either here or there, one of the faithful is one of the faithful. Consequently, soon the muezzins of Fez will give the call of the night. You know it or you do not know it, that from one country to the other, from one continent to another continent, there are differences in time, but at any rate this night all of the Muslims of the earth will pray. Now, what if I told you that there are five hundred million Muslims in the World?"

He took off his jellaba, and threw it an arm's full length. Without needing to turn around, I felt the panting of the human mass behind me. Even I was getting feverish. I had gone up to the first row. I went beyond it, let my green rug fall, fell down on it very close to Si Kettani, almost at his feet. He did not even look at me. I put my babouches down very gently.

"Half a billion," he went on, "you businessmen, salary earners, idlers, those with private incomes, unemployed workers, you disabled, you are used to the obligatory conversion of everything into terms of money, and a half billion francs represent a thousand years of work, a telephone call, or a state budget for you. You give weight to it: several kilograms; a utility: a villa, car, women . . . and a sense: I desire, I pay; I am the King of Kings, king of eaters, king of sleepers, you know the series. So, five hundred million men, what do you say to that?"

He threw down his tarboosh and stepped on it. The puffs of breath rose to break against the dark vaults of shadow.

"Five hundred million men who have the same God that I do, and are instructed in the Koran as are you, and who, like those after the Battle of Poitiers are dead like you and me. Five hundred million men turning toward the Black Stone of Mecca awaken tonight and once more have balls and brains. Because this is the Night of Power, because until dawn, Power belongs to every one of you, and not only to you, but to all the reigns of creation, hyenas, grasshoppers, rocks, the sands of the shore, and to all the demons of hell as to the angels in heaven. In a few moments, the muezzin in his minaret will cry out. I know him. I got his job for him. He was a gravedigger before, and he didn't like that work. I tell you that soon that muezzin will cry out to the four winds, and he will be the first to have the Power. Then we will all get up..."

The chant of the muezzin began.

"...and each one of us, however little he knows of the Koran, will come to lead the prayer. And so..."

We got to our feet. The swell that was released indicated to me that the mosque was totally full.

"And so...and so...a little silence," roared Si Kettani..."and so in my capacity as descendant of Mohamed, as *cherif*, as a religious leader and the commander of *zaouïa*, the religious center, I am going to begin."

He turned toward the alcove reserved for the imams and faced the wall.

"In the Name of Allah, the Compassionate, the Merciful..."

Thirty thousand voices repeated: "In the Name of Allah, the Compassionate, the Merciful..."

And the Thin Line took hold of me.

I recalled the teachings of Raymond Roche: "An object will not be an object until the day that it is given a fitting name and a definite use. The Thin Line bothers you? Try to define it. Above all, do not explain one abstraction by another abstraction. You'll become an abstraction yourself."

Listen, Monsieur Roche. One day a man said to me—because my father employed him as a farm worker at thirty francs a day, because that particular day at the farm I was basking in the sun and was watching him sweat, I had never spoken to him, I did not know him, you have been in Morocco long enough not to be unaware of the brutal jealousies and envies—that man stuck his spade into the ground that he was turning over and asked me in a hoarse voice I can still recall, "Can you make a needle?"

"A sewing needle? (He shook his head in affirmation.) Of course! Give me the steel, a spinner, a drill, in other words the raw material and the necessary materials.

The man smiled: "None of that," he said. "If I got you what you are asking for, where would the creation be? So you can't make a needle."

I understood, Monsieur Roche.

That the Thin Line appear here in this mosque constitutes a datum. This twenty-seventh night is another, the state of my soul, a third one. It released itself sooner or later, and I probably understood nothing.

Kettani no longer had a stomach. I could only see his back. Even had I seen him face to face, he would not have had a stomach. He was no longer ugly, he was no longer bestial. He recited in a high voice and chanted versets from the chapter of the Throne. Here and there a saint, or the Prophet, or the eternal were mentioned. And the whole mosque stirred restlessly in the undertow of choruses and of fervors: "May Allah bless and honor him!" or "Glory be to Allah!"

I should have enjoyed a normal balance. The Lord had sent me to Fez? Here I am. So that I could evoke a holy man, a marabout? Very good. I closed my eyes: "Marabout, no matter which one, I invoke you. My father is ruined. Do something." I opened my eyes again. I had not ceased to be shaken by the Thin Line.

The Thin Line is clear at present. Everything got misty in front of my eyes so that it would be clear. It said to me: you are a black. You are a black from generations back, crossed with white. You are about *to cross the line*. To lose your last drop of authentic black blood. Your facial angle opened up, and you are no longer woolly-haired or thick-lipped. You were the issue of the Orient, and through your painful past, your imaginings, your education, you are going to triumph over the Orient. You have never believed in Allah. You know how to dissect the legends, you think in French, you are a reader of Voltaire and an admirer of Kant. Only the Occidental world for which you are destined seems to you to be sewn with stupidities and ugliness you are fleeing from. Moreover, you feel that it is a hostile world. It is not going to accept you right away, and, at the point of exchanging the box seat you now occupy for a jump seat, you have some setbacks. That is why I appear to you. Since the very first day I appeared to you, you are nothing but an open wound.

But no! I turned to Kettani and tapped him on the shoulder: "May I?" There was certainly everything that the Thin Line could signify, but there was also my high-pitched sensitivity to a dead rat or a Chinese poem, so high-pitched that Roche compared me to a bagpipe.

If earlier in the crowds and the lights and the noises I had been able to find enjoyment, what was there to sanction? My emotionalism. Yes, sunsets, the rising of the moon, winds, storms, heavy thick heats of August, I was still receptive to all of that, and that prepubescent base of first joys still lived on in me, something that no reading, no suffering, no dogma had succeeded in snuffing out in me.

Si Kettani whirled around. Starting to sing the overture to the chapter *H hard M*, I entered into the *mehreb*. The Thin Line entered with me.

"*H hard M*!"

"And these are the verses of the Book:"

"We have chosen an easy lesson so that you will understand;"

"For Us the importance of it is great, and the field vast."

"Is it necessary in passing to remind you that if you are a people without a goal with spiritual content, how often in past times have I sent prophets to you?"

"And with the coming of each prophet, he has found always that a mocking public awaited him."

"On those peoples We have caused calamities to fall, and the example of other times has disappeared..."

Yes, Allah Mine, You speak truth. You see I still accept You. You speak through Your "legate," of whom I hear that he is honest and good. You find the necessary words and even when You thunder out Your maledictions or detail for us the punishments of the Last Judgment, You explain Yourself in incantatory rhythms. You see, Allah Mine, Hajji Fatmi Ferdi taught me to love You, in fear for the body and the desolation of the soul. He applied Your law, to a woman whom he has tortured, tortured so thoroughly, serious, punctual, worthy, that, without this torture, she would fall into dust. To sons that he tied up and bound, cut up, and crushed, duty and honor, he says ... I still love You. And so, although from You to me, from You who determine for me what is determined, a prayer would be useless, cause me to love You for a long time still.

These versets that I chant in Your house and in the ears of Your faithful, I say them as of spasmodic flesh, because—but it would be derisory to explain to You anything whatsoever, to You who know all, even what escapes us—because You ought to be something else than the Allah of the Koranic school and shackles. I repeat to You that I am shackled. Blinders, bridle, gee up, stop, start up, there's the manger trough, here's your trough. I said: good. Why not? Starting from nothing, it is quite possible to make a sewing needle.

"If you ask a son of Adam: who created the heaven and earth? he will answer you: He who created them is the Supreme Being."

"He who, by His will, caused the water to fall from the sky, water that We have utilized to make fertile the sterile earth    thus did you come out of the earth—"

Someone nudged me with an elbow. What's the matter? I'm not through ... thank you ... I took the blue paper ...

"He who for the male the female, for the female the male, universally has created ..."

"I have searched for you in fourteen mosques, your mother is half dead with fear ... I don't know how to read ..."

"And to spare you effort has provided you with the felucca and the beast of burden for your travels."

"Thus can you, from the security of your mounts, thank the Lord!"

I keep quiet.

Behind me there was silence, to such an extent that I could have thought I was all alone in that immense mosque. I turned around. My uncle was looking at me. There was something like sadness in his eyes.

I could hear myself swallow my own saliva. The paper I held in my hand was a telegram.

Rows of heads were looking at me. I could make out the details of some of them, a swollen head, a *hirsute head*, a minuscule head ... three pairs of eyes surprisingly staring. Si Kettani had disappeared. So had the Thin Line.

I opened the telegram and read it. I reread it. The strange thing was that neither the amazement nor the pain bore into me. I can still remember how a whole network of chills in undulating waves rose from my left leg into the left half of my skull, then the left half of my face, and the left side of my chest. Action had begun.

"I'm going on," I cried. "And from the security of our mounts, we will not thank the Lord. Why should we? Does He have need of anything? ... Pardon?"

The third disappearance was that of my uncle. Oh my ear, you have heard nothing. Without a doubt.

"You say? ... Gentlemen, no; I am not a blasphemer ... Nor a Communist. My name is Driss, son of Hajji Fatmi Ferdi and the grandson of Omar Zwitten. You know both of them. One is a tea merchant and the other is a marabout. That does not keep me from saying that since it is the Night of Power, you have just given me Power, oh my God. I thank you for that, but I do not know where that power will take me ..."

The whispering became a blast. There were no longer any rows, any chandeliers, any columns, or any vault before me. Suddenly I was the center of a vacillating circle of anger. I was not thinking. I plunged, banged a shinbone, tickled an abdomen, twisted about, and fell into an empty space. Then I sat down.

The hordes of people came and went. With their contorted faces, their red eyes, and their hands that mimed a quick and certain strangulation. I stayed quiet for several hours. Then I picked up a pairs of bootees that looked like my size—I had lost my babouches—and I left.

I found my mother prostrate before the fountain. She got up as I came in.

"Hamid," I said.

She collapsed. Five years later, I heard a sack of logs fall. That was the noise she made when she collapsed.

I knelt down and held up her head. As I noisily slapped her face, I could smell her: the odor of acid sweat and the sickly innards of women in labor.

My uncle was washing his hands in a tub. Kenza, standing in a doorway, with one leg up against the calf of the other like a stork, was sobbing. I stretched my fingers out straight and hit strongly. My mother opened her eyes.

"Good."

I took her by the wrists and got her to her feet.

"The train?"

"If Allah permits..." my uncle began. He had begun to wash his feet.

"He will permit. What time is the first train?"

"It has already left. You'll have to wait till evening."

"Well, get up then. You're going to Si Kettani's with me."

"Why?"

"Because he has a car."

"Do you think he will..."

"Yes."

"But I am doing my ablutions."

"Get up!"

He got up, waving and wringing his hands.

"Kenza," he said reproachfully, "I thought you had quieted down. A towel."

I grabbed him by the shoulders and dragged him outside.

Si Kettani received us in his bathroom. He had his arms crossed, his head bent down, and his eyes half-closed. A young Berber was anointing him with oil, using his bare hands.

"Si Kettani..."

"Yes, my child?"

"You have a car..."

"Four of them, my child."

His breast was flabby, and his legs were hairless.

"I have just received a telegram telling me to return to Casablanca as quickly as possible. The first train that I can take is not until this evening, making sixteen or seventeen hours of waiting."

"And so, my child?"

"Will you please let me borrow one of your cars?... I repeat that it is a question..."

"No, my child."

He repeated, as I counted twelve gold teeth and four drops of sweat on his nose, "No."

"I'm not surprised," said my uncle.

"Unless..." began the faqih.

His legs suddenly and purposefully opened. The sponge that had served him as a kind of loincloth fell aside. I had not been wrong: a member like a bull's.

"Unless beforehand, a quarter of an hour is sufficient but necessary, we come to an understanding."

He lowered his arms and caressed the Berber's head. The Berber shuddered.

I yelled, "You bastard!"

He pushed the Berber boy away and came toward me, thick, heavy, dripping with oil. He came right up to my face and said, "Just beneath your feet there is a trap. That's where I throw sons of whores like you, and forget them. There are three tame chimpanzees down there to rape them. Get the hell out of here."

My mother had not budged. She wasn't even standing straight on her legs, and I recalled that when I had helped her to her feet, I had done so very quickly.

"Hamid?" she said.

"Dead," I said.

This time I did not see her faint. I bent down and pressed my thumbs into her temples. My joy was gone, replaced by waves of fear I did not want to recognize. I heard myself say, "Kenza, hit her. Hit her hard. If you don't get any results, use a pail of water, and then an onion."

I stood up and began to run.

Perched on a mattress folded in three, my uncle was winding a wall clock.

"Uncle, is there a bordello in Fez? If so, where?"

Outside it was the beginning of the morning. A beggar was chanting his hunger on a bitter flute, and the hunger of his children and of his wife who was giving suck to the newborn, and his mother who was being eaten up by gangrene. An old man, discreet and very thin, was turned toward a boundary stone with his hand on his stomach, and vomiting something red, more like blood than wine, and with the deep cough of a heavy cold. A bit farther on, a half-naked child was lying, teeth white and eyes white and dead, on a heap of scraps of watermelon. Pigeons cooed, public ovens shone red, windows shined with luminescent rags, and in the distance, the incandescence of the dawn could be seen on the horizon. No one could say that there was no more life. Life is there, swelling up at every step, with every bit of dung that my feet dragged with them.

I was figuring things out like an old woman. One night out of two, Julius Caesar had told me: "one night out of two, you can find me in Bousbir." He told me that three days ago. Three days ago he was here. Yesterday he was at Bousbir. Tonight he is back in Fez. But where? Unless he's at Moulay Abdallah's, Fez's bordello.

He was just coming out as I was about to go in.

"Greetings," he said in a shrill voice.

He wasn't at all drunk, he had used up his supply of sperm, and he needed forty-eight hours of sleep.

"Where is your bus?"

"My Chevrolet? Wait."

He kissed me on both cheeks, laughed a weak laugh, so tired that I thought he was crying.

"Old buddy, I went to bed with a little Negress . . . we went up to her room . . ."

"Your bus?"

"Can you believe that at the moment when...yep...she said to me 'move your knee...move your knee,' she thought it was my knee."

He saw that I was not laughing.

A quarter of an hour later, the Steam-Horse charged off into the rising sun.

# 3. THE REAGENT

*Grass must grow and children must die!*

INTENSITY does not form part of my tactile and painful sensitivity, but belongs to that whitewashed wall on which I trace a distracted finger and a flabby palm. You might say it was granulated cement, coated by who knows what kind of tool of human creation except the trowel.

I said to myself: it's my mother. One of her responsibilities is to whitewash the walls once a year. Clumsily, stubbornly, courageously, she labors, but finally the house is white. And no doubt I should be inclined to indulgence. No doubt! I form my hand into a fist which I scrape against the wall with such force that blood spurts out of it in furrows, because all pain is dead in me. Then I shove the hand into my pocket. The blood will coagulate, the skin will close again.

The room where I am standing is for junk. The junk has been removed. Hamid has been stretched out there with his mattress. Hamid died on that mattress. Camel and the Lord picked it all up, one in front and the other in back, like two stretcher-bearers. When it happened I was still in Fez, but I can imagine how they put down those bones and that straw-filled bundle. Nothing more than garbage. The law says: what is dead is corruption, no vigil, or sober and expeditious services; the refuse collectors will soon come by.

The Steam-Horse had devoured space. Afterwards, perhaps a couple of hours had gone by. As soon as I had stopped in front of this wall, however, time had ceased to exist. Perhaps because it had become too amplified, too intense, too present. And I am searching desperately for some sort of equilibrium.

Everything appears to me clear, sharp, and material. Like the images that animate a screen. As soon as the projector is turned off, the screen will become nothing more than canvas and bits of wood. The blood will coagulate, the skin will close again, rub your fist, and make up phrases.

The sobs tear the house apart, and perhaps the hearts of the passersby, because the windows are open. They are of an inexorable tonality and frequency, as much as the Lord has permitted. They will go on as long as the time he has allotted them. I can distinguish between them: the exaggerated sobs of Madini, the desolated ones of my mother, the forced ones and those that are mere echoes of the others, and above all, those due to Nagib, precisely because the herd screeches. I can place them: my mother squeezed into a corner of the walls like a little rat panting with terror, capable of leaps and powerful flight, but not moving at all; someone has closed himself into the ground-floor toilet; someone else is searching through my papers. I don't know where the Lord is. His hour will sound.

The windows are open. A woman has stopped, our neighbor has told her what is happening, and the woman has gone on her way, saying, "One more or one less in that battalion!"

I practically leaped outside and hit her with my fist. She hardly budged, only her head jerked back.

An open knife has been placed beside Hamid to ward off evil genies. It wasn't for sticking in the gut, but I recognized it: the Lord used it to clean the callouses off his heels. If he has given it up, it surely has some symbolic meaning which I cannot understand. A candle has been stuck in the mouth of a bottle and is burning. It has been calculated that this candle will last until the time to take away the corpse. The sun strikes straight down outside.

I must resist all pain, reject all emotion. I bring this death back to a simple verity: it is action. I see it as a breach, however small, in the citadel named the Lord. And I must make use of it right away, before my flesh and my nerves demand their debt of suffering. This reckoning renders me inhuman. I know that, and I take delight in it. I also know that I will weaken soon. Saints of the Greeks and the Russians, let it be as *much* later as possible!

Naturally I had telephoned. That is not a substitute. Sublimate? If you wish! But my opinion is the following: it is a question of one of those things that does not happen every day, and for someone like me who has been waiting for something of this kind to happen for nineteen years, of excessive character like an infectious departing visitor.

"Monsieur Roche?... Hello! Monsieur Roche?...yes, yes, it's Kraut-head... fine, thank you, and you?... Of course!... three, one of them collected in Fez...yes, I have been to Fez... I'll tell you about it in detail... then a certain Julius Caesar arrived in Fez, I think the story will be very interesting for you, it's a heavy and primitive irony... What? What did you say? an abnormality in my voice? I am glad that you noticed it... No, quite simply just a death..."

I reminded him that Hamid had never been to school. We had had our own little world, we two, hidden away, charming, and frag-ile. He recited with me: *Rosa alba, rosam albam, rosae albae...* Or, our eyes half closed and our hands crossed, we sang German verses:

> Ich hatt 'en Kameraden
> 'En bessern findst dù nicht...

Because I was learning German and Latin.

I had a collection of pipes, fourteen of them. Hamid emptied them, polished them, arranged them. Tobacco? I didn't have any, as the Lord gives me no pocket money. Consequently Hamid slid under the Lord's bed and brought me back cigarette butts because the Lord smokes cigarettes in bed before going to sleep.

There was a whole sum total of little things that were forbidden, not a part of the norm, but which meant living to us. I would light the night lamp, he would bring up a chair and sit facing me, looking at me in silence. Once my homework was done, I tidied up my books, notebooks, and papers. Hamid could climb up on my work table and sit cross-legged like a tailor. Then the two of us looked at the Larousse twentieth-century encyclopedia.

Hamid was beaten up by my brothers because I gave him the keys to my room and he would not let anyone go in. He would cry and threaten, "Driss is coming, and I'll tell him you beat me up. And Driss knows how to box. I'll get to see you pick up your teeth one by one."

He was free to go into my room, but I never found my papers disturbed. He put his eye to the microscope, but moved it away afterwards to delicately wipe off the lens.

One day Madini slapped him. Hamid's gums were bleeding. He took up a piece of paper, made a little pocket of it into which he spit and then put it in his pocket. That evening as he told me the story, he showed me the blood as a proof. I went downstairs and, shaking with anger, I broke down the door of the toilet where he was hiding. Several bricks fell down with the door. The Lord ordered me to pay the damages. Hamid prepared the mortar, and I rebuilt the wall.

Because he was the frailest, the weakest and the smallest of the Lord's household!

"The grass must grow, and children must die!" Roche had said.

Who said that? Victor Hugo. Victor Hugo, shit all the same!

Whoever is in the toilet has to flush: he decided to urinate or to defecate, but he's still sobbing. Whoever is going through the contents of my drawers up in my room is furious: he hasn't been able to find the little creature that probably kept us up at night, Hamid and I: he also is still sobbing. The candle is half burned down, the flame is flickering, and now a current of cold air blows across the floor, a wind comes from who knows where and that would smell of hydrated whitewash if it has not already smelt of melancholy. A few more small changes, some new contributions, and time will go on. The calves of my legs are already knotted with cramps. Only my mother's lamentations have stayed the same.

I shake myself the way a dervish shakes his lice. Everything must continue to be intense. Otherwise the breach will risk being filled up, cemented, sarcastic. The knife that protects Hamid from evil spirits has a longer blade, brighter than mine, mine with the switch-blade that I never go without. I exchange the two and patting the cheek of the dead: "See you later! I won't be long," I say out loud.

The courtyard is empty. A couple of butterflies are flying around there, coupled one on top of the other. The door of the kitchen is open as if someone had just pushed it, a kettle is simmering, a casserole is boiling, and a broom is waiting in the corner for a pile of peelings. The oil jar is full. I draw off a ladle-full. Allah accord me the Power!

When the Lord had his house built, he wanted a building that would last. The stairs that I climb are of concrete. I feel as if I were crushing the bones of my feet—I'm barefoot but no one will hear me come up.

As I stepped out on the landing, I remembered that the Lord was ruined. "How many hours," I asked myself, "how many minutes have I ceased to think about it?" I barely modified my step. That and nothing more.

Nagib was sitting in my favorite chair. He was crying. He had my microscope on his lap. Sprawled out on the table-desk, Abd El Krim was looking through the Larousse. He was not crying. I stopped before the open door. Had I appeared just at the moment of the relay? Nagib stopped crying, and Abd El Krim took it up. As I went in, I understood to the very marrow what their intention was: the dictionary was open to the letter S, and under the lens of the microscope were a couple of glass slides. I hung the ladle on the coat rack. They saw what I had done more than they saw me myself, and began to sniffle in unison. Their eyes were fixed on the knife.

"You see this knife?" I said. "Don't move."

That was the moment the cat appeared. I don't know why I saw it as thin and half-starved. It was probably bald in spots with blisters on its stomach. It howled to the heavens, and I identified its cry with the screeching of an old owl. Then as soon as it had given its cry, it was quiet.

I took the slides from under the microscope. The only thing on them so far was a bit of spit, phlegm, and blood.

"You should have told me," I said in a sad voice. "You should have come and found me, taken me by the sleeve and said to me 'Driss, we're curious. We have been for more than six years. We found the keys under the door of your room, found the dictionary and the microscope. We want to make an experiment, Brother Driss.' That's what you should have done. I'm not mad at you. Why should I be mad at you? Now that we're here, we might as well twist that unhealthy curiosity by the neck. Nagib, on your feet!"

If the cat hadn't meowed again, I think my fist would have come down on Nagib's head, because he hesitated whether to obey me, but the cat did cry, and I said softly, "Please get up."

Perhaps it was also because of that mewing that Nagib did get up. I turned my back to him and leaned over Abd El Krim.

"Just look at that!" I said. "You haven't even found it yet. SPAD, SPAR...Turn a few pages more, well turn...we're getting there... SPEC, SPEF, SPER...there...*Sperm*: That's the word you were looking for, wasn't it? You get up too."

I poked around in a drawer and handed them each a piece of blotting paper. Then I sat down.

"I'm waiting. I have confidence in you. You're going to be quick, for three reasons: the first is that you're in full adolescence, the second, that you're used to doing it, and third, because it won't be long before they come to get the body. Now it could be that you won't want to do the deed in question or that the secretion of your glands is cut off for different reasons. In that case, take a look at this knife. I'm moving the cutting edge along the nail of my thumb, and you can see! It cuts to perfection. The master of the house could come in and surprise us. In that case, you will remember that three days and several hours ago, I had in my possession a knife that I did not use. Right now, I can assure you, that if the Lord walks in, that very knife will fly out of my hand like an arrow."

I methodically crossed my legs.

"In order to be sensitive to your sense of modesty, you can face the wall. When you have finished, please use the blotting paper that I gave you. Don't spatter the furniture or the wall or the floor."

Do cats suffer when they give birth? Maybe it's a cat in labor, or in heat, or maybe even as only Allah has knowledge of such things, someone amused himself pulling the cat's hair out hair by hair, like a tooth-puller on Benghazi Square—delicately. I didn't go to the window. I didn't shrug my shoulders. The window was protected with bars through which came the wailing, and the heat, like a couple of blows of a fist.

My room was small, square, and with a low ceiling. The walls were white. I like the heavy dark-colored furniture, the creased leather of the armchairs, the lumps and hollows of the sofa, the agedness of the books on the bookshelves in the corner. Roche had spoken to me about London as a good old town where everything was maternal, with softened noises, sleepy facades, and an indulgent fog. A little bit of London, my room, in the raw house of the Lord.

And these two dolts, my brothers, had come in there, scraping their nailed shoes over the wood floors that I waxed every evening, opening the window wide, with the half-light and poetry outside! For we're in Morocco, infringing on the warm nest of the seats that, in the time that I have been sitting there, have ended up taking on the shape of my behind. They're pointed, my buttocks, thin, but they're mine, and there, pipe in my mouth and a book on my knees, I curled up for hours with whatever kind of young girl type of reverie. I know also that my personal diary has been deflowered and polluted. There was no lack of winks and of obscene smiles, and I am certain that a spider becomes homicidal when it has finished weaving its web, confecting the contours with delectation only so that a broom can tear it down, and you were overjoyed, poor little creature!

As I contemplate my masturbating brothers, I have a kind of impression of loss. One of them has almost tried to run away twice, and the other one turned around and crossed his arms. And both times they have encountered my eye that was neither sad nor hard— animated with an absolute indifference. When they got their task underway, I wondered if they would have preferred looking into the black and shining pupil of the Lord's eye.

There is still the cat. I'm certainly not the person who stepped on its tail or who tickled it. If it mewed I don't want to know why. What's essential is that it did, until it became part of a drama. It cried three times, and then gave no further sign of life. I'm on the lookout, like a victim of water torture.

"And you?"

Abd El Krim cautiously hands me his blotting paper.

"And you?"

"Well," cries Nagib, "I still haven't..."

"Hurry up!"

Buttoning his fly, Abd El Krim sized me up with a somber look. He had conscientiously masturbated. As far as he was concerned, my order had signified what the proverb says: "Strike the hound with a leg of mutton and he'll be rather contented." Now the spasm was over. Afterwards he gave me a dark look. I honestly interpreted this silence: rotten swine, lousy shit, asskisser of Jews ... and the customary insults used by young men of good families.

Nagib moaned briefly. His knees had weakened, shaken by a slight trembling. I was careful not to budge. I knew that if I did budge, Nagib would twirl around to grab me by the throat. Among all the foetuses of hate, he hated me with a solid hate. I saw his back stiffen. As long as the masturbation was going on, he had been strictly carnal; now like an old remorse, he recovered his sorrow and the need for sobs. My impression of loss became ever stronger.

Nagib sank heavily to the floor and, with his head now in his hands, began to study me. It was really strange. For years we live among people whose slightest interior shiver is perceptible and familiar to us, and then one day we perceive that we are incapable of affirming whether they have blue eyes or not, or a pug nose.

As Nagib was squatting on the floor, I was not amazed that he had a nervous reaction, a reaction of brief impulse, but I was startled to suddenly realize that my brother was a long-eared bat with a remarkably pronounced mastoidal apophysis. That discovery made me think. For a moment I wondered what could be the second angle to the problem; if I was simply the black sheep for my brothers: was the sheep black? From that very fact, every other identifying detail becomes useless, and what would their stupefaction be if they found that I had limbs, a torso, and a face … and, like a sounding in a marsh, there were the others, those whom I loved or admired, and those envied or to whom I was indifferent—then all the vast accumulations of other things that have neither weight nor measure, only a name, a name: is it because of such an order of relationships that one of the faithful, speaking of a toothbrush would say "it is a pear" if, as ill luck would have it, the Koran has made a judgment: it is a pear?

I went to pick up Nagib's blotting paper. His sperm had the character of apothegma: dry and angular. As I was getting to my feet, Nagib quickly slid on his back and stuck out his right foot toward one of my tibia. Exactly the move I expected. I dodged him, and accidentally crushed his hand under my foot, for a long time, surely, until his face—he didn't cry out even once—went from apoplectic to ashen. Meanwhile I asked myself: why did they hate me? And why was it that I could not hate them? I regretfully lifted my foot.

Abd El Krim was resting his elbows on the windowsill. I tapped him on the shoulder, asking him to mix the sperms. I watched him carefully. He was familiar to me too, but those red spots, how long had he had them on his face? He had cut off a bit of blotting paper and was using it as a spatula.

He held his head down as he mixed. Where did he prognathism come from? The Ferdi never lowered themselves, and neither did the Zwitten. The Lord was an example: "Plant chickpeas and chickpeas will grow; and if, for good measure, you get some raffia, give praise to the Eternal One. Our old Mother Nature is a helluva trollop." Looking straight at me, so spake the Lord.

Abd El Krim was beating the mixture. He was beating it the way woodsmen would. He smelled of cheap perfume from Marseilles, of reheated sweat, and of basic idleness. I was thinking of the mason from Mogador who had built our house. He went to find the proprietor. "Your house is finished, Sidi. What can I do now?"—"Tear it down." Which was done.—"And now?"—"Rebuild it." It seems the

mason never understood that in the case of houses, he was construct-
ing potatoes on a grand scale, and I would say that if contests, prizes,
and records were inaugurated in Morocco, the United States would
be quickly dethroned. And so I know an old *taleb* from Sousse who
never consumed beans of the variety denominated Saint-Fiacre's
Runner Beans.

"Don't tell me that life is a lot of rubbish," I remarked. "I would
agree with you. I watch you turn and re-turn those sperms and you
wish you could finish me off, and I'd like to see you finished off. You
tell yourself that the one who is downstairs on his mattress does not
deserve to be on his mattress. Others should have died in his place.
I agree. Why him and not you, for example? Turn, dear brother, turn!"

He had a few hairs on his chin and his grin was painful . . . I am
on my feet. I am sick of it all. Leave me alone! . . . Nothing is uglier
than the senility of someone young.

"Stop!" I cried out. "It's mixed enough like that, and I have no
choice but to be your brother. No, you see, what disgusts me is that
you too . . ."

Over my shoulder, I suddenly flipped my right fist. I struck the
hand of Nagib with conviction. He had gotten up surreptitiously
when I turned my back to him and had got a hold of the knife. He
dropped it and went back to where he had been squatting, rubbing
his fist.

"What disgusts me," I went on, "is that you too, you have to be
my brother. And you too, you admit that obligation, and are disgusted
with it. Since that's the way things are, go sit down or stay standing
or make an attempt at flying, if in your little cranial box in the form
of a lump of sugar and of which you are so proud it is written that
you will absolutely not obey me."

He stretched out on the divan. I smiled: his instincts were still
puerile. I place two cc's of sperm between the slides of the microscope.

"A little while ago," I said, "when I came into the room, you, Nagib
(he seemed to be cold), you had this instrument on your knees, and
you were examining a bit of spittle. You, Abd El Krim (he was scratch-

ing the inside of his thigh), you were consulting the dictionary looking up a specific word. You aren't going to tell me that you went out
of your way for all of this out of kindness. You might tell me that
with that dried spittle and that specific word, you were going to
quietly wait for me to respond to you: I am an authentic crankshaft.
I knew quite simply that you would not dare to. So in I came, and I
helped you, perhaps a bit too harshly for your taste, but do you merit
anything striking arguments, that I ask you? Now that the work is
ready, and what fine work ... I almost feel like laughing. All you have
to do is satisfy your curiosity. Here is the microscope, and here is the
sperm. I have everything ready. And I think now I'm going away and
leaving you. If by some unlikely chance, once the examination has
been finished you don't notice anything really strange: is that what
it is? ... that's all there is to it? ... in that case, call me. I'll be downstairs. I'll come up, and we can discuss until we resolve the dilemma:
or throw this damned microscope into the wastebasket or mash your
face in. In the meantime, I think you will have seen that it could not
have been a question of sperm for Hamid and me. Whenever we
opened a book it was not to look up some filthy expression. What
united the two of us, what made us two companions—two brothers?
I told you—it was not the microscope or the dictionary, nor the pipes
nor the prick sharpener, not even the desire to talk about you who
spied on us, you rotten pair of testicles! As for this door..."

I took the ladle off its peg.

"I left my keys there, and you opened it. Keep the keys. That way
you can go in and out whenever you want, as many times as you please.
Even come in at night. So you can contemplate one Driss Ferdi, son
of the patriarch, grandson of a saint and that a dark destiny—may
Satan be cursed and his eyes put out!—turned into a Christian.
People say that those who sleep are close to death, and even I, the
Christian, when I sleep don't exactly know how. A Christian is subject to astonishment. Consequently you will watch me sleep. Then
you will inform me if I snore, if I fart, or if I have nightmares. Also
verify the adage 'A Christian who sleeps is a swine.' I also beg of you

to smell me, if I stink at night, as you never know. As for this door, as I said, you must have noticed that when you opened it the lock worked with difficulty. Given that fact . . ."

I made a rough arch with the ladle. If the lock profited from this watering, blame fate.

". . . put some oil on it. Look! Now the key turns . . . like in a lump of butter . . . and no noise. I'm clearing the way for you, getting rid of the obstacles, and ironing out the dirty little tricks. So you'll feel right at home, and because I love you."

I picked up the knife.

"I'm taking it back. It has been useful to me, but to tell the truth, the person for whom I'm keeping it has not shown up yet. Goodbye!"

As I was leaving the room, a hand came down on my shoulder. I knew it was Nagib's, and I quickly prepared for the attack. The wolf gets screwed twice, then he gets furious. I was furious.

I turned around, and Nagib's eyes pleased me. I had never seen his eyes that way before as long as I can remember. Maybe I was wrong. Maybe I was in too bitter an emotional state not to wonder if I was not making a mistake. His eyes were coactive, and the hand that I grabbed was fraternal.

"Driss," whispered Nagib, "count on me. I may be a square peg in a round hole, but you can count on me."

His face tightened. I shook the hand that a little earlier I had crushed. I let go of it.

He added: "I'll tell you everything. How Hamid died, what brought it on . . ."

That was all. The broad outlines of my plan were underway. Not one single time as I traversed the patio did the idea come to me that Nagib was behind me shaking his fist at me.

The padded door panel that I pushed was hard to open. I kicked it hard a couple of times, with increasing interest. I expected it to fly open, but it was my mother who came to open it.

"What's the matter," she said. She realized as she said these words that she had lost several seconds that were owed to tears. She slapped her palms and wrung her hands.

She was wearing a many-colored obi in place of a belt. I asked her in whose honor. She lifted her head and, if she noticed something in my look that was unusual, she certainly drew some silly conclusions from it.

"Driss, my son . . ."

"Driss your son is here."

The "Steam Horse" had left us off, the two of us, at the end of a turn on two wheels, before the house of the Lord. She crossed the threshold of that house like a catastrophe, preceded by disordered veils and abandoned by the babouches with thread of gold that could not follow her. Before she could throw herself on the corpse, the Lord had restrained her, first shaking her like a sack of nuts and then carrying her like a sack of nuts up to the conjugal chamber. Stay there and cry if you want, scrape your cheeks with broken glass if that's what seems right to you, but no outbursts. We have spoken.

"Driss, my son," she repeated between hiccoughs.

"I tell you that Driss your son is here."

I began to comprehend. I was balancing the knife in my right hand, balancing the ladle in my left hand, while I tried to balance myself on my two feet. I was concerned for the fate of that cat that had cried out only three times. For my taste, three cries were not enough, and I supposed that whoever had had fun skinning the cat had not had enough patience.

"Why are you wearing that obi?" I asked her. I perceived the softness of my voice, and I was surprised.

"Driss, my son . . ."

"Well what, Driss, your son?"

I used to kiss her hands and her feet. She hid the conjugal handkerchiefs under her mattress, and when I found them, she hurried to explain to me: I had a cold tonight and I had to blow my nose—and I chanted: those-are-the-handkerchiefs-where-mama-blew-her-nose! She would have blessed me so I would not suffer.

"What is that all about?" I said with emphasis, pointing to the belt.

Something strange was in my voice as well as in my eyes. That upset her, and that was detestable. She was waiting for the open arms of Driss her son in which she could find refuge. I would have assured her that the death of Hamid was a cataclysm, that I was a soul without body and bleeding flesh, and that her own pain was at least that of Christ on His cross. Instead of that, I stood balancing myself on my two joined feet and asked her questions.

I judged her to be weak and awkward, eating, drinking, sleeping, excreting, having intercourse. Respecting the menus established by the Lord, the Lord's tea, five times a day, or two times a day, and according to the wishes of the Lord. In the interval, you cook clean, sweep, do the washing, sew, darn, mend, knit, bake bread, kill the mice and cockroaches, mill the wheat, sieve it, keep a "mental budget," embroider handkerchiefs, beat the tambourine and dance barefoot, and chase the flies away. That I could admit.

"I had judged you to be weak and awkward," I said, "eating, drinking, sleeping, excreting, having intercourse. Respecting the menus established by the Lord, the Lord's tea, five times a day, or two times a day, and according to the wishes of the Lord. In the interval, you cook, clean, sweep, do the washing, sew, darn, mend, knit, bake bread, kill the mice and cockroaches, mill the wheat, sieve it, keep a 'mental budget,' embroider handkerchiefs, beat the tambourine and dance barefoot, and chase the flies away. That I admit. What I don't understand is this obi. Why are you wearing that obi? As far as I know, today is not a holiday. And your lips painted with poppy juice? And your eyes made up? And why the powder and the fingernails like a bordello? What's it all about? Will you tell me why you're sobbing?"

She took my hand and put it to her lips. She made such an imprint of distress there in the form of a kiss that I reacted strongly.

"Driss, my son..."

"Driss your son asked you a question, and you must answer it."

She did so spontaneously. So spontaneously that I had the impression that it was unintentional; of a kind to make the response unintelligible, and that created a confusion in me so that I had to have her repeat herself, but in the interim, either the resonance would have established itself, or else I had become slightly adjusted to what she said.

"He was my little one," she said . . . "Now I want to replace him."

Those words, and as if to underscore them, the mewing that spurted forth lugubriously and then was spread out like a leitmotif of three notes, short, long, short, with a stingy little silence between two notes.

Still swaying back and forth on my feet, I smiled. With a smile whose grimace was painful. While the cat mewed, my mother trembled, and outside, under the sheets of sunlight, animals and people were inert, I searched for the succinct terms and a cruel enough tone to fling at the person holding my hand.

I cried out: "Just a receptacle for pregnancies!"

Then I repeated: "Just a receptacle for pregnancies!"

And I turned on my heels.

As I was going down the concrete steps, the mewing stopped, and I remembered what I had recalled a few moments earlier, that the Lord was ruined. How many hours, how many minutes . . . Hardly this derivative. Time had recovered its movement.

In the kitchen, the broom, if it is still on its pile of rubbish, seems at fault. The handle has slipped a little bit, moved by who knows what whim of weight. The oil in the jar gurgles when I put the ladle into it, then it smooths out as the former round bubbles expand. I uncover the cooking pot. The water in it has boiled and reboiled, then became inert even though the fire underneath it is still intense. I let fall an abundant bit of spittle on it. If you ascribe that to my subconscious, I'll quickly applaud you.

A little while ago a coupling pair of flies buzzed about in the courtyard. They are still there, coupling and buzzing. I suspect they've climaxed half a dozen times at least, but I'm not sure. Just as I can't certify that Madini has emptied his guts to the very phlegm or if he's just constipated. Kicking on the door of the toilet, I ask him the question. He stops sobbing.

"Ha! . . ." he gasps, "what's the matter? . . . It's occupied."

I transform my heel into a snout and the door gives way.

"Excuse me," I say, "it's for a bit of verification."

The candle now measures four fingers high. A dried tear clearly lines Hamid's face. I have left him perhaps no more than a half hour, but that time has been enough: he has become rigid and has stretched out longer. No doubt he wants me to know that he is good and dead, and that he is nothing more than a cadaver. I accept that fact. I called him my little bird.

I am immobile. Suddenly there is silence. Several doors open or close. Some grass is burning, giving off an acrid odor. I know. That very odor is sovereign, purifying, and chases away the odor of death. Just as soon as Hamid and his mattress are hoisted onto a horse-drawn hearse, dozens of buckets of water will be poured all over the house, my little bird.

My little bird, I shall remain standing by your bones and your mop of hair until the last centimeter of the candle has been transformed into a smoking bit of sputter, until the droning passages from the Koran will have drowned out the silence.


Along the fronts of the houses, the crowd stretches away in two lines. Just as we are going down the steps carrying the mattress, there is a hubbub. I evaluate what they are saying: "That's Hajji Fatmi Ferdi. They say he killed his son . . . blows to the head, I think, but evil tongues are never idle, and I can't guarantee you anything . . . The other one is Christian. Even for his brother's funeral he stays in Christian clothes . . . They say that he . . ." A few seconds later and the crowd begins the Chant for the Dead.

The sky is dazzling white, so white that I can't make out the sun. Behind us a door has slammed, a door against which the fists and forehead of my mother beat, for the Law forbids her presence at the funeral ceremony. Her cries are frightening . . . Saints of Islam and of Mohammed, I have not invoked you, you have taken your revenge, you've taken my little one away from me . . . Saints of the Greeks and Russians, I did invoke you and you have answered me. You took away my little one . . . Saints of the Jews and Tartars, they say that you exist: why would you not exist? Then open me that door . . . If you want, I'm a Jew, if you want, I'm a Tartar, a dog, rubbish, shit, but please open up that door! . . . At that moment I think I could have crushed her in my arms.

Suddenly the sun lashed out against the white shroud until it reflected like a mirror. Slowly, carefully we go down the steps and, as he is ahead of my going down steps backwards, the Lord has lifted up his arms. Consequently Hamid has stayed in a horizontal position, and I almost feel gratitude for this gesture.

On the last step, I encounter the cat. It is rust-colored with gray spots, a rosy nose and wet eyes. It is half-buried under a heap of gravel, stones, and tin cans. It lies still and beaten, as if it had had every kind of rubbish fall on its head. It tried to pry loose, it struggled, cried, sweated. Now it's worn out. It knows it's going to die soon. As I stepped over it, it didn't even look at me. It waits patiently for me to throw a stone at it.

I told Julius Caesar to be there. And there he is. He waves to me, and I nod back to him. I asked him to find something, and he found it. The Steam Horse snorts, jammed to the very top with happy folk, one with a guitar, another with a tambourine. Sitting on the bumper, Julius Caesar has the half-bored half-indulgent air of an orchestra conductor who is waiting for the audience to quiet down. As I go close by him, he lifts up his head. His eyes are very black and very frank. "So?" he seems to say, "we're going to stick it to that bastard father of yours?"

My father has seen nothing. He does not know those people. Even though he's going backwards, he moves straight ahead with his head high and his features cut out of rock. His shoulders may have moved a little bit, but it is undoubtedly the effects of the weight that make him stiffen. And I could be mistaken as the luminescence is such that everything has lost its contours.

The Chant for the Dead intones: "Oh God! Praise be to God! Only God is eternal. God is the Most High. The power and the glory are only God's. Misery is our misery and perishable are our bodies." Sweat runs down every face and I swear the voices are fervent. There is a deep silence as we place the mattress on the carriage, then the horses set off, and the chorus begins again.

The fronts of the houses are high, their windows protected by iron grillwork behind which immobile heads intone the Chant for the Dead. The telegraph poles are decorated with the swastikas and equivocal propositions, and at their feet the micturations and excrement spread out like little islets. The odors sui generis have long since evaporated. That's no doubt why a dog, a fat and well-cared one, sticks his nose into the sludge with his tail beating a little pile from the day before in one of the drowsy little pools.

We walk along behind the horse-drawn vehicle, the Lord and I. Some dozen sensitive souls detach themselves from the crowd and follow us. I put their number at twelve, fifteen at the most, perhaps less, by the sound of their steps. Julius Caesar and his riffraff end the procession, and I hear from them the grating of a violin, a sort of try-out. I can imagine why it is no more than a try-out. The emotion that I feel has gotten to them too. Misery is our misery and perishable are our bodies.

The man who walks by my side is my banner. We love the banner under which we fight—just as we can also hate it. One foot in front of the other, his babouches finely made, his step supple, he walks on. His hands are of particular interest to me. They most surely came down on the skull of the boy we are taking to the cemetery. They closed his eyes and gave him his last tidying with hot salted water, palms caressing and fingers expert. Then those same hands, joined together, august, somber, blessed him. "You were the fruit of one of our legitimate couplings, Hamid: misery is our misery and perishable are our bodies. So be it!" Without a single tear, without a shudder on that worthy face.

He swings his hands as he walks along. He does it so naturally that one would say that they belonged to someone out taking a stroll. If he intones the Chant too, it is because he has taken on the role of officiating priest. And if he feels any suffering, his shoulders show no signs of sagging, his back is straight, and his mask is stamped with the rigorous dosage of customary impassivity. He is his own confidant and his own judge. Suddenly my hand grabs his hand and squeezes it.

"Father, I am so— "

"Walk!" he said.

I was waiting for his big firm hand to press mine. It did. Buildings go by, then open fields, and the pavement shines.

"Father, if you knew— "

"Walk!"

The cemetery is quiet. I don't know where it comes from or how it exists, but there is a soft wind there that rustles the trees. The *talebs* are still howling their Koran. They are always in the cemeteries, permanently. Augmented by those the passage of the hearse had raised to their feet as if by a spring, they *sleep their lives away* in recesses of doors, on cornices, the length of ditches and only awaken to go to howl over a tomb. Later on they'll go back to their lethargy, hardly interrupted.

The gravedigger's pick shines each time he raises it, for the grave must be dug. There is no priest. He goes: "Hi! Hi!" and his torso bends and unbends, the sweat no longer pours from his bare pate: it has all poured out. He works hard, he makes an honest grave, not in the soft soil, but in the firm part. He knows he's dealing with a rich man.

Seated in a circle on the ground and keeping time with their hands, those who screech the sacred versets find the work slow. They encourage one another. Every time their voices go down a tone, one of them jumps to the following chapter, and the voices and spirits rise. There are twenty or thirty of them, and their eyes are shining. Soon they will have a good plate of couscous.

The hand of the Lord rises and falls so quickly that the two gestures are hardly distinguishable. Bending down to earth, the gravedigger has lowered Hamid into the grave. Without coffin or covering, just in the white shroud. He has propped up his head with a stone that the pickax has broken into two pieces. Other stones have fallen on the corpse, and the red earth fills in the hole.

I had fallen to my knees. I got up. A lizard wriggled in the undergrowth; a pigeon cut through the air with a sonorous wing. The most conscientious of the *talebs* were still seated, undecided, still jabbering the last words of the last verse. I got all the way to my feet, and saw, standing immobile and bareheaded, the Lord. He was smoothing his black beard with his index finger, and a veinlet had appeared under the ring beneath his eyes. It was twitching spasmodically.

From that moment on, events unfolded smoothly, without a wrinkle, with a sure and rapid rhythm. As if the burial of Hamid had suddenly transformed these grazers with feet of lead into fiery steeds, shooting their rump fill of vitriol.

At the entrance to the cemetery there was a fiacre.

"Are you coming with us?" asked the Lord. "We're going to Aïn Bordja."

The *talebs* murmured that it was very hot, that this was the hottest day of Ramadan and that they would be happy to hear the sound of the cannon shots that evening.

"At Aïn Bordja," explained the Lord, "they're holding the market of cereal grains. The new moon may be born in a few hours, and so tomorrow would be Aïd Seghir, the most holy religious holiday that every pious believer should observe by a distribution of wheat or of barley to people in need. A gesture we judge to be adequate to give thanks to Providence that has had us fasting for twenty-nine days. We will utilize this fiacre to go to Aïn Bordja."

Swearing in a low voice, Julius Caesar walked around his bus. Head down, he examined the ground and then took a step. Could the ground be mined? With application and method.

"As you wish!" said the Lord.

He climbed into the fiacre and then added, "You'll take care of the *talebs* then. Give them some couscous. We told your mother to prepare some, but don't have them inside the house. They would find a way to still be at the house when we get home! Strike up, driver!"

A kind of truncheon that was once a bicycle tire came down on the horses' backs, and an instant later a cloud of dust hid both coach and coachman.

Julius Caesar was standing still.

"Can you…"

"…get the *talebs* in my bus? Of course! Guards!"

Four men surrounded us instantly. Julius Caesar presented them to me: "The *Kilo*, so called because if we took his word for it his genital apparatus weighs that much… *The Ass that Laughs*. I don't know if you've ever seen an ass that laughs, but, by God, just look at this guy!…This one here is *Stalin*. Why Stalin? I wonder myself. Perhaps because he doesn't have a single cent, no roof over his head and no law. And he's got a hand in our pocket and screws our women. He calls that 'communism.' I still don't understand very well… And finally there's *Victor Hugo*. He recites Victor Hugo's poetry to us, but what does he expect us to do, lechers and tramps that we are? Victor Hugo's poetry!"

The guards took care of the *talebs* whom they pushed in the doors, accompanied by many an insult, and the Steam Horse took off like an arrow, with Stalin astride the roof and Victor Hugo stretched out on a fender.

"A funny group of guardsmen," said Julius Caesar as he shifted gears. "They're all four good-for-nothings, troublemakers, and braggarts, but they're devoted to me, and that's what's essential."

He was driving very fast, as always. Seated right beside him, almost on his knees, I could see his hands clutching the steering wheel and his nostrils flair.

"Are you mad at me?"

"I don't know," I said.

"You have a right to be," he said strongly. "Get the friends together, do a circus bit, learn the *Te Deum* in record time that we would have sung at the grave… and the result? Nobody budged, not even me. Can you explain that to me?"

"I don't know," I repeated.

Some new executioners must have stopped before our doorstep. I took their measurement at the volumetric extension of the mound of stones. Only the head, one paw, and a bit of tail of the cat were still visible. It had not died yet. It watched me good naturedly as I went up the steps.

"Well what then?" I cried. "What are you waiting for to follow me?"

They all wanted to obey me, but I only had Julius Caesar and his guard come in.

With his hands in his pockets and with a meditative air, Nagib was standing on the landing.

"What's that racket all about?"

"Just so! You're going to go down and tell them to shut up. Once they've shut up see if you can get them all in a circle so that a fifty kilo weight thrown over the wall of the terrace will land without bludgeoning anybody. Then you will wait to see what happens. Ah! ... if you see a cat three-quarter done in near the doorstep, don't finish him off. He's reserved for me."

"Right."

Still with his hands in his pockets, he hurried down the stairs.

The latch that closed the door to the storeroom was made of wood. Instead of pulling it, I knocked it off. Kilo let go a whistle of admiration.

"Well, well!" he said. "When it comes to provisions, that's something, some provisions, name of a virgin's cunt! In all of my damned life I've never seen such luck. If only I'd known this winter ... Cigarette?"

"You would have served time in prison," I said to him. "Or you would have been half eaten up by worms by now, because my father the Lord does not like thieves. As for the cigarette, I'll take one. I'll take several if you don't mind."

I precipitously forced the smoke out of my lungs of the one I had lit up.

"So what are we doing?" asked Julius Caesar. "I admit I don't understand why you had us come up here."

"It's a very simple matter all the same. Just Listen. I'm a Muslim, and the Ramadan Fast may be over tonight. That's one part of it. On the other, there are some friends and some thirty *talebs* outside. You aren't going to tell me that there's a single one of them that won't eat with an appetite, are you?"

"Agreed, but I don't see..."

"So here are these provisions."

I said nothing more, with all my joy of smoking. All of a sudden, he jumped to his feet exclaiming, "Ah good!"

I turned over an empty box, placed it in a corner that was not too sunny and sat down on it. When I finally got up, I had smoked five cigarettes and the storeroom was completely empty.

"Perfect," I said. "That's a fine piece of work, and I'm very satisfied. One thing more to do: clean up. You're going to go downstairs and clean the street and the area. I don't want to find a single wisp of straw of a single grain of wheat. But don't be too meticulous. That could give warning to the master. Then break up your group and leave."

I had thrown my cigarette butt down and put it out with my heel. Julius Caesar picked it up and reshaped it with his fingers.

"Give me a light," he said. "Don't you think the neighbors might..."

"I don't think so," I cut in. "For two reasons. If you've heard people talk about the Lord, you've also heard about his Wall of Silence. He has no neighbors. And if by some extraordinary chance some charitable soul should try to say something to him besides the usual *salamalec, Lord!*, you can be sure that he'd go straight on his way. There are no neighbors. Secondly, he is too well known for anyone to suppose for an instant that the emptying of his storeroom into the street could be done in any way except by his orders."

He didn't seem convinced, but he held out his hand to me.

"Goodbye," he said.

"Goodbye."

His handshake was brief, and he seemed in a hurry to get on his way.

"Naturally I can count on you?"

There was a silence. I added, "If I still have need of you?"

"Always."

Because from one minute to the next, I may need you."

"Always. Goodbye."

"Wait."

I suddenly caught sight of troubled waters.

"Where can I get in touch with you? Tonight, for example if something comes up?"

He delicately batted his eyelids and violently shook his shoulders.

"Well it so happens that tonight I have an invitation. One of my cousins who's getting married. And tomorrow at the crack of dawn I'm off for Fez. I can't lie around too long. No matter what..."

"No matter what, you're scared. You mean that you want to be a rebel but just up to a certain point. In complete tranquility. You smuggle barrels of gunpowder, but you don't want to be the friend of the son of Ferdi, even knowing full well that the barrels had nothing more than chalk in them—I verified that—but that my father could cause you trouble. If you consider yourself free of obligation, there are some people here who are without guile, my brothers, and who aren't named Julius Caesar."

He shrugged his shoulders again. By the frank way he did so, I understood that the list of those who did not like me had just grown longer. I lit up another cigarette.

"You're wrong, Driss."

"I hope so, but tell me, is it useless to remind you that I asked you to clean up the street?"

"It is useless."

"Goodbye then!"

Kilo was the last one to leave.

"Me," he said with a smile, "I'm ready to give you a hand."

"You?"

"So? Maybe one day you'll call me to carry off the furniture and everything else in the house. You never know. And I like you. Here are my different addresses."

Out of his pocket he pulled a seal, a stamp pad, and a notebook. He tore out a page and put the stamp of the seal on it.

"I don't know how to write," he said by way of excusing himself.

He handed me two packs of cigarettes. "I think you don't have any tobacco."

And off he walked rubbing his hands.

My mother was waiting for me seated on an ottoman. She had parted her thick hair in regular headbands; it gave her face a pinched look and pulled taut the skin of the forehead. An incense burner had been burning for about a quarter of an hour, hardly even a quarter of an hour.

"I'm fully in agreement with you," I said. "Hamid is dead and buried, some Vandals invaded the Lord's dwelling, and a cigarette is dangling from my mouth."

I knelt at her feet.

"Don't say anything," I went on. "Above all, don't say anything. If you were to talk, the very hair of my armpits would turn white. Because if you have anything to say to me, I know what it is, and misery is our misery, I have already heard all that. And if you have anything to repeat to me, you would do so with the same monotonous lamentation that you never deviate from, and that I know very well. So just be quiet, give me your hand, and don't be afraid."

Those who come forth from the womb of their mother know what they are doing. Just like me, one day they will seat themselves at her feet, take her hand and ask for an accounting.

"Everything went well," I continued. "That is to say that he has a decent tomb, a meter deep in freestone set between a small fig tree and an aucuba, the only shrubs in the cemetery. In other places there is undergrowth, palms, and couch grass. I'll take you there some day, preferably under a roasting sun like today's and we'll sit down, you under the fig tree and I under the aucuba, because the fig tree gives more shade than the aucuba, and you deserve that, given your age and the fact that you are my mother. You deserve it also because of the pain which would become even stronger, and it would be more fitting for it to find expression under a fig tree that an aucuba. On the whole, then we'll walk all around the cemetery with its sixty thousand tombstones to look at in the undergrowth, the palms, and the couch of grass. And the sun, the blessed sun, plus the gravedigger, or his brother or his replacement, half-visible in the red grave. So much for Hamid. God surely has his soul, and the verses have already nibbled at the derm. Let's talk about something else, because seated at your feet and holding your hand, I am here precisely to speak of other things."

Those who have decided to ask for an accounting from their mother have certainly made up their minds to do so. And as they start to do so, they find themselves pulling. My mother was going to take me on her lap, fill my mouth with her breast, and talc my behind. Then later on she would tell me the story of that episode in her life, and it would be transformed into a fantastic intricacy…Yes, my dear one, I'm telling you that I was seated on an ottoman in the conjugal bedroom one late afternoon…I must tell you that that day Hamid, well, you know very well! Hamid…then Driss came in…For a moment I thought he was joking…and then I said to myself that the pain… but I'll never forget…he was speaking like a madman, yes, dear one, like a madman…his eyes were haggard, and he held my hand till he almost crushed it…above all, his eyes frightened me…

"So you have given birth to seven sons. One of them is dead. There are six left. Let's talk about them."

I was counting: three transversal wrinkles on the forehead, one middle one, two grins. Normally she was pale-skinned. She had brightened her face with a poppy-colored rouge. The lines were naturally yellowish and benign but with the makeup, they stood out brick-colored and deep. Horses sleep standing up. The day they sleep differently, they become a circus attraction. The illustration comes from the Lord. If I comment with a fart, I'll be accused of being irreverent.

"Those who sow and those who reap, are of no interest to me," I went on. "The essential thing is that between the two the grain resigns itself to growth. The same with you, having left Fez at the age of fifteen with your tenderness and the perfect secretion of your glands. Here you are the twenty-ninth of Ramadan functioning as to glands, by reverberation, and as to tenderness, by the reverse. In the interval, the earth has turned around the sun twenty-four times, and seven times your womb has ejected. Let's see the results. A cadaver, a drunk, two looneys, two shadows, and me. Plus a master and the hope for a new pregnancy, and this hand grown callused through servility."

I struck a match violently against it. My cigarette had gone out a long time before. If the hand was quickly withdrawn, the mouth stayed closed and so dignified that I almost reached to twist the lips. I went on in a fitful manner, "That's right. Do not talk. Not because I asked you not to, but because you are invoking the intervention of the Lord with all your strength. Too bad! He is at Aïn Bordja, and I have a good long moment ahead of me. And, if you please, express a bit of interest for my words on your face. Or is *madame* terribly bored? She has paid her tribute with tears and cries. A little later on when the cannon goes off, she will find herself once more before a plate of beans, with the same beggar, the same waiting, the same trapeze . . . She has become cuddly, daubed and perfumed herself so that with a little luck her husband may discharge some copulative secretions tonight. And life will go. I tell you: it is impossible."

I got to my feet and lit my eleventh cigarette, threw it on the rug and stamped it out with my foot. Her mouth had contracted: filthy little brat, I thought you were crazy, and you're only spiteful . . . And I perceived Nagib leaning against the frame of the door with his hands in his pockets and straw in his hair. He had come in quietly and was waiting. He was waiting until my eyes met his to announce:

"The *talebs* have left and so has the bus. Can I stay here?"

That was spoken very slowly, in a quiet voice. An ant warms itself in the sun; or: the Atlantic Ocean has dried up. He had certainly been there for a while already.

"Not quite," I answered. "What's Camel doing?"

"He's dead drunk."

"Abd El Krim?"

"Sleeping."

"Madini?"

"Just sitting."

"And Jaad?"

"I don't know."

I beat the air with my arms.

"Have them come up here. Put some mattresses behind this door.

What difference does it make if they sleep here or somewhere else? I'll give you the sign, and you'll have them come in one by one."

He disappeared, scratching the pockets of his trousers.

My mother had barely shifted the center of her dignity. She looked at me from between her eyelids without lashes. As I stretched myself out on the *seddari*, I heard the tic-toc. I raised my head and saw the clock. The pendulum was regular in its beat, the tic-toc was centuries old. I knew that my mother was counting the seconds. She was so tense that she seemed to want to hurry time along.

"Because," I went on, "what I have just told you had to be said. But it's only the beginning. In the first case, it will be useless for you to comprehend what's going to follow. In the second case, you'll comprehend all the same. Because in both cases, the only thing you can do is listen to me. Listen! I am going to tell you a story."

In desperation I made every effort to bring my quantum of emotion to full play in my voice. I was probably the glimmer of a candle in full sunlight, but it was worth a try. If I could win my mother over to my cause—and nothing is more difficult "unhinge" than a mediocrity—the rest would become as simple as a simple minded person.

"The story takes place one winter's night some fifteen years ago. We were living in Dar el Chandouri in Mazagan, and the only children then were Camel, Abd El Krim, and myself. Camel was sleeping, and Abd El Krim was in his crib. He had just had the measles, and you had anointed him with olive oil and smeared him with honey. You were drowsing over some work on a tapestry you had begun at the beginning of the measle attack, because it had been paid for in advance so that you could buy the olive oil and the honey. What did your Lord and Master say? 'If it were written that one of our children...'"

"Driss, Driss my son, I beg of you..."

"Will you please let me speak?"

I had won. For which I could not congratulate myself just yet. The hose had to be shoed at full gallop.

"He always had despicable rules. He was out that night. It was one o'clock in the morning, and while you were working on the tapestry, you were reminiscing about the city where you were born, fairy-tales, you made up riddles for me. Poor mother! I knew them all by heart, and it was above all the monotony of your tales that kept me awake, as if I were waiting for some variation or theme not yet touched on. Finally I would fall asleep."

"Why bring up these memories? I'm suffering enough. Why make me suffer more?"

"Why? There are dogs that do nothing but yap. The system is to give them a hiding now and then. Then they can really yap."

Then I fell asleep. Somewhere in the house a shutter was slamming with regularity, pushed by a wind that blew in gusts. More than my hunger, that shutter helped me to fall into deep sleep.

What woke me was the silence. The wind had fallen, it had rained or it had not rained, and nothing could guarantee me that I had slept only an hour or two—instead of three or four days. I opened my eyes.

My mother, besotted by sleep and her back bent over, was pinning together some banknotes of tens and twenties, then making a pile of them on the matting. The Lord, a yellow pencil behind his year, was counting coins with a sound of metallic rivulets. His lips were moving, and his fingers were black from handling the nickel and silver. He stacked them into piles, jotted the amount on the white wall and put the pencil back behind his ear. That went on for a long time. Then he gathered up the money in a purse of heavy canvas, put the banknotes into a bag, and stuffed them down with his right foot. Bag and purse were thrown into a coffer with locks and chains. He put the string of keys back around his neck and went out to do his ablutions. He came back in, said his evening prayer, went to bed and farted loudly. A few instants later, eyes half-closed, he began to snore peacefully.

My mother went over to tuck him in. I saw her standing in front of his mattress for an instant, looking at him intensely, her chin trembling and her hands folded in an expression of suffering, on the point of fainting. But nothing happened. She slowly turned around, almost regretfully, took up a candle, lit it, placed it into the neck of a bottle, unfastened the lamp to fill it with carbide, and left the room. She also did her ablutions and evening prayers. She remained on her knees on the prayer rug to say her beads and to stammer the litanies in honor of Moulay Idriss, the patron saint of her home town. Then she snuffed out the candle and stretched out on the bed nearest mine.

I couldn't sleep. I could hear her soft sobbing until dawn. I wasn't quite sure of it, but the next morning my mother's eyes were more deep-sunken than ever.

Those eyes were now looking at me. They were so large in that small head that you could end up by not seeing them, and so *bare* in the midst of the makeup that I closed my own eyes. They no longer expressed anything, neither reproach nor desolation, not even indifference.

"That is the night that your son Driss was born," I concluded. "Flying the flag of love, I have never ceased to love you and to support you. Never stopped listening to your adages and the least of your pipe dreams. Unilaterally. Which is to say that if you have received affection from me and comprehension, will you tell me if even one single time you have asked yourself if I also was nothing more than a lost dog? With a head to be patted, delousing all over his coat, to stroke rather than to pummel, because that's what I expected, pummelings, I always expected them, and I would have raised my paw and shown off, or bitten and snapped at, I had need of it, too much energy and no outlet . . . And then when I accepted the fact that I could not curl up again on your lap, when the hand I had not liked pushed me away: Go away! Get out! You'll come back tomorrow and I'll sob out the rest of the serial . . . Then I would go off, a little boy to my straw mattress in a dark corner where I would cry out my distress and the distress of my distress. A bit bigger, I'd stammer out a string of words against Camel's breast. He was patient exactly two minutes and then he'd push me brutally away. Damn and double damn! I can't take a single step without the company of that blow-fly . . . Then, an adolescent sitting in the hollow of my armchair near my desk in the familiar semi-darkness, I would open a book I had read and reread, fill up a pipe with old tobacco, light it, my whole self drained to the point of distress . . ."

I paused, less to catch my breath than to make my point. A pause serves as a trampoline for underscoring the dramatic. You can consider what has just unfolded, and you can sort of step back to leap ahead in the minute that is going to follow. That's what I did and I lit up a cigarette. My eyes were still closed.

"For years," I shouted. "Whether the sun rose or did not rise, I wasn't aware. Time was divided into the following: chow, prayers, waiting in the evening. So functional they were that if I tell you I did not know whether it was day or night, you have to believe me, just as you have to believe this: Driss your son is fed up."

All the same I opened my eyes. And if I perceived a prostrate form, I verified: in the direction of the door; I calculated: in the direction of the Lord who would enter by that door, I raised my voice still higher.

"Driss your son is dead. Dead for you, dead for this dog's life. He's going to leave, but before he does, just imagine an oak tree sawed off at the base. I will have cut down the Lord my father, and you, I will have treated you like some kind of imbecile."

I got up and went towards her, picked her up and grabbed her by the collar.

"Some kind of imbecile," I repeated quietly. "The oak tree is unsound, do you understand? You have to cut it down right away. Or would you—there are passions like that—prefer to remain a human wreck? Because in the latter case, tell me, and instead of treating you simply like some kind of imbecile, I'll also treat you like some human flotsam."

I still hold her by the collar, then I sit down.

"Didn't you ever think that I could be proud of you, a person who could be a mother and is nothing more than human flotsam? Or do you suppose that the moment you got me the hell out of you with three or four hundred grams of placenta, that I was going to spend my life blessing you? Nothing doing! . . . So?"

I wasn't sure: if she was totally submissive to her master, from me she could not accept that *so*!

"So?"

Nevertheless I was conscious: At least by a default of optics the

Lord had been completely reproduced in me. And I had the right to cry, "So?"

With the enormous difference that he would have contented himself with a single interjection and that I was acting like a young rascal.

"So?"

I released her.

"Good!"

And I opened the door. "Next one!"

I was exhausted.

"Sit down. Your name is Abd El Krim and you are my brother. Before anything else, a question of principle: have you also decided to pack your bags?"

He had sat down, but he hesitated to reply.

"Next one!"

My exhaustion became stronger.

As I kept on talking, it grew even worse. To the right, to the left... the disc of the pendulum was of yellow leather. It took on tones more tenuous, then paler or changed into dark brown through the effects of shadow and light. I went on talking.

I had had them all come in. Some of them had sat down. Camel was snoring, Nagib was still in the doorway, on hold between two decisions: to come on in and applaud me or to take a step backwards and shrug his shoulders. He was, however, the only one listening to me.

The quarters, halves, and the full hours sounded. The pearly panes of the windows had turned yellow, reddish, and finally were disappearing. The smoke of my cigarettes had dissolved, dilutions in the dark corners, inert tuft before each window. Outside, still in the distance, the first waves of beggars were underway. I desperately needed sleep. I fell silent. Nagib closed the door.

"I'll try to answer you," he said. "Our father has been enfeebled on two points: the ruin of his commercial enterprises and the death of Hamid. So be it! Second stage: from there on, you spent close to three hours trying to persuade us—reminding each one of us of a memory of our own that was particularly hurtful—that we had to act, to carry out a sort of coup d'état. When you finished what you had to say, you declared you were stupefied that the only result from us was silence and a lack of comprehension. *Now*, brother Driss, if I said to you—and I speak for all of us—that we ourselves do not understand *why* you wanted to persuade us."

In two bounds he came over and sat down beside me.

"I know. You are the product of the same sphere, but why in the devil do you believe that *we*, staying here, suffer here and suffer by being here? Either you are wrong or we don't understand one another anymore. I don't know how to explain myself the way you do, but I think that these few words will suffice for you. But tell me, if you really are suffocating here, why don't you just walk out through the door?"

"I am sufficiently complicated," I was satisfied to answer.

"I see! You want to start the revolution? Do what you want, but leave us alone . . . At least, I promised to tell the circumstances under which Hamid met his death. Listen."

I was still listening when the door opened and I saw the Lord who was disburdening himself of a sack of barley. As he sat down, he declared, "The one who brought you all together here had a good idea."

The cannons of El Hank bared their first salvo.

Our colonizers? They would colonize the Sahara desert where they'd live like Metropolitans. A problem reversed, why be surprised by a marmoset in a zoo? If it's still a marmoset, only the background has changed.

Of course the trapeze against the wall only has four hatchings, but consequently they have spaced themselves out, and the trapeze is there. Pacified in their attitude, glum eyed, silent, mean. On the Lord's right, Camel. Drunk, that I know, but neither his face nor his body show that he is, apart from the fact that his creator knows it. Just as he must have seen the three or four mattresses that served as a waiting room. And he smelled perfectly well the stale tobacco and perceived the origin and the sense—just as he must have sniffed out the strange atmosphere that greeted him. That is why, as soon as his ritual phrase falls, the last salvo of El Hank and the explosion of the muezzin's concert, he says: "Is everyone still in a state of purification?" (I was seated on his left); after doing a somersault, I attack: "No."

"Who is not?"

"You."

I suddenly understand why little donkeys sometimes turn on their backs. That lessens the itching on their spine, of course. They stay in that position for hours. The sky, where their eyes lose their way, is above them. If only their hooves could imprint themselves upon that vault of blue innocence that pours a continuity of suns on their donkey's back as long as a donkey's life goes on!

Me? And why not? A little donkey, nineteen years of age. And for nineteen years with my father astride me. Consequently, please comprehend why I lash out.

If he had bellowed: what are those mattresses doing there? Or else: So now you give yourself the right to smoke? And in our room? Or anything else of the sort, If he had beaten me, I would have done anything or said anything. I would have eaten my beans and have gone off to bed. Very few beans, a catalepsy. That, I assure you. But . . .

He is fully aware of everything that went on in his absence. He has come to the following conclusion: signed Driss. And his Lord's brain has worked, suppurated, sanctioned. His broom is too clean to consent to dirty it on my excrement. So be it! I explain myself: "Because the problem is badly put, admit that . . ."

"*We* admit nothing."

"As you wish. But badly put it remains. This little phrase like the sound of a gong is to be heard every evening: 'Is everyone still in a state of purification?' From you to us, from you the theocratic and the immaculate to us a priori subject to blemishes. I say: by what right?"

The curtains, carpets, silks, sparkling gildings, arabesques, and chandeliers, every object has taken on depth and vivid tones, those objects that normally are dormant. Would they like, in their language of objects, to explain their participation in the drama? Including even the bag of barley crouched on the floor, that ought to denote, and does not denote. The air is very hot: for a moment I thought it was going to get cooler, and I was exulting over it, but then it got very hot.

"Go on."

And how!

"And how! Like a double-edged blade. But first, the dead being buried, life must start up again, and your law goes on. Speaking of that, you must have a long-winded speech to make to us, don't you? After the prayer customarily it would be more solemn. Then no other morality tales on the program, no parables, no philosophical discourse? No, really? Let's move on! ... At the end of the evening, a dish of beans, I remind you ... Ah, good! You know? Let's move on ... And so, in truth, you feel that nothing has changed?"

"The other edge of the blade, please?"

"Later on!"

He is polite, very polite. I would like to be obscene. "I seated Beauty on my knees, and I found her bitter, and I insulted her." Oh yes? And she let you do it? By all that's holy!

"Later on. Are you in a hurry? First of all, did you kill him with your fists or did you use a club?"

"Chastised him, not killed him. Two clouts were enough."

"You should have used a club. He might still be alive right now. Nagib!"

I clapped my hands, but Nagib did not move. The cat may have whined again—or had I at that very instant expected him to do so? "Hajji Fatmi Ferdi, you have been a *hadj* four times, I have been to Mecca one time," but the beggar is there near to our window, with his leather skull and shining cheeks, his full set of solid teeth and his stentorian voice.

"That's all right, Nagib. It's natural for you to be scared stiff, and I'll speak for you. Father, two days ago you ordered me to get ready to accompany mother to Fez, and you went off to bed. Father, when you awakened, you ascertained that we were already on the Imperial

Highway. You also must have noticed the disappearance of some money from your billfold. I'd left a laconic note: 'Father, I took money for the trip. I didn't want to disturb your sleep. Bye-bye, Driss.' Someone must have told you that I had an accomplice: Hamid. Someone that you are looking at right now: the second hatching of the trapeze on my right."

"I didn't do it."

"Yes, you did, Nagib," I said quietly.

"Go on!" said the Lord.

All the same! The plaintive voice of the beggar has added a few new couplets. He utters them with hesitation and discordance. But surely not! I'm sure tomorrow he'll bellow them out in perfect style.

"Hajji Fatmi Ferdi, now that a part of sleeps beneath the earth;

"Do you hear me? Do you hear me?

"Now, don't be ashamed, may your strength be lightened;

"Hajji Fatmi Ferdi, do you hear me?

"Then throw me some wheat bread, half a pound of tea, or a joint of lamb..."

"Go on? How cynical you are. Do you know what your two clouts signify? Trauma, cerebral hemorrhage, willful murder: you are a murderer. Unfortunately, I can do nothing. The forensic surgeon is too late: a Noraf's cadaver, typhus or plague, what difference would it make to him? I said nothing to him. I would have said to him: Monsieur, it a matter of a crime, and just as fast I would have been on my way to the insane asylum. Your word carries weight."

"Quite right."

"Quite right that you are vile."

I know. The minarets have been illuminated, the steps perfumed, the facades adorned and everybody goes around saying that Ramadan is dead. A patriarch will go into the mosque in a little while and will read the Sura of the Cow. "In the name of Allah, the Compassionate, the Merciful, we give thanks to You for the fasting which you have just had us observe..." Translated, this means: "Good Lord! For twenty-nine days we tightened our belts, we didn't get drunk, and we didn't fornicate, out of respect for damn fool tradition. Now, in God's name! how we're going to eat, to drink, to fornicate! ..."

I jumped to my feet.

"First paragraph finished," I announced. "Before going on to the second, a little interlude."

The beggar outside bellowing furnished it to me: he is there by necessity. He may feel like going to have a round at the brothel. A beggar can fornicate, that I can tell you.

"A little interlude in honor of that beggar, Lord. No shake of the beard? Half a barley bread? Or perhaps the idea of alms must obligatorily come from you? In that case, you have the time. While we're waiting..."

I lift up the sack of barley and undo the string, empty the contents out of the window between two bars of the grill. It took me all of a couple of seconds.

"So there!"

I sit down. A yellow butterfly has come in, flying from one chandelier to another. I glance at my mother. Her sash is less vivid in this light, and her eyes look at me without seeing. She is asleep.

"This sack multiplied by sixty—I counted them—three of sugar, fourteen cases of tea, tomatoes, dates, peppers, rice ... Your storeroom is as empty as this bag. The *talebs* of the cemetery, you remember them? And the riffraff that you didn't even deign to look at. They carried everything away. Consequently: the club, the clouts, the malediction and indifference pure and simple? As for the club, I can break it. The clouts, I know how to defend myself. The malediction, what can that do to me? But let's talk about your famous indifference."

"Happiness to My Lord!" yells the beggar. "Glory to My Lord! Long life to My Lord! By the flabby gut of my mother, all that grain? ... May Saint Driss the First give you healthy foot healthy eye ... May Saint Driss II give you good harvests ... Shit! Still barley! ... Jew of a Jew, miser, pig..."

The Lord got to his feet.

"Such would be our desire," he said. "But just look."

The clock showed ten o'clock. I did not hear it strike.

"Prayer first!" he responds. "And we think that your words have infested this place and the whole building around it. A mosque is a necessity now. We shall purify our ears on the same occasion. When we get back, we shall have the pleasure of responding to this conversation."

"No kidding?"

I listened carefully. I'm no dope. He was well and truly cornered.

"I'm no dope. You are well and truly cornered. Go to pray in a mosque? I would remind you that this evening began with the word: you. You are not in a state of purification. Why a mosque? You aren't in a condition to go there. Even here, you are impure. The second blade edge you asked for a while ago, father. And in order to get into details, sitting or standing? Make up your mind. Me, I'm lighting up a cigarette."

I light it. He has accepted the challenge. He has bent over and covered his knee with his tarboosh. He sniffs at it distractedly. His skull is of a delicate rose color, almost white, of an ovoid shape. He has some sweat drops on his forehead.

"Perfect! We are listening to you."

There I am the puppet again! The rugs are of heavy wool, the dyes come from Izmir, and the incense that was burning a while ago is perceptible once more—along with the stale smell of tobacco.

"Well?"

Well, lay the blame on those who have given a denomination to affective conditions of second or third order. So authoritatively that these derivatives have become effective for those who were perfectly contented with their elementary conditions. For me, for example.

"Well, lay the blame on those who have given a denomination to affective conditions of second or third order. So authoritatively that these derivatives have become effective for those who were perfectly contented with their elementary conditions. For me, for example."

"What does all that mean?"

"Just wait. I'll explain myself. Suppose you were an oak tree. Let's say thirty meters high. Imposing, venerable. Me, I'm the woodcutter. That fact that I have the *capability* to cut you down gives me an intense feeling of pride. Not everybody gets the power to cut down this edifice, this grandeur and venerability, but for me to *cut you* down, that's something else again!"

"Metaphors!"

I put out my cigarette.

"You don't like metaphors anymore?"

"What does that all mean?"

"I'm coming to the point."

My butt is still smokable. Three or four puffs make little difference to him, and will do me a lot of good. I light it up again.

"We can still come to a compromise. I am ready to forget everything that has happened. What am I saying? I have forgotten everything. I'm ready to eat my beans, to stay awake if you so deem, to allow your wife the transcendency that she is hoping for. Just look at her. She rejoiced—and tomorrow your son Driss will be reborn, your son and Driss, your slave. On condition..."

"Conditions? Conditions to us? Who is being ridiculed or what?"

We both rose at the same time. Nevertheless while his tarboosh rolls and I put out my centimeter of cigarette, I wonder if the beggar has gone away, why the clock does not strike anymore, what time it could be, and if the cat has decided to die.

"On condition..."

"No conditions. No blackmail."

"Do you think you're going to blow on me and reduce me to ashes? I don't believe in the thousand and one nights anymore. On condition, I tell you, that you resign yourself to transforming your theocracy into paternity. I need a mother, a father, a family. As well as indulgence and liberty. Otherwise my education should have been limited to the Koranic school. Beans, waiting, prayers, servility, mediocrity. A slight reform that you could grant me without undermining your authority as I will still be under your tutelage. The little donkey has grown. He now needs three sacks of oats. And don't try to persuade me that *precisely* you have never ceased to be an unusual father, something that I have never ceased to recognize. I would answer you that that tarboosh that separates us is a pumpkin. So?"

"Otherwise?"

"Otherwise, the second edge of the blade. Seated or standing?"

"Standing, dog."

"Dog if you wish, that is going to bite. But think first. You are intelligent, very intelligent, too intelligent. And I know that you do not tolerate, not the idea that I have risen against your authority (I have done so since the age of fourteen and you know it and have accepted it), but that this insurrection has come to term. Muslim theocracy? The fourth dimension. Nevertheless, you must have heard of Ataturk. If you continue to cloak yourself in your intransigence, there will be a second one, from Ataturk. Here and now. Do I make myself clear?"

I mangled my words, shouting them or whispering them, I don't give a damn, and that's what's essential. Fifty-eight years old, black beard, bald head, a good appearance, reduced to himself alone, I like him. In Europe he would have ended up a mediocre grocer, or an upright bureaucrat.

"Are you through?"

"I think so."

"Leave."

That little word ejected from his pursed lips as if he'd spit it out.

"Throwing me out? Simply throwing me out? I was expecting it. And do I have to obey? In the Name of Allah, the Compassionate, the Merciful!"

I began to laugh, even though I didn't feel like it. That curved ceiling over my head is a witness to it: he desired it.

"You don't lack courage. You don't lack anything except modesty. That's how you've driven me into a corner and you stand up to me? And you tell me 'leave' and I'm supposed to leave?

"Get out!"

"I can still give you another chance."

"Will you get out of here?"

"What about your innate imperturbability?"

"Will you get out of here?"

We begin to turn in circles. Only a few centimeters separate us. He walks toward me, I back up, and we both turn in circles.

"I thought the other edge of the blade interested you."

"Will you get ..."

"You hear it all the same."

I immobilize the hand he has raised. What if I were to tell you that that hand that I had supposed to be of steel was actually puny against my fingers. The whole thing was to be bold. The hands of the clock indicate that it's about eleven o'clock.

"You want to go to the mosque, do you? And why not? You say your five prayers a day, and your prayer beads weigh a kilo. Everybody respects you. You have the beard of a patriarch. You are a man of Allah. I admire you and am devoted to you. I bow to your saintliness. You are a saint. A direct descendant of the Prophet, Allah bless and honor him! You're going to the mosque? I happen to be going that way too. Give me your prayer rug. It seems to me that you carry it with a certain difficulty. You don't want that? I understand you! Well hidden inside that pious felt bag *there are a hundred grams of kif.* The spiritual and the temporal at one and the same time, isn't that right? That's life. Allah is great!"

I see him grow pale, standing there beside the door. I have freed his hand, which he examines attentively. Made for money-making, for correcting, for commanding, for blessing, how could it take hold of me to transform me into chopped meat? Indifference is no longer acceptable. I have to act.

"You are looking at it? It is made for money-making, for correcting, for commanding, for blessing, and you wonder how it could take hold of me to transform me into chopped meat. Indifference is no longer acceptable, and you have to act. I shall furnish the means for you by pointing out the famous second edge of the blade of another argument. Do the rest of you hear me?"

They hear me. They don't scratch, don't sneeze, don't cough, don't belch, don't fart. But they hear me perfectly well. "Is this business going to go on for much longer?" Camel must be asking himself. "Damn and double damn! If I'd known, I'd have stayed at the bordello." And my mother. Her lips sealed. Saints of Hell and of the Abyss, I was taught I had to invoke you! I invoke you. Please have the earth swallow me up forthwith—or let it swallow up this maniac.

The butterfly had disappeared. Why had it not stayed? All the same, I accuse it of having some nerve to have spent time in our midst.

"You hear me. You don't scratch, don't sneeze, don't cough, don't belch, don't fart. You hear me perfectly well. 'Is this business going to go on much longer?' Camel must be asking himself. 'Damn and double damn! If I'd known, I'd have stayed at the bordello.' And you mother, your lips are sealed, which is to say: 'Saints of Hell and of the Abyss, I was taught that I had to invoke you: I invoke you! Have the earth swallow me up forthwith—or have it swallow up this maniac!' I understand all of you. A little while ago you bombarded me with silence. Just as long as you have your beans, what the hell do you care about ideology? I know: go knock on Hitler's door, or Musso's or Roosevelt's and say: there's a way to put an end to this war and you, then you present to them, to the aforementioned, a kilo of hippopotamus shit. Why not? You'd be given a Nobel prize. Whether I talk about liberty, sovereignty, reform to these Arab heads, I get silence, contempt, distrust, and flagrant lack of comprehension. Furthermore, I have just taught you some things that should have stupefied you. You sit there in your trapeze, *sitting drunks*, lips sealed. Those famous beans, of course! You have seen your Lord grow pale—but you, only your retinas. Who can take pride in seeing the moon wearing sunglasses? If he turned pale, well!, by Allah, the Kaaba, and Beelzebub, that doesn't turn him hot or cold. And that's not going to change your beans into hashed meat made of sparrows' tongues. Agreed, Lord! I continue?"

His look has hardened. The little vein that I'd noticed earlier at the cemetery stands out and is throbbing. He opens and closes his hands, and it seems to me he's having trouble breathing.

"Because there is still time. You make a gesture and I'll be quiet. Ready to fall to my knees before you, ask for pardon and forgiveness. I have renounced my demands, and perhaps—you who are so strong, so noble, I do not like to see you suffer—I'll finish up this evening by speaking to you in affectionate terms, the way I once did a long time ago when I stammered out my first syllables. Father, I beg of you. Make me be quiet."

"Too late," he said.

Those words. The little hammer of an auctioneer, a mass in a deserted church. There are suns that rise disenchanted—so that beggars born sightless will sing *ardently* with their bagpipes.

"I don't deny that. I am still persuaded ... And so shit! The proof of what I've asserted? Here is your prayer rug. I open it, and here is the kif. Take my feverish gestures any way you wish. I am at the end. Secondly."

The muezzins cry out again.

"Secondly, second impurity. You of whom we are function, adherents, and an extension, what does it signify? Your farm at Aïn Diab is planted with tomatoes. These tomato plants, a little worker from Khouribga—I checked this out—the girls from Khouribga are very precocious—I checked it out—thirteen or fourteen years old, ties up the plants during the day and attaches them to their stakes with sprigs of palm. And at night, what does she do? I have checked it out: two bastard children—thanks to your caresses and bites on her firm breasts. I haven't checked out, but I've seen the one who makes you forget the flabby breasts of your legitimate spouse under Islamic law, those breasts that have nourished seven children. Amen! How the beggars howl!"

They're howling both because the night is fully dark and because it is time for the evening prayer. Let those who are lying on the body of a woman rise and say their prayers. Alleviation is illusory with the body of a woman, whereas ... and so on. The new moon is born. The muezzins must be placed in the category of the poor. A measure of wheat or of barley would probably be most welcome. And, of course, Allah is sovereign in heaven and on earth.

I repeat: "Amen!"

I notice a spoon on the tea tray. I pick it up. "If all the girls in this wide world" wrote Paul Fort in a little round. What has become of her! Dead letter. And if I add: "no comment," I will have made one all the same.

"A spoon." I pick it up and take several steps. Here I am before the library. Venerable books with gold page edges, papyrus, bookrolls of silk. The meditations of Hajji Fatmi Ferdi, his nourishment and his introspections. All the people of Mohammed are there, philosophers, theologians, metaphysicians, historians. I don't give a rap. The mechanism that makes all this dusty sanctity is what interests me. Because there is some device to make it turn. Consequently I utilize the spoon. I shove it into the slot and turn at it methodically.

I really forced it. There was a cracking sound, and all I had to do was pull aside the paneling.

And to announce: "Vermouth, Martini, Saint-Raphaël, Cinzano... Chablis, Gaillac, Monbazillac... Burgundy, Geizman champagne, cognac, Napoleon brandy, port...'White wine determines the dance of Saint Guy'—isn't that how it goes? 'The dance of Saint Guy! And red wine is common to many peoples: whirl and to the devil with the rest!' I am only recalling your irony the other evening. What brand of wine do you advise us to buy, son? You have your choice, father."

I do not look at anyone as I go toward the door. Why should I? There are suns that rise disenchanted—so that blind beggars can chant *disabusedly* on their bagpipes.

"Old vintages, old reserves, old wines. Or perhaps it's nothing more than grape juice? Made venerable by age. A hadith, a storyteller from Abou Bekr, the Truthful, teaches: 'you think you have just farted. But reflect on it, people of Allah. Has your anus ejected a single ounce of feces? No? Then calm yourselves: you have not farted.'"

I opened the door.

I had provided myself with a bottle of Old Lady. As I opened the door, the neck of the bottle struck the heavy latch—and burst. I took a long swallow.

"Grape juice, no doubt about it. If the label says: Scotch Old Lady, it's a damned lie. Camel can testify to it."

I threw him the bottle and left.

There was a man with the beard sitting on the third step. I greeted him, and he hastily told me that his mother had died that morning, his grandfather yesterday, and that his wife had just been hit by a Jeep, and that his aunt was on her deathbed. He must have been sixty years old. His smile was as jovial as could be.

He was rolling a cigarette, which is to say he was *beginning to*: I insist on that detail. He was spreading the tobacco on the cigarette paper with his index finger.

Meanwhile, I was leaning over the cat. I cleared away the debris with both hands. After I had lifted off the last stone, it sank down and its head fell to the last step between the bearded man's feet. A streetlight was glowing at the corner of the street.

"In the Name of Allah, the Merciful, the Compassionate," I recited as I stood up. "Father of the Universe and of the Last Judgment!"

I lifted up a paving stone to the height of my sternum and let it fall freely. At the same fraction of a second, the bearded man (he was still smiling) said: "Amen!" and the eyes of the cat became florescent. I recognize that one was frightened and the other was dead.

Someone had turned on the sixty-three bulbs of the chandelier, which created areas of shadow in the sheets of light. The first thing I ascertained was the Chant for the Dead. Then I saw the Lord seated in the middle of the room.

"Let everyone rise and spit on us!" he said.

Camel was laughing epileptically. I lit a cigarette.

"Lower than the hoof of a mule, viler than a Jew of Tel-Aviv, reviled, *miserere*! To this we have come. You will arise and you will spit in our face. That is an order."

My mother's lips were trembling. Outside someone was crying thief. My cigarette went out. I relit it.

"Hajji, we are no longer a hajji. A father we have never been. Lord, our throne is now a pile of excrement, pig and dog excrement. We await your spit."

I put out my cigarette with my heel.

"A philosophy of desperation," I said. "Have you ever heard of Sartre?"

He did not answer. My brothers had stood up.

"A matrix calculation," I went on. "Have you ever heard of Einstein?"

Nagib had gone up to the Lord, looked at him, and passed by. Madini took his place. Spittle rolled down the Lord's forehead.

"Einstein invented nothing," I went on. "Neither did Sartre. If they had been present to see this, they would have kicked each other in the ass."

Madini spit, then went over and sat down. Outside someone shouted that it was a only a woman who had just been raped.

"Hajji Fatmi Ferdi attains his power. By the way, how is business? He could recognize his faults and make honorable amends. No, sir! He needed a seigneurial gesture. Gandhi is not a Muslim."

Camel spit twice. He staggered, and his fist pressed against his stomach: he was just about to vomit. As an afterthought, he spit a third time. Then he ran over and vomited on the tea tray.

"You had made a calculation: the most spectacular act would be self-abasement. And you all sat down. From those of us accustomed to servility to you, the all-powerful over our bodies and our souls, spittle can only be a glorification. And tomorrow your yoke will be stronger and surer than ever."

Jaad spit. Abd El Krim spit. When it was mother's turn, she sobbed.

"Spit!" cried the Lord.

She obeyed stealthily, then knelt before him. Outside a public crier looked for a child that had disappeared a week earlier.

"Only I am left," I concluded, "because all this comedy is for my benefit. The most sensitive, the most violent of your children, Lord."

He looked at me. Only the eyes stayed intact in that head covered with spittle and phlegm. They looked at me with a *tone* that was a renouncement.

"The one you have instructed, for whom you reserve happiness in the other world, and your scepter and your crown. We perceive a coming explosion in you, you said the other evening. And you hoped that that explosion would not be for me anything more than something to make of me a modern man and above all a happy man. Shall I spit also? You look at me and you say: he will not spit. He is, however, going to do it. And, as I am not spiteful, I'll aim at the eyes."

I spit, he got up, shook my mother and pushed me violently away.

"Now for the two of us! At the beginning of this altercation, we said: get out. Get out!"

Sixty-three light bulbs went out.

"If I leave, I won't be back."

"We hope so. You go first."

The great door closed with a slam behind us. The doors of the past must slam that way too.

"I'll keep only my hatred from the past."

"Better still: my curse."

He turned the switch. The patio filled with shadows. We began to descend the cement steps, me backwards, he waving his arms and hastening me from one step to the other. I could feel my heart pound wildly. I was smiling.

"You will leave accursed. You thought you would triumph and crush us and dictate conditions to us. We cannot tell you how great the disgust is that we feel. You were in our heart, in our blood, and in our mind the favorite of all our sons."

"Your eyes are streaming. Is it tears or saliva?"

"But, as the poet sings, it is not a bad thing to know which grains to give to each fowl of all the fowls created by Allah. We bestowed our confidence and our love on you. We do not know at present if you even merit our contempt. You were not unaware, however, that your future was more precious to us than gold and that that situation among the rest you have lost. You rebelled? Then be happy like rats in the sewers, because your life is nothing better now."

We walked along the corridor. He turned out the light in the stairwell.

"Speak to me about your ruin."

"You were a blessed being. You had everything to expect from the future. You are no longer our son, and we are no longer your father. Do not think of us or of your brothers again. You are a disgrace to us all. Don't murmur to yourself the name of the mother who loves you so devotedly, that we know, and, struck by the same grief that we feel..."

He opened the street door and crossed his arms. I could make out his eyes in the dark. They were blazing.

"...curses you as many times as there are leaves on the trees and bushes of the world, as many times as there are grains of sand on the beaches and in all the deserts, everywhere that sand exists, as many times as there are fish in all the rivers, in all the seas, in all the oceans of the globe. In the name of the Lord-On-High, the All-Powerful, Father of Benevolence and of Punishment, we all curse you. Amen! Goodbye."

The door hit my back as it closed. I went tumbling down the steps, and I distinctly heard the Lord conclude: "We have buried two of our sons today. Misery is our misery and perishable are our bodies!"

# 4. THE CATALYZER

*The Counterfeiters.*

I GOT TO my feet.

"Finally my aunt died," says the bearded man to me.

He was leaning against the lamplight, more lying than sitting, and he was smiling.

"And I just heard that my eldest son has enlisted in the French army," he added.

He stuck out his tongue. *Then he conscientiously wet the gummed edge of his cigarette paper...*

―――――

At first I thought she was crazy. She burst out of the carriage gate shouting at the top of her voice, "Too bad!...Too bad!..."

A skinny little woman, so small and so skinny that she would have fit easily into a shopping bag. Once I'd thought about it, I caught up with her and took her by the shoulder, "Yes indeed, madame. Too bad, as you say!"

She turned to me. The lamplight revealed what teeth she still had left: four blackened fangs.

"You saw him?"

"Saw who?"

"My dog, of course! My dog Too Bad."

"Ah, so!... No."

She was swallowed up by the night.

———

Then I placed myself in front of an open window.

A candle was burning in a room next door where two Negroes were sitting. One was stirring a ladle in an earthen cauldron, while the other plucked at the strings of a guitar.

A straw matting, some cushions, a leopard's head, a lot of steam, cockroaches and spiders' webs. I smoked two cigarettes.

"I don't understand. These green peas have been on the fire for more than three hours now, and they still aren't cooked."

"Pass me a ladle full," said the man with the guitar.

A few arpeggios and then: "We can wait," he declared. "It's a question of green peas . . . and not even complete: You cooked them *in their pods.*"

The guitar set into a Berber dance.

———

As I turned the corner of the street, I was almost knocked over by a bicycle rider. He put on his brakes, begged my pardon and began to scream:

"My whitings! My whitings!"

I dusted off my clothes.

"So? I see them right there, tied one to the other by their gills by a piece of string. A sort of necklace that you've hung from your handlebar. I count three whitings or I'm all wrong."

"There were fourteen of them," he said to me in a soft voice.

Had he spread them around on the way?

A red light in the night.

———

That is how my first minutes of liberty were filled. Comical. I stopped another passerby.

"Pardon me, sir."

He was smoking. I opened a pack of *Favorites*. He tapped the end of his butt with his finger to knock off the ashes, took a couple of long puffs and gave me the glowing end. I lit a cigarette from it.

"Allah relieve you of this sin!"

"And you too, my son!"

He walked away. Tall, stiff, and skeletal. That and nothing more.

To tell the truth, I was well-supplied with matches and if I stopped him, it was only to ask him if, in his opinion, it was cold.

The second passerby that I made a sign to had two hats, one on his head and the other under his arm. I went up to talk with him. I saw a cigarette dangling from the corner of his mouth.

"A light, please!"

He had taken off his hat and was waving his headgear like a beggars bowl. Resignedly I dropped my box of matches in, and my cigarette butt. He put on the hat that he had had under his arm.

"Allah relieve you of this sin, my son!"

"And you too, my father!"

I walked away. Tall, stiff, and skeletal. That and nothing more.

Two mistakes, two evasions, I felt accursed and I was accursed. Sui generis, there I was, good clothing, my digestive apparatus empty and the sapid oil that my pores perspired and the half-savage, half-frightened expression of someone who has had the door slammed behind him, then goes out into the desert of the street and of the night. By chance I stopped a third passerby. I was cold.

"Sir, I have no matches, and I don't smoke. Do you smoke?"

"No, I am a faqih."

"So much the better. According to you, is it cold?"

"Where?"

"Here."

"When?"

"Now!"

He stared at me.

"Let me go get some information."

He rushed off. I learned thereby that there was a heatwave hot as hell. That was when I really felt cold.

I saw small smoking lanterns, groups of people gesticulating, donkey carts with wheels circled with steel and rolling along with the sound of metal, sacks of cement, watermelons, fowls and gravel and manure, figs, reeds, straw, a happy donkey, a pensive donkey, thirty, forty, and dervishes that ate their soup in a corner or smoked a *sebsi* of kif—a long *sebsi*, a bitter kif—talked to themselves, or vomited. I also saw turns of the street that I cut across, and with every turn a new type of life, noise, lights, and a violet sky touched with silver that seemed about to embrace me or to scoff at me. There were phonographs playing at full volume, the song of the Nile, Antar and Abla, Matrah Matrouh, and the inevitable Koran, here and there a boil, just like a boil on the skin of a woman to bite, a killjoy. I was cold.

I went into Derb El Kebir. I said to myself: "Just like an American. If he loses his toothbrush, he loses his jaws. The night is vast, Driss, as vast as your hunger, as great as your fatigue and your desolation. Where are you going like this?"

I went to knock at the door of Berrada, number seven, Derb El Kebir. He came to the door in his pajamas, chewing chewing gum, smiling, satisfied, affable. On the doorstep.

"The new moon was born tonight," he said.

"I haven't noticed it," I said sadly. "But it seems so."

"Yes, it has been," he insisted.

Then he spit out his chewing gum, right between my side and my right forearm, just as I was holding out my hand to him. He shook it in both of his. Warmly.

"Hi! Can I come in?"

"Hi! I was just getting ready to go out, but since you're here, just wait a minute for me, the time to get my clothes on, and we'll take a walk together."

"I don't think you understand."

But I was beginning to understand. Dry your shoes on my beard, I intend to go to the Turkish baths.

"Wait a minute. I said: can I come in? That means, can I spend the night at your house?"

"Huh?"

"Berrada, you are my best buddy, and I'm very upset. I'm cold, hungry, thirsty, and I need sleep. You are my best friend and I'm coming to ask you for a piece of bread, a blanket, a jug of water, and a night's hospitality. You can interrogate me later on, I'll explain everything."

"Listen, Driss, I'm ..."

"No?"

I hauled off with both my fist and my foot. They landed respectively on his smiling mouth and on the door which he was forbidding me, the door that flew open onto a corridor with black and white square flooring that a floorcloth had just dampened. I even caught sight of the aforementioned floorcloth in the hands of a woman who disappeared screaming: stop the crazy man!

Berrada had sunk to the floor. Heavily, spitefully, I sat down on his thorax. He began to work my sides over with fists and nails, with application and method, without saying a word except for several savage interjections when he lost his breath. The old woman reappeared with an old club. She gave it a twirl, supposedly to bring it down with more baraka on my skull, but I disarmed her, and she ran off again screaming: stop the demon!

By the time I got to my feet, the street was teeming with people. There were neighbors, kids with extended stomachs, women baring their breasts to newborn babes, but whose faces were Islamically veiled, beggars who came gathering together, even one on a bicycle. You never know! All with suppositions, commentaries, orders, counterorders, marginal mentions, what heat, he's a Christian ...

"No, I'm not. The new moon is born. I have seen it."

"It-is-born!"

One single clamor that covered me like a cloud of wasps as I pushed my way through the crowd. I took longer strides, took the side street, another and then another. I wasn't at all cold anymore.

A carriage came out of the shadows. It was hitched to an old melancholy horse and gave off an odor of fresh paint. I hailed it.

"Ho!" went the coachman.

The horse stopped. What else could he do? Even in Morocco, horses are trained.

"I'm going to the European part of the city," I said. "I could make the trip by foot, but I'm tired. Only..."

"Well?"

"If you'll trust me, I'll pay you later, because I prefer to tell you now that I don't have a blessed cent...However..."

"Gee-up!" said the coachman.

And the horse started to trot away. What else could he do? Even in Morocco, horses don't stay put for every long.

"Wait a minute," I yelled

"Ho!"

"I'm the son of Hajji Fatmi Ferdi. I think you..."

"Get in!...Gee-up!"

What slap could sting more? Once I was installed on the seat, I began to recite the tale of my rebellion to the sturdy back of the coachman, to the thick nape of the neck, to his shoulders. Did the latter shrug one single time? I don't think so. But the night was still very dark.

"Ho!"

"I thank you very much..."

"Gee-up!"

One day, Tchitcho had talked to me about his dog Youki. It was a bulldog that slept from dawn to dusk, but that conscientiously fulfilled his duties as sentinel at night. That means that if he sniffed a prowler, he either began yapping or barking furiously. In the first case, the prowler must have been a European; in the second case, it had to be an Arab. Then my friend Tchitcho's father had a choice: he could either come down in his pajamas and his nightcap and talk quietly with his compatriot, or he could open a bull's-eye through which to aim the barrel of an authentic German rifle.

Youki came to sniff at me as I was ringing the doorbell. I had never seen him, and he did not know my odor. Not quite Arab, not quite Christian...Perplexed, he growled a few growls, which I compared to the Golden Mean of Aristotle.

Tchitcho was going over his studies. A manual of philosophy, algebra formulas, traced with chalk on a slate, a small dormer-window open to the night, a small clock to spin out the time. The face of Tchitcho asked for explanations.

"Berrada," I said. "You know him, don't you? I just broke one of his ribs, two teeth and a watch that he had on his wrist. I am evil, I am brutal, I am crazy. If you want to ask me questions?"

There was a slight cough.

"Yes...why?"

"As if you didn't know! Did he telephone you too?"

"Who?"

"Come on, Tchitcho! You're doing the second part of your *bacho* diploma and you're still playing at riddles? Answer me: Did he telephone you?"

The beginning of a slight cough.

"Yes."

Then he went on quickly: "I want you to know that I have no feelings against you and that I'm not here to judge you. If you've had a row with your father, I can't play the role of either supporter or mediator. If you ask my opinion about the actual situation, I would point out to you—if you don't know it already—that as the son of a consulting barrister and of a Corsican countess (a titled line dating back to the Empire), I was born, have lived and will live no doubt in a carefully delineated circle of people, with dimensions, limits, savor, color, and the whole bit, I mean, a circle so well delineated and so self-sufficient that..."

"...that?"

He emptied a bottle of beer. The moment's pause was necessary. The gesture was superfluous. I could easily have terminated his sentence, but as a matter of fact...

"...that," I went on briskly, "an element that would survive *outside* the circle, *externally*, would be something you would not try to comprehend. Not even recognize its individual existence. Rubens and Michelangelo painted. Picasso? Never heard of him! Have you finished?"

"I don't like that tone of voice. Bitter, surly, accusatory, and just when I greet you pleasantly..."

"Put me down for a pound of it, Tchitcho! I'm an imbecile, of course! You're going to talk with me—pleasantly, as you affirm—and anoint me with balsam because you see I'm covered with bruises, and recite Ecclesiastes to me because you feel I need comforting. After which you'll close the door on my pointed shoulder blades, on my pointed buttocks. All the same, I threw out that imbecile. Where was I in my studies?... Oh yes! 'the idea of liberty according to pragmatism...'"

And I sit down. A stool or an armchair, what difference does it make? I sit down.

"Monsieur de La Vitrolle François, surnamed Tchitcho, look at me. This face that you see is my face, covered with sweat. On the one hand. On the other hand, I can make out some little drops on your forehead and the bridge of your nose. Also sweat? Let's not generalize. Just simple perspiration. *Me*, I sweat. Give me a cigarette. You don't have any? Well, I do. You want some? Or did you stop smoking?"

I smoked silently for several seconds. There was nothing but that to do: smoke, talk, use my fists. Then the street and the night again. My stomach? Nuclear physics teaches us that once the quantum has been passed—however inconceivable that may seem—movement becomes inertia.

"So be it! I made a mistake. A mistake in believing as certain as dogma that you, a Christian and a Frenchman, a classmate for the past seven years, my buttocks and yours sharing the same benches, taking pretty much the same class notes, having the same taste in philosophers, in poems, brands of tobacco, *phraseology* between two courses, harmony between us, I copied your neckties, and you adopted my undeceiving way of walking back and forth... So be it! I told you that Berrada had an excuse to turn away from me, the fundamental jealousy of Arab for Arab and the fear of trading off his position as secretary-interpreter in the Pasha's court for a firm detainment for some sort of nonvalid reason, but one that would become valid if the Lord judged it good. Because—excuse me for talking so fast and in such a choppy, complex, dry manner: I am tired and instead of being in a comfortable bed, there are seventy-two hours without sleep that are crushing me … I am sitting down … on a stool or in an armchair, I have no idea, and I don't even want to know. It's not a bed? So? … And I have to talk!—because such is the Lord's threat. He phoned Berrada. To summarize briefly: 'Berrada, you have a good position. You must know who we are and that we have just thrown Driss out of the house. Think about some fundamental facts. Now you either shut your door and you continue to get sixteen thousand francs a month or you suddenly acquire the soul of a Saint Bernard and you will consume two hundred grams of *kesra* in a prison in Souss. Of course, I have no advice to give you. Peace be with you! *Salamalec*!' Now let's talk about you. You are, as you pointed out a while ago, the son of a barrister and of a Corsican countess … Between parentheses, I didn't really get what you said about 'nobility dating from the Empire.' I'm just an Arab pure and simple, excuse me. But you, don't depend on either makhzen or on Allah. As far as I know! And if I've understood the terms of the Protectorate, some Moroccan potentate (be it said in passing, the potentate in question is completely ruined) can not in any way impose his will on a young Frenchman of twenty years, the latter being the son of a barrister and of a Corsican countess whose nobility dates back to the Empire. Let's take an example: you're in the act of making love, I *suppose*! Suddenly a fly begins to buzz around the room. If you get up to swat it, tell me, for what reason did you come to Morocco? Our friendship is now severed, of course! (We can talk about that some other day.) So, in your soul and in your conscience, what did my father *order* you to do on the phone? To turn you into a coward? … And give me that bottle of beer. You've had enough to drink … *What*? I-tell-you-you-are-not-thirsty-any-more! I am. Now speak up!"

I could have gone on like that for some time more, have entered a room, demanded explanations, gone out. The circle of my friends. Report to Tchitcho the conversation that I had with Berrada, to Lucien the one with Tchitcho … plot. With the perfectly useless intensity that makes a single bead in a rosary stand out, its one distinguishing feature. Dense, I was dense. Under ordinary circumstances, satisfied by a plate of lentils, I would have acted otherwise. Come on! What would I have done? When the door slammed behind me, it made me stumble down the doorstep. I got to my feet and sat down on the step or on a flat stone, holding my head between my hands. I might have ended up falling asleep. Those who begin by going to sleep are wise ones.

I found myself once again at my point of departure, as a *mokkadem* with a tambourine howled that it was two o'clock in the morning. The winds of the *cherqui* had begun to blow. I was told that it was a wind that blew from the East. I don't think so. The *cherqui* came from everywhere, even from the sky. It was laden with sand and urine, heat and dryness, with an edge like metal and wholly unique. Salutation, oh master of French literature, you who found yourself in this wind one day and who had the gall to produce forty pages describing it! I have read those pages. You have said everything there is to say about the *cherqui*. I illustrate two phrases from it, and the wind swept me along like a great broom, as far as the bordello.

I had trouble getting Kilo out of there.

"Give me the key to your cabin. I see on your timesheet that you've set this afternoon aside for me (it is Friday) 'Friday... from two to ten in the morning: in a cabin once a urinal, Tolba Street...' The key! And go to my house. There is a street lamp there. Make use of it. Land on the terrace without making any noise and pick up everything that can be sold. Fifty-fifty. All right?"

He yelled: "all right!" and set off at a run.

The cabin contained a bottle of red wine, some beans mashed into a pulp in a mixing pail, and a straw mat. I drank, ate, and went to bed. The *cherqui* snored its sonorous insults.

I must have slept for some time. It was after dark when I opened my eyes.

"Twenty hours," said Kilo. "It's Saturday, eleven o'clock at night."

"And the wind?"

"It's blowing somewhere else."

He had turned the pail upside down and was sitting on it. Even though he was smiling, he looked peeved. The mashed beans spread out between his feet in an unwholesome geometry. I had not eaten everything up the night before, and Kilo had not emptied the pail outdoors before turning it over to use it as a seat. He was peeved.

"So?" I asked him.

"So, not much. Two cops were on guard at your house until dawn. I think they were waiting for you. Then your father came out, installed himself on his prayer rug, and began to give out money, as everybody was holding a hand to him . . . *Ten* francs!"

"That's all?"

"Of course not."

At the same moment, he lifted his heel and brought it down hard. A kind of brown pulp spread out around it, plus the tail of a lizard.

Kilo repeated, "No."

Then—I had thrown off my covers and was sitting bare-assed—he added, "Not bad, those accessories of yours!"

I quickly put on my undershorts.

"Accessories, you're right, simple accessories, but you had something more to tell me, I think."

"Yes."

On my feet, I take stock: Distractedly he was covering up the lizard pulp with the mashed beans, shaping it into ridges, then leveling it off and tamping it down. I noticed that he was smoking a short pipe with an ebony stem, after what series of tribulations to end up stowed between his teeth, I wonder. Let's not dig anything up, as I am in a hurry to hear.

"Look at this denture," he said.

Four incisors, two canines, two premolars, of eight hundred fifty gold. The denture looked familiar to me.

"Your father the hajji took it out and placed it in the hollow of his palm so that he could scrape away a little piece of meat that was hard to get off. Did I ever tell you that I was a pickpocket? There's the denture."

The hillock was transformed into a compact mass, clay or dirt to be modeled, and it had the form of an immense penis complete with attributes. Kilo got up.

"The Jew," he said.

"What Jew?"

"It makes no difference which one, the one who will buy these teeth from us. Fifty-fifty, remember."

"That's right ... but what time must it be?"

"Around midnight. Why? The Jew's never closed."

The Jew's name was Haroun Bitoun. He was stocky, dressed all in black, covered with hair from his head and his beard. When he saw the denture, he grabbed it out of my hands, placed it in a strongbox, pushed us outside and pulled down the metal grill that covered the front of his shop.

"How much?"

Now that he was in the street, he feared neither Hitler nor thunder and lightning. The vegetable is too expensive, sang Hyspa, and the Prophets denounced King Achab.

"At one hundred fifty francs per gram," proposed Kilo, "it ought to bring..."

"Not per gram," interrupted the Jew, "gold in bulk. Your piece of gold isn't worth more than two thousand francs."

"What did you say? I'll teach you, you lousy..."

"It's not worth a fight," I said. "He's the one to teach us. Two thousand francs?"

"Yes, Monsieur," said Haroun.

"I accept."

Haroun was unmoved.

"Monsieur, you have no guarantees, and this denture does not belong to you. Consequently I can only pay you in Spanish pesetas."

"In pesetas?"

"In pesetas. These pesetas, I know a *brother* who will exchange them for English pounds...Wait a minute. Another Jew will give you Indochinese piastres for the English pounds..."

"I don't understand."

"It's easy to understand. You can convert the piastres into rubles, the rubles into dollars, the dollars into Italian liras, and finally the liras into French francs."

"I assume this series of operations will not take place without including..."

"Yes, of course, there will be included some charges for the exchange service, Monsieur."

He rubbed his hands and became very serious.

"Charges of a thousand francs. That is what you can expect. I am ready to give you that much right now, just to save you time and effort, but if you really want to be paid in Spanish pesetas..."

"I prefer it that way."

He counted it out, and Kilo grabbed him by the fist, with neither brutality nor gentleness. Like a natural function, but the Jew understood immediately that that fist that was holding on to him had something in it similar to the curse of Jehovah.

"We'll all go together to take care of these various exchanges you've told us about," I said. "First of all, you're going to take us to this *brother* whose job it is to change pesetas into pounds."

We did not let Haroun go until the sun was up in the morning. He was outraged. "My beard I'll pull," he groaned, "my cheeks I'll line with the scratches of my fingernails—the Hebrews have been kings, and Issa, the king of the Heretics, was crucified for his efforts. Now an Arab is outwitting a Jew—and in the exchange of monies, oh Moses!"

"Now," I said to Kilo, "we're going to 'Neomi's Place.' Of the twenty-two thousand eight hundred francs we just ended up with, I think you would agree with me to divert a part of it. The warrior's fatigue, one might say, and I need to think a bit."

"'Neomi's Place?' Don't know it. A whorehouse? If that's what it is, I'll lead the way. If not, I'll follow you. In any case, I trust you, but tell me, Ferdi, how did you get the idea of all this stuff about the exchanges? I didn't know you had a business sense like that."

As we walked along, the sky began to pale and some pigeons cooed (let's say, duos of love). From the medina came a slight odor of something rotting (at awakening, savor a woman, savor a city). I explained to my companion that if a sum of money in Spanish currency would come to the half of its value in French francs, nothing was more simple than to ascend the chain, and that is just what I did, with the help of Haroun Bitoun, stupefied or not, from whom, after all, I did buy back the dentures, in pesetas.

"And the cost of the exchanges?" Kilo asked me.

"Were reimbursed. Do you know how to use a toothbrush?"

"No, but I'm going to become a moneychanger as of tomorrow."

"Why do that? Aren't you happy as you are? Just remember that it was your innate simplicity that drew me to you. Do you think that for me it was a question of sociability?"

"No propositions! Thanks all the same. Why? To have a lot of money, and to spend it on screwing."

"That's where we're heading."

Neomi put a bulb in a socket. The vestibule that smelled of onions and tobacco disclosed to us, like a photographic negative, an ancient Negro who was munching on an onion and puffing on a pipe, first a bite and then a puff. He was sitting down, but at first glance I estimated that he'd stand well over six feet tall. He looked inoffensive, for now.

"The light switch won't work," said Neomi. "The young ladies will be coming downstairs, so come on in, Gentlemen, good day, Gentlemen."

She pushed a button and took a look at Kilo's head. It was typically Arab, a thousand pardons, madame.

"That no!" she screamed. "We have rules and regulations here!"

"Rules and regulations?"

"These right here."

She pointed to a signboard. The Negro had put his pipe on his knee, then put the onion on the bowl of his pipe. He was paying close attention.

"You're all right," explained Neomi. "This Arab isn't. My lodgers don't have to take up with Darkies, and I can swear to you that that's the first time one of them dirties my door—and by Darkies I mean Darkies, Arabs, Yellows, Redskins and all that stuff that isn't Occidental, right!"

I didn't ask her if she was racist on principle or simply for economic reasons.

"This man is with me, and that's that."

She seemed relieved. She opened the door for Kilo. He disappeared, bent over, fatigued, chewing not on who knows what injuries, but with some bulky expectoration that would ease his feelings far from this brothel—in good old Bousbir probably.

I followed Neomi into the parlor. It was furnished with an armchair in which I installed myself, a bridge table, and a dozen young women who were smiling, enticing me, and very desirable. Neomi told me their names... Françoise... Paula... and some first names that I didn't know such as Annalia, Thorla, names I would have said for rare birds. They gave a little bow with the points of their breasts and took refuge behind their smiles.

"And so?" Neomi asked me.

She was smiling at me also. She was waiting for me to toss out a name, Françoise or Thorla, first I would set myself a quarter of an hour and then would go off with the girl of my choice.

"And so?" she repeated.

"From now till noon?" I said, "How much?"

She began to pout.

"That will cost you a thousand francs... plus the tip. So?"

"So here are thirteen thousand francs... Count them."

I grasped Thorla by the neck.

"This one will be the first, Madame. Show me the way, Madame."

It was Annalia who gave me the final kiss.

"I'd like to see you again, away from here. You are refined and you stand out. Can we meet?"

"Certainly we can, but you are too romantic, my darling."

"Monday?"

"Monday if you wish. That's my day off."

I knew I'd never see her again. I asked her to go downstairs to fix me a cup of tea.

"Impossible, darling. There hasn't been any tea to be found for the last two days. Not even on the black market."

Roche had talked to me about a priest named Father Blot. The next morning, Sunday, I went to ring the bell at his vicarage. He ushered me inside and had me sit down in a rattan armchair, then listened to me. I was abjuring Islam. The Catholic religion tempted me. I was asking for counsel.

"Obviously, it's a difficult problem to resolve. For three reasons: first of all, because it is badly stated, secundo, because I have not experienced it, and third, because I see it with the eyes of a European and a priest."

I don't know exactly what he said to me. The physiognomy that I am looking at intrigues me, and I try to understand to what point the problem that I have submitted to him is of less importance than the one that he himself poses for me. I stare with amazement at his regular features, so handsome and full of ardent life. He must be thirty years old. When he opened the door for me, I saw that he was tall and that when he seated himself it was gently, with a supple and feline grace, accentuated by a calm toss of his head against the back of his chair. This priest emanates such calm, such an animal magnetism of which he himself is conscious that I wonder what tale of love, what series of circumstances, what aggregation of coercive measures relegated him to the level of consoler of souls, this man who I feel, who I know, was destined uniquely for the satisfactions of the flesh.

A metal ruler that he turns about in his hands and that reflects the daylight that comes through the window to which he has turned his back brings me out of my distraction. Father Blot now has his elbows on the table and holds the ruler across his forehead.

"... to the highest pitch that you have kindly revealed to me the conditions of life growing up as a Moroccan child. There have been missionaries who have come here in their day. I don't think they ended up with a dozen conversions all in all. That doesn't keep us from ..."

And suddenly…

Suddenly, I felt my testicles grow hard. The church organ drew out some resonances that were already slow, and the priest was whispering. What was he whispering? I have no idea. He was whispering. His lips had the rhythm of a newborn babe as it suckled, sure, regular, heedless. For an instant, as if I were looking at him through field glasses and as if, as I looked through them I was regulating the instrument, they appeared to me protuberant and quivering, filling my optic field. That field grew darker and suddenly went black. *I became nothing but my hand.*

The right hand. I knew I had placed it gently on a shoulder, a shoulder of blue-green organdy and of connective flesh, as soft to the touch as the thigh of a pigeon. A shoulder! I know. A stream of blond hair that has the scent of a newborn adolescence appears a few centimeters before my face. I know how powerful my nose is, and how it could and would submerge itself in those tresses and draw out all the nectar. I know of concavities and convexities ready to unite and my aortas to harden. "The bones of the earth will moan the last day of days, and on your skulls, impious people, they will rain down like hail." My God, pardon me: I am a sinner, and I want to repent. "The bones of the earth will not moan the last day of days: Man has transformed them into cement."

Consequently, my God, surrender this shoulder to me. It belongs to a young woman, homely or beautiful, or even asexual, I don't care, behind whom I placed myself as I entered the place of worship. I would have gone back of a column in the church or any other object of creation, but she was there. And do you think I am going to interrogate myself on the series of circumstances that determined that I would…? One day I threw an onion to a hungry dog and he ate it right up.

It is a shoulder on which I placed my hand. To place it there, I closed my eyes. A blind man is the master of touch. Do you feel it, that hand? You were there, and I bless my luck. Luck is permitted to those who are in the know. But me, I'm not in the know. You were there, and I am going to make you an offering. Later on I will go away, then you will go away, you perhaps intact, but I with an abscess open to the very blood. Then, much later on, the lips of a husband or the teeth of a lover would make you shiver with pleasure. My hand? You probably do not even feel it. Nevertheless, in that hand as in a kind of refuge, I shall transform everything, flesh and wound and avatars and grandiose complexes, into delirium. I have told you: *I am nothing but a hand*.

First of all, accept my dream. Call it latency or whatever will define the real or $\delta \psi (M) dt$, I see nothing inconvenient in that. Who is concerned with ratiocinations at the moment that Destiny swoops down upon us? Listen to my dream, and do not be afraid.

That dream of mine, undefined, takes wing with the flight of green spheres under the familiar wind of future shadows. Tomorrow? ... Tomorrow will be the knell for open windows that were brutally closed for crazy reasons. Tomorrow will extinguish the stupid sound of stupid voices that bellow the terror of normal yapping; and spleen as it smokes will spit on our snouts from its hookah the drunken odor of shit or of fuel oil.

And do you know, I constructed giant ports with giant cranes that lifted mankind's worlds and torrents: I stayed useless, spineless, and alone on the dock.

And do you know, when the last ship with all its apostles had sunk, I cried out: "I am going to create others"—and calmly I began to laugh a laugh that was unctuous, bitter, and gay.

I have told you all of this in anger, young woman with the blond hair, blond as wheat and blond like the stars. You heard nothing, but had I spoken aloud, you would probably have hardly batted an eye.

Listen a bit more. I'm going to be even more violent. You were in front of me, my hand grasped your shoulder, I presume it is already black and blue and, if you have not moved away, any movement would have sufficed, a shudder would have sufficed, it is because you have been shaped by principles and propriety, good principles, good proprieties—how old could you be? Sixteen, seventeen, maybe less ... fifteen-sixteen-seventeen years of shaping!—or perhaps I imagine that I am violent: because I like violence. Yes? I am also sadistic. At first there was pride, pride as far as repression, then suppression as far as sadism, and sadism to consciousnessless. But do not be afraid. I assure you that it is only a question of an offering. The person making the offering is in distress, a poor little distress. Listen to me.

Once upon a time red suns pulsed in the temples of poets and of conquerors. And as water had more value than gold, they drank their perspiration and thanked Providence. But the sea itself would not have satisfied them. Out of the horror of the nadir was born the horror of vampirism. The law of the survival of the fittest found its justification. Nevertheless, the blood that was spared was sucked up to the very last drop by the victors. Resistance grew stronger; in their veins blood cured blood of any traces of civilization. There were those who, readjusting their mask that had fallen to the lowest level of torment, took their communion in the tabernacle of anger. Others laughed because others were weeping, but undeniably it was the advance of the strongest. Even monotony had no meaning except through the burning braziers and the burnt skulls. There was no more heaven, or somewhere in the heavens, the sun: but even without an interstice of blue, there was a blazing irradiation of thousands of suns.

And above and beyond the panting hornets, the votive saltings, and the gravel breaking open cracks in bare feet, above and beyond the flashes of guipures, and a need for a brutal male gratification predominated.

Then the cerebral convolutions that had been revealed from the very first horizon cried out like nerves stretched toward the infinite contrast of a slight chill.

It was only a stroller on a beach warmed by an August sun, a stroller whose muscles, cooled by a recent swim, need the kisses of those who have gone astray out there on the sand, those whose thighs and arms can annihilate to the point of asphyxiation all notion of reality.

In my soul and conscience I have felt the identical call of solitary bellowing bulls.

In my soul and conscience, I have told you, young woman.

Byzantinism and willful Byzantinism, young woman, in self-defense of my pride. Or is it quite simply no more than a mask for my mediocrity? In the main, I clasp your shoulder a bit more strongly.

Remember that in the beginning there was pride! Every being is born proud. Is not birth itself an act of pride? And I add: passivity is a quantum of pride. Gandhi.

Mister X will write: "... And I call truth everything that is continuous." Mister Y in his role of critic will be astonished: "What about falsehood? Is it not continuous as well? There are a thousand examples I could cite." That sound criticism would have buried Gandhi.

I call pride the possession of one's self. A few kilograms of flesh, blood, skin, cartilage, bowels, nails, a hair system, glands for making love, *dura mater*, gray cells, contours and forms, tares, avatars, beliefs, a critical sense, and appetite for believing, the five senses, kinesis and the world that one discovers, translates, adapts to one's self so perfectly that it becomes our own property. That was my pride, young woman, my ego, my portion, my contingencies. I took nothing from anyone.

Years have gone by. Here I am, clasping your shoulder. As a continuation of what? I'm going to tell you what. A story of teas, a brief trip to Fez, Hamid's death, and my rebellion.

"Perfect!" concluded Roche. "Keep that inside yourself, anchored deep in your memory. Study every fact of it, every incident. Later on when your vocabulary contains some eight thousand words and when distance has sufficiently well sharpened the contours of this rebellion, you can make a novel out of it."

*A novel*. A novel, do you hear? The ingredients would be: a story of teas, a brief trip to Fez, Hamid's death, and my rebellion. If only I could still laugh, young woman!

But precisely until the moment that I placed myself behind you I have not ceased to be a puppet in my novel. And at that very moment, I emerge from that role, I escape from it. That is why I spoke to you of an offering that I extend to you although I cannot assign a place to you whose face I have not seen and who will walk away without anything more. You stray from the path a moment more. You stray from the path a moment to vomit, and then start on your way again either feeling better or else a bit more ill.

I was telling you about my initial ego. It began to disintegrate one day. Day after day, it disintegrated more and more. Tender gestures were refused me, mute suffering was detected and condemned, my enthusiasms stifled, games forbidden, separations quickly brought to a halt. By dogma, for dogma, in dogma. I kept quiet and dutifully followed the Straight and Narrow. And I would have continued to follow it had it not been for a sudden incident.

One day a schoolbag was substituted for my slateboard, and a European suit for my jellaba. That day my ego was reborn. For a very short time. Other commandments came to take over the older ones, and I who had obeyed the latter, had to obey the former. They were as follows: "There is no Divinity but Allah, and of Allah we are the representative on earth. If we grant you the right to breath in a certain quantity of air, a certain quantity of air and nothing more is what you shall breath in. And if you permit yourself any dissoluteness, Allah shall surely damn you, but we will already have strangled you with our own hands."

There were as follows: "The world has changed, my son. The first person who loves a man is the man himself. However, if he has children, his greatest desire is that they be better than he in every way. We are going to reproduce ourself in you, perfect ourself in you. We are from the century of the Caliphs, you will belong to the twentieth century. If we have installed you in the camp of the enemy, it is so that you will familiarize yourself with his arms. That, and no other reason."

I call sadistic any being capable of exuberance that vegetates and wants nothing more than to vegetate. I call his other faculties, tendencies and potential. I was both one and the other, and I was satisfied to nourish my hatred, abetted by the example of *my intelligence that European education was developing, to the detriment of all my other faculties*. Second stage, that I also disdained. I did not nourish myself with literature.

The third stage is one I am trying to go beyond. When my brother died and was buried, I left. It was a pretext—one day or another I would have left anyway—a sort of exteriorization, to be transformed into acts, into words to be put into concrete form. I left in order to stake my claim. Listen to me, young woman.

"I cannot take you in," Tchitcho said. "Not even for one night. My father is a lawyer. Your father entrusted him with the tea business, with fabulous fees. If I gave free bent to my friendship, your father would take another lawyer."

"My father is the manager of a textile corporation," said Lucien. "The principal stockholder is named Hajji Fatmi Ferdi, but I'm not telling you anything new. Now, I want you to understand me, Driss, if I ..."

"... if you gave free bent to your friendship ... Oh yes! Goodbye, sir!"

"I am a cosmopolite," Roche said. "I am at home everywhere, and nowhere do I have a home. Take you in? Take you in where? And why? If you were still passive ... but you only want to be active ..."

"Why, Monsieur Roche, what about your teachings? Your critical dissections, your amusing stories, your thrashings, your anarchism? ... I considered you to be my true educator ..."

"And so? I'm going to confide something in you: this country needs anarchists. Who knows? Perhaps one day the disciple will eclipse the master."

And Father Blot, young women! This priest who officiates, who looks at you, who listens to you. I visited him this morning in his vicarage. I was the first one there. I was sincere, I was good, I was pitiful. Ready to offer myself up, a monk or a latrine cleaner for Christianity. And you know what? (I weep as I tell you that, weep tears that you cannot see and that you cannot hear, silent hard tears.) Of my whole being, my whole wounded being, do you know what Father Blot retained? *His priest's perspective.*

"Of the greatest interest what you have told me about growing up as a child in Morocco. In earlier times ... it's no matter that ..."

A Counterfeiter! All counterfeiters! Lucien, Tchitcho, Roche and that nasal-voiced priest. Every one of them saw me from his own perspective. Me? I'm a beefsteak passed from one hand to the other, weighed, examined, sniffed at, and haggled over ... Ho! A beefsteak!

Then it's my turn to see things from the perspective of my ferocity. Fabulous fees? The principle stockholder? Cosmopolitanism? A childhood in Morocco? Who do you think you're talking to? I'm not the handle on a frying pan.

Let's get to the core of the matter: you do not accept me. I cannot be your equal, because that is your secret fear: that I become your equal, and that I come to demand my place in the sun. Oh yes!

I know there are those who rubbed their hands with joy when I rebelled and when I rejected the world of the Orient.

"That is not all," I said. "Move over. I'm going to sit down too."

"*How's that?*"

How's that? Did you think that I was going to consider my revolt as a good conduct mark on my report card? That I should store away that energy without giving it form or utilizing it? That I should be static? Take a post as superintendent for Rights of Entry or secretary-interpreter, a kind of no-man's-land?

"And so, dear friend, you have not yet gone back home? ... No? ... You are a cretin, dear friend."

More than they think. If I had reflexes, sensations, sentiments, and ideas while I was at the Koranic school, neither one nor the other were the first ones. Victor Hugo, Kant, and the Counterfeiters turned them off course. So far off course that they helped me, me who had rebelled and candidly considered my rebellion like a deliverance—*for delivering me from this rebellion.*

"And so, dear friend? This little game of yours can go pretty far. Have you come to any result yet?"

Young woman, I have communicated this result with my hand. The beefsteak has become an authentic sole of a shoe, and the ego of which I was talking a while ago, because it was still in a false situation, became very determined. Determined to live as the sole of a shoe, and it is as the sole of a shoe that one day or another—I am set on this goal—I shall disembark in France, and up in the heart of France,

Paris, me the sole of a shoe, balls and brains, sadism and good will. Lucid, do you hear me?

"Let me go!...You're hurting me..."

Oh yes!...Young woman, time I believe and I hope, will take charge of determining my absolute. As it already has reminded me that I am no longer an Oriental to give me permission to cut off a slice, to stabilize it in a neutral position, to find refuge there. As it reminds me that I am only the character in a novel. Too bad, young woman! I thought I had been liberated from all that.

"Let go of me...will you let go of me!"

There...there...The character will be reinstated in chapter four...

"What is all this mixture of essay and of novel, all these agglutinated terms?..."

I have let go of her. She turned around toward me, still shaking her shoulder. No doubt she saw my eyes. She fell in a faint.

I left the church, and Tchitcho offered me a cigarette.

"I'm reminding you that the testing for the baccalaureate certificate is tomorrow at eight o'clock."

He didn't say another word and started to go away. Like a road sign that is found to signal a detour. Chat? Let's be practical: I asked him for a light for the cigarette he had just offered me. Then I went back to my hotel room, shaved, drank a cup of coffee, and slept. I dreamed about the girl dressed in organdy, the girl who had the power to empty me—as the girls in Neomi's place had made me ejaculate.

He was drumming a tattoo on my door. I got up and opened it. He was wearing espadrilles. He seemed to be thirsty. I handed him a carafe of water. He drank, gave me a cigarette, and helped me get dressed. We went down the front stairway. The cool morning air stung me and made droplets of perspiration form on my forehead.

"The stomach, Tchitcho," I said "or at least the liver, controls good health."

"I know," was all he answered.

He made a grimace that was almost a smile. He was tall, taller than I, very thin, thinner than I. He was a bit stoop shouldered and walked like a crab. The sky was clouded, a few dogs rummaged through garbage, the macadam stretched out in front of us, shining in places where a car had pissed its oil and where the sun hit it.

I wanted to say to my companion: "I am touched. You want me to take the test for my diploma. You chased after me in my hotel room. I think you are my friend, and I was wrong. I treated you like shit and you've already forgotten it. Forgive me!"

I said to him: "Have you any news for me from home?"

"No, but it won't be long before you go back there."

"Why?"

"I presume so. In any case, it's preferable."

As we were going through the gate of the school, he handed me a carefully folded newspaper.

"There's an article in there that could be of interest to you. I marked it off with red pencil."

I sat down at a desk, before some thirty backs, before a blackboard on which a piece of chalk had just elegantly written out the subject of the essay on France: "Liberty, Equality, Fraternity." The boots of the monitor sound a coming and going that reminds me of the pendulum of the clock of the Lord. Noisier, no doubt, but just as regular and clearly defined. Pens scratch, coughs are repressed while the sun up in the sky has moved with its accompaniment of clouds, and I have awakened.

A short while earlier, seated under a chestnut tree in the playground, I read the newspaper article, without enthusiasm. An affidavit, but it did wake me up.

Liberty, Equality, Fraternity, no, I never underestimated the power of the Lord. *"No one knows how the phenomenon came about, but there is not an ounce of tea to be found in the markets."* I like such clear, clean terminology.

Most of these backs are unknown to me. Why unclothe them?

Better to leave them covered with their eczema, and their shoulder blades and spines sticking out. The habit makes the monk, and illusion is something to be cherished. If the man who was my father was capable of juggling events, by heavens, what else can you expect of him?

Liberty, Equality, Fraternity. I am thirsty for words, hungry for incantations. "A stay in prison," the Lord taught me, "makes a just guard of a convict and a convict of the just guard. The important thing is to be one or the other from the very beginning. For us, the choice would be to be a convict."

I wept, and he slapped my face: "He is bad" when what he wanted me to learn from it was: "Be tough." Liberty, Equality, Fraternity. One day you will find yourself face to face with the ruin of your enterprises: energy or your poems? My poems, father, my poems!

The blackboard is an assemblage of boards, in short, the boots against the floor sound quite different, if I were to wear them, with application and method, stamping on my latest excrescences—but who was it who talked to me about symbiosis? "The symbiosis of the Oriental genius, of Muslim traditions and of European civilization..." Vague, very vague, which is to say: Let's do some demolishing there, and amiably smother the matter. There may be shit at the bottom of the pot of honey. Symbiosis, yes, but: the symbiosis of my rejection of the Orient and of the skepticism that the Occident is creating in me. That is called a poem, father. I dipped my pen in the inkwell and began to write.

Liberty, Equality, Fraternity: *hic* the subject.

Apropos—An American periodical informed me recently that some chemical engineers at Harvard University, specializing in the study of plastics, had succeeded in extracting an appreciable quantity of acetyl-polyvinyl and of chewing gum of very good quality from a pumpkin that was picked in Sidi Bel Abbès, Algeria, and sent to the U.S.A. That means that the slogan of the French Republic "Liberty, Equality, Fraternity" would furnish material for:

*Fixing the boundaries of the subject.*

a) A good novel of the old type: Morocco, land of the future, of sun, couscous, wogs, a male Noraf on a donkey and the female walking behind, the souks, the shantytowns, pashas, factories, dates, muezzins, mint tea, fantasias, *khaîmas*, jellabas, haiks, turbans, snake charmers, public storytellers, pidgin French, *méchoui*, *kesra*, drought, grasshoppers—is that all? No!...the tam-tam, the sorcerers, the dug-out canoes, the tsetse fly, the savannah, the coconut trees, the banana trees, poisoned arrows, Pluto, Tarzan, Captain Cook...What in the hell does the slogan of the French Republic have to do with all of that?

"Just so! An old monkey is going to mix all of that up, between two cocktails, between two farts, between two yawns, *is going to make a novel out of it*: a comitragic love story with local color and with such themes as: Morocco-the-land-of-the-future, of sun, couscous, wags, a male Noraf on a donkey and the female walking behind..."

"What about the slogan? The famous slogan?"

"Keep your hat on, gentlemen! The monkey is clever. Just like an old Ford in the hands of a good mechanic, your slogan will come out of this novel running smoothly, repaired, checked out, 'like new'—to such an extent you'll wonder if it ever had more clout."

b) A good whodunit novel: Callaghan, Fantômas, eroticism, crime, mystery, adventure, sudden developments, theatrical effects, flying saucers, a potato, another potato, a third potato...

"But, sir, what about the slogan?"

"Sirrr, I am a monkey!"

c) A poem in verse and in Alexandrines written in the manner of a Negro baptized three times and of whom we ask something about the condition of Negritude: "Me no yet White, but no more Nig: Liberty!"

d) a song for a singer;

e) a politico-economic treatise;

f) an algebraic illustration for the Taylor series;

g) an octavo of history;

h) a *modus vivendi*;

i) a *casus belli*;

j) a registered trademark;

k) and, if I were an American, a railway guide.

Let us fix the boundaries of our subject. I am neither novelist nor poet nor economist nor mathematician nor singer nor historian nor practical joker. I am simply a young man nineteen years old sitting on a bench before a student desk. And here is what is essential to my meaning: the factor of being a *candidate*, the one who is going to write on the subject.

I know very well, gentlemen examiners, that a student's copy ought to be anonymous, without a signature, name, first name of any kind of mark that would indicate who the author was. I also know very well that the canvas reveals the painter. That is to say that some time ago you penetrated my personality: I am an Arab. So allow me to write about the aforementioned subject as an Arab. Without a plan, without a technique, gauche, belabored, but I promise you I will be frank.

Let's be more precise. As I was coming here this morning, I met an American in the Military Police. He stopped his Jeep.

"You French?" he asked me.

"No," I answered. "An Arab dressed like a Frenchman."

"Then ... where are the Arabs dressed as Arabs, speaking Arabic and ..."

I pointed in the direction of the old Muslim cemetery.

"Over there."

He set off.

Why tell this anecdote? It tries to show that the author of this treatise is an Oriental with a vocabulary of some three thousand words, half educated, half rebel and for the last forty-eight hours in a bad situation both materially and in morale.

*Getting into the subject matter.*

An aged bonze named Raymond Roche, a friend of mine, said to me last night: "We French are civilizing you Arabs. Doing it badly, in bad faith and without any pleasure in it.

Because if by chance you become our equals, I ask you: with regard to whom and to what will we then be civilized?" The subject is "Liberty, Equality, Fraternity." I am not fully qualified to speak on the subject. On the other hand, I can easily substitute another subject to replace it, one with which I am familiar: "Muslim Theocracy." Using such a theorem of similar triangles, I presume that the result will be the same or at least very similar.

*Development.*

The five commandments of Islam in order of importance are the following:

Faith;

the five daily prayers;

the fasting of the month of Ramadan;

annual charity;

the pilgrimage to Mecca.

As for the first commandment, everyone believes in Allah although the "average Moroccan" does not respect the corollaries: you can swear and forswear, lie, be an adulterer, and drink, but faith is secure, and Allah is All Powerful and All-Merciful.

As for prayers, only persons of a certain age say them, even though for most of them it is a matter of habit or merely for show. Consequently, the person who is a believer in Allah fasts during the month of Ramadan, avoids wine and pork, says his five prayers every day, and pulls the Devil by the tail, as long as he has reached a certain age and wears a heavy string of prayer beads around his neck and has a thick beard.

My grandfather became a saint posthumously, because he was poor, pious, and a lunatic.

Fasting is usually a part of the beliefs and is followed everywhere as a ritual dating back a thousand years. Which is to say that except for those who must work every day to provide for their needs, people stay in their beds until noon and get together for interminable games of poker or lotto to kill time and to deceive their hunger. Games of chance are forbidden by law, and Ramadan is a month of meditation and prayer. I always saw my father in a particularly foul humor during the month because he could not smoke. He would go out and take a little walk around midday, then would come home and exhaust every subject of conversation and every occasion for an argument. In the evening, he would become the pleasantest of men once more because he had smoked, and he would not converse because he smoked until dawn.

When the Prophet Mohammed preached fasting, it was so that everyone, rich and poor, young and old, would all suffer alike during a set period, from dawn to dusk, from the hunger from which the poor suffer uniquely and eternally. It was also for the purpose of persuading everyone to maintain a character of equality everywhere and in all circumstances, so that their abstinence from food and drink, from sexual or other kinds of pleasures would forge character and, by purging mind and body, would predispose people to spiritual matters that would elevate them toward Allah. And finally, it was to make certain that life, with its monotony of day to day routine cut into by a complete change of daily habits for one month in twelve, would not turn men into robots.

The fourth commandment is defined by the following laws:

A tithe of 2.5 percent of one's goods should go obligatorily to the poor;

this tithe is annual and must be as precise as possible;

non-revenue producing real estate is not liable to taxation.

In Morocco, the Day of the Year of the Hegira has been adopted for the enrichment of the poor. Actually, I have always seen a distribution of coins, figs, and dates by grocers and shopkeepers on the particular day. The rich take their precautions in advance, transforming their liquid assets into fixed assets which, according to Islamic law, cannot be taxed. That way, they have nothing to give to anyone and don't have to give an accounting to their conscience or to Allah. The Prophet had not foreseen such subtle dishonesty. Furthermore, assets and real estate acquired in this manner can increase tenfold in a very short time. That is one way to explain miracles in business affairs.

On the other hand, there may be some poor who get together a tidy little sum on that day. They'll be beggars again the next day due to having sent all the money they collected back to their little village to buy a patch of ground or some livestock.

The pilgrimage to Mecca is a pretext for rich Moroccans to visit countries of the Middle East. I cite my father's case as an example. He was away for three years, supposedly to plunge himself into meditation at the Kaaba, the sacred Black Stone. When he came back from the pilgrimage, he distributed dates from Medina and sandalwood to his family and friends, all happy to receive so much as a grain of dust from the sacred land. My mother still licks at one of those famed dates on the twenty-seventh night of Ramadan, the Night of Power when "angels and demons fraternize in paradise on lawns covered with rose petals." My father extended his right hand in a magnanimous gesture, and everyone kissed it and is still kissing it while bestowing its possessor with the title of Hajji, which is to say, someone who has been to Mecca. Later on, he was to apprise us of the fact that the greater part of his fortune had melted away in the fleshpots of Damascus and Cairo, but that he had truly meditated before the Kaaba and so had a right to his title. Glory be to Allah the All-High, the Father of the Universe and King of the Last Judgment!

*Conclusion.*

Man proposes and time disposes, but not even a shoeblack from Medina would so acknowledge, and that is what gives Islam its strength.

There is still the theorem of similar triangles spoken of earlier, but I am confused about this. You gentlemen who are doing the examining should not establish a parallel too quickly, too exactingly. I still have something more to say—about which

I want to impress you to take notice before ending this. The report that I have just written up in the form of a treatise could be considered a kind of rejection of my antecedents. Not wholly so, however, as I still have many strings to cut, many memories that need to be sat on, but that is not the fundamental question. What is important is my present situation, of which I am not fully conscious, as if it were a convalescence—nor fully satisfied. Even though I am still shackled to my tormented past, and to my bookish learning and the counterweights, and to the dressage training and sweetened teas, I have committed myself to your way of life, gentlemen. I have not entered into the marriage as a *virgin*, but as a spouse "who has greatly suffered." Consequently if I say: "Liberty, Equality, Fraternity: a slogan as rusty as ours is," you will no doubt understand me. Nevertheless, as I go along, I still dare to hope that those words will be cleansed and refurbished, regaining their impact and the seductive power that my books communicated to me—for ever so slight a bit of optimism which your humble servant so deeply needs, and for the greater glory of France. Amen!

I was daydreaming on a bench in Murdoch park. A hand grabbed me by the lapel of my jacket.

"On your feet, *hallouf!*"

It was Tchitcho. I followed him—or to be more accurate, he dragged me as far as the playground of the school, the two marching quietly along like a pair of soldiers. Tchitcho kept nudging me with his elbow. He was excited about something.

"Look at this, *hallouf.*"

He pointed to a signboard. A list of candidates who had passed the exam was fastened to it with thumb tacks. My name was on the list.

"Look here! Driss Ferdi... Passed with distinction."

A voice sounded behind us.

"Monsieur Ferdi!"

It was Joseph Kessel. A man of letters, the great traveler?

"No, the licentiate in letters, and the sedentary, and I'll say nothing worse. Your examiner, Monsieur Ferdi. Please come in."

We went into the headmaster's office.

"Please sit down. Cigarette? ... So you are the Moroccan Martin Luther? You really made me laugh, you did! To take a look at you as thin and pale and timid as you are ... Mademoiselle Uller, a maiden lady and a colleague of mine, laughed too. That skill, the erudite tone, that 'serious' violence, and despite all the barely disguised puerility throughout your treatise ... You've heard of Vannier, haven't you? He was an ace. Now I've put on some stomach and belong to the teaching profession, but I can remember. You listening, Ferdi? Vannier and I, you weren't even born yet, two slender determined young men, two high school students on vacation ... we decided to set off at random, and we opted for Morocco ... Really, that way of making a clean sweep of everything before, Uller, Mademoiselle Uller found very exciting, but I didn't. At any rate, you had to do it sooner or later. And so, my dear Ferdi ... apropos, what does the name Ferdi mean? Well, Vannier and I, he has since died, poor guy, cancer of the prostate I think—we did some flying. That was the good times. But you, dear boy, you don't know what you're missing, this sun, this sky, but it's a new country with promise ... Casablanca was not called Casablanca but Sidi Belyout. We were pioneers in the delivery of airmail. You've heard of the aerial postal system? The pioneers! Of course I've not returned, but seems like yesterday ... Overflowing, indeed! Really it hasn't changed: factories, buildings, garages, roads and all the rest, but the Arab himself has not changed. I'm going to tell you something. In 1938 I published a whole series of articles on my journeys entitled 'The Maghreb, Land of Fire.' Local color, that's what interests the European reader, like a painting of the veiled women and the casbahs ... Uller, Mademoiselle Uller, wanted to send your essay to a Parisian newspaper, but I thought about it a while ... So, dear friend, what do you think about your relationship to the Noraf? You, of course, have evolved and are an exception ... The disturbances that certain so-called Nationalists brandish on high are disturbing, don't you find? But in final analysis, they're just a bunch of musketeers, all good guys, because if we French leave, it is clear that some other nation . . . After thinking a bit more about it, it would be possible to place your essay if you wish as a kind of today's thing. But tell me, what about the Sultan? Just between the two of us, he seems to be very conventional. Let's face it, no eagle . . . I've never really seen him. To get back to your essay, original, but Uller, Mademoiselle Uller was shocked. You have to comprehend her, my friend, she expected you to conclude . . . How shall I say it? It's very simple, I marked you a ninety-five, the maximum, because it is very clear that youth, true Moroccan youth, is right there in that essay. You know very well that the policy of the Protectorate is precisely to bring out . . ."

The telephone began to crackle.

"Hello! . . . One moment, dear friend. Hello! . . . Hello, for whom are you asking? The *broufizour*? Do you mean the *proviseur*, the headmaster? How's that? You say you are an Arab? Well, my friend, when an Arab telephones the headmaster, he does so with the help of an interpreter, *that* I can tell you."

He hung up.

"Things never change! But remember, the policy of the Protectorate . . ."

The telephone rang again.

"Hello! Hello! Yes! The interpreter? What interpreter? Yes . . . and then, *what do you want of me, you two?* Speak fast and clearly. My time is precious . . . *What?* . . . yes . . . of course."

He put the phone back on its cradle, suddenly acting very serious.

"Yes, my dear friend, we're going to have to end our conversation for today. Yes, a reception I must attend. Oh, the obligations, the . . . even in this Land of Fire . . . *Tell me, what are you going to do now?*"

"That is to say," I answered him, "that if you had wanted to talk with me, let's say to get to know me, it was what I would call a tourist complex, for lack of a more academic term. I myself was the receptor. That's also to say that I have not reacted in the way you wanted me to and that you know at present what conclusion to give to our conversation. I'm going to put you at ease. What am I going to do now? First of all, get up."

I go up.

"Then ask your two favors."

"Go ahead! Go ahead!"

His tone had changed. And to say that the Arab had remained exactly the same, ever since the advent of airmail service!

"The first thing I ask is that you take a look at the furnishings of this room. I was listening to you so intently that I didn't even do that. But now I'm going to look ... Let's see, a mahogany desk, highbacked chairs, a collection of Berber artifacts, the usual piles of paper dear to headmasters, the shutter closed—an old habit—a siphon of soda water on the small table, the bottle of pastis is somewhere in the wall cupboard ... and a few flies, a smell of wax, of hot cardboard and of very old mice. Understand me! I am obliged to *assign places*. Pardon me, sir!"

I pushed Joseph Kessel's bulk aside and went toward the door.

"The second favor is to have permission to leave. Goodbye, sir. Very happy to have met you."

"Ferdi!"

I turned around.

"You have something more to add? For example, that I am a boor, that you have honored me by treating me in such a familiar fashion, and that you are astonished, even outraged by my attitude? ... That I am not of sufficient stature for revolutionaires? I know all of that ... And that consequently, the best thing for me to do would be to go back home, the home that I never should have left? That's what I'm going to do. I'm going right now. Anything else to say to me?"

"Just this, Ferdi ... (his stomach trembling, his jowls trembling) this: I made a mistake in your case. I should have given you a good round zero, but I'll be waiting for you at the oral examination, my friend ... and I'll see to it that you're booted out, my friend."

"Agreed."

Tchitcho was waiting for me in the yard. He seemed more upset than ever.

"So?"

"So, so long, Tchitcho, I'm going back home... *Yes!* I say so long to you because, of course, I'll see you again."

The fake palm trees of the Boulevard Victor Hugo welcomed me and escorted me. It was decidedly bizarre! That French poet Hugo is everywhere, even in Morocco, even in my distress, and I happen not to like his work. I did once though. I was moved by his epics, his prose, and his Biblical tableaus. Then biographies revealed the man to me, not a deception, basically impulsive. Politely I led the burglar back to the door, with a thousand excuses, I advise you to go to the jobs-wanted office. Roche told me that over and above real life, every man carries something of dreams inside himself. I wonder if that very part, in Victor Hugo, was not precisely the outcome of the mediocrity of his life.

I strolled along the boulevard feeling exhausted. There were great heavy clouds moving overhead. To the south-southwest, one of them, solitary and gray, remained strangely fixed in place. Hidden behind it, it must have been the sun, I'll chase away the blues, and will illumine the harvest fields, I lifted my eyes toward the tops of the trees. Not a leaf was stirring. The air was heavy, warm and static, a little short of the air that my bronchial tubes had need of.

I lowered my eyes and saw Roche. His arms were dangling, and his mouth was open. When he got up to me, his arms opened in a gesture of welcome, and his mouth confirmed the gesture.

"Kraut-head?... Of course it's Kraut-head! Hi! What's become of you?"

A Jeep filled with bricks suddenly appeared, grazed the sidewalk and backfired off into the distance.

"Monsieur Roche, either we have met fortuitously or you have been following me."

"I've just been taking a little walk," he protested.

"Perfect!" I concluded, "then go on with it. This stop is to no avail. In the future nothing of this kind should happen. I have known you for a long time. Our paths have separated, and I'm convinced that their divergence will become even greater. Life inevitably provokes such ablations. Why in the devil should an individual, even if his function is that of a stimulus, be stuck to our ass to the very last chapter?"

"You've learned from my lessons," he said. "I'm pleased about that. One question, however, before we go our ways: are you going back home?"

"I'm going back home."

"Regards!"

His white baggy trousers were billowing as he walked away. They brightened up the gray sky for a moment and then became a part of it.

"Regards!" I said.

I began walking toward the Lord's house again.

Everything came together to make me go back, my illusions that had burst like soap bubbles and my rebellion that was as sterile as dried shit, the newspaper article, my success, Joseph Kessel and his phone call, Tchitcho and the fact that he had waited for me, and Roche who had come to find me, despite his saying he was just taking a walk—it's clear, I am a billiard ball.

Even to the symmetry. My first minutes of liberty had been characterized by funny incidents. The symmetry was established when I went out into Benghazi Square. Between the two boundaries a difference of potential had certainly been produced. I would have had to be prepared to subjugate myself. What does that mean, I asked myself. Better to give me something to eat. The statism of the present, and I was as cold as a fisherman's behind.

As I went out into Benghazi Square, a door fell shut. That door had its history.

Three Berber brothers have a shop. There is a single pair of babouches to shod the three of them. One of them does the selling, another does the cooking in back of the store, and the third is out doing shopping and gets to wear the babouches. They change responsibilities from one day to the other. Most of the time they get their nourishment from bread dipped in olive oil that they get in the following manner: in transferring the oil to the customer's receptacle, they use a funnel. After each transaction, the funnel is placed in the mouth of a bottle. As oil is very much in demand, the bottle, which is empty in the morning, is only half so by evening, and there they have their meal well earned.

Everybody in the New Medina knows that store where you can get everything, from kitchen salt to gunpowder, not to mention lemonade and white mice, and that has always been open for the last twenty years, day as well as night. The building in which they are housed has changed hands many a time.

"The facade of the building was restored," said an onlooker. While they were shutting the door of the shop to paint it, it fell down. The hinges were so rusty that they had held together only out of habit.

---

Two streets further on, I heard a child crying. The impatient voice of a man muffles the cries.

"You know what it is now? Here are a hundred grams, here are fifty grams, here are a hundred grams, do you understand?"

The two voices come from a store that is closed and from which show some slender strips of light.

"It is a man who is trying to teach a child to learn weight," a passerby says to me.

For a child to be beaten is a daily occurrence. No crowd gathers. People shrug their shoulders and go their way.

I go up to the store. I look through the crack. There is a child on the ground. His buttocks are bare. So are the man's. There are no scales for weighing anything, nor is there a whip. Just simply a bowl of oil that the man sticks his hand into. Maybe that's how he'll get the child to stop crying

---

Hajji Moussa of the Small Stomach, feet bare and hands joined, ran along behind his donkey that was piled high with bundles of mint.

As it trotted along, the donkey turned its head and snatched a bunch. The man cursed it.

"Hajji Moussa..."

He stopped.

"Yes, my child?"

"Hajji Moussa, there's something I promised to tell you a long time ago. It's this. The front of your house is covered with grapevines, isn't it?

"Well, from morning to night, the naughty kids of the whole neighborhood bombard it with rocks to make the clusters fall."

"So what?" he said. "I don't even water those vines."

Then he saw that the donkey was already far in the distance. Cursing my ascendance and my descendance, he ran off.

———

Bachir, called Trippa, the butcher, was washing down his stall. When he saw me go by, he stopped dead still, sponge in hand and cigarette butt stuck to his lower lip. A few instants later, he grabbed hold of me, walked along beside me without saying a word, sponge in hand and butt on the lip, all the time staring closely at me. Then he turned back and I heard him cry out to himself, "So lamb is two hundred francs a kilo? Well I sell it for fifty. Fifty, you hear? Who wants meat as fresh as water from a well, as red as blood... fifty francs, come one come all!"

Bachir, called Trippa, the butcher, was going to make use of the return of Driss The Accursed—a fine story and a fruitful bit of gossip to help him get rid of his stinking merchandise.

———

Ahmed ben Ahmed the beggar, with his fists gripping a walking staff and his abdomen on his fists, was bellowing his hunger.

He had his torso almost horizontal, his feet spread apart, and his face turned up toward the Lord's window.

"Hajji Fatmi Ferdi, throw me a load of bread of tender wheat, not of barley nor of corn nor of rye: of tender wheat. Your son is dead, your other son ran away—do you hear me? Do you hear me?..."

I pressed my index finger against his coccyx.

"Fifty kilos of barley weren't enough for you? The sky could fall down and you'd still be begging. Why do you beg?"

He stood as straight as the organ of a zebra. He seemed surprised. He smelled like a wet dog.

"I'm going to tell you, son."

He handed me his staff.

"I have some papers to show you. Can you read?"

He hunted around in his jellaba. He fished out an immense billfold. I twisted the staff in my fingers. Night was falling. Suddenly it was dark, without an intervening evening or twilight. One moment it was still day. Now it was night.

"Begging is not demeaning, with all due deference to those who do not beg but who are demeaned all the same. In this *choukkara* there is a whole life, as I will show you. Beggars have their history."

I had no need of that. I looked at the staff. Bringing it up to eye level, I examined it attentively in the light of the streetlamp that had just been lit. At almost the same time, thirty or forty others had lit up from space to space—and that had created two lines, two rails of sparkles between earth and sky.

"You're looking at my 'third leg'? I've had it for thirty years. It's a branch of walnut that I cut myself when I was a shepherd. Yes, shepherd! My father had vast domains...These papers...You'll see..."

I had no need of anything more. I gave him back his staff. Very sad. A walnut branch! "Third leg," during thirty years! Held at the same place, faithful and sure, so atrociously that *the hand of Ahmed ben Ahmed the beggar had worn away the wood and had made a deep imprint on it.*

"And the French Army has capitulated on the Tunisian front?" yelled the bearded man. "Good news! My son remains there, riddled with bullets, bad news! All the same I've just learned that my niece got herself fig-figged by some American blacks, so things even out, if you will…and why not? All the same, The Eternal One is immovable and we wait, plants, animals, and people, until the sky pisses its rain."

His beard had grown thicker since my departure, with ringlets and crazy locks marked here and there with a spot of brown. *He had lifted his cigarette to his mouth and lighted it.*

"A mathematical progression," I said, "or else an absurd absurdity of our poor world? You are going to tell me that it is a question of the same single cigarette? The one that…"

He quickly pointed with his finger toward the Lord who was standing on the doorstep.

———

"I have come back."

"Who said the contrary? Come in."

No belligerence, no. Quite simply the door opened and closed behind me. A switch was turned, and the vestibule appeared coldly mosaic, raw and without life. Like hotel rooms rented for a quarter of an hour to couples who are in a helluva hurry, or those antechambers for petitioners…

"Come up."

"I'll come up," I said. "You were the nipper-in-the-bud?"

"We were. Come up."

"I'm coming up. And the interpreter?"

"Camel."

Time can wrinkle, dig into a face, an old theme, an old religiosity. Steps, shoes, tanks, where they pass, they leave their mark. I look at the cement steps as I ascend them, regularly, one by one. Where are they worn, these steps? Can you please tell me what time means for cement? Certainly anyone who breaks against one, like tide against a cliff. The eternal gnawing? The triumph of the abstract.

The Lord had lit the stair light, a stairwell that ascended toward the darkness, like the maledictions of creatures toward their creator, like an uppercut to a smiling jaw, like a penis toward the female sex. Right on! I climbed the stairs resignedly, lifting myself up not from one step to the following one, from one time span to another time span—a life to start over? another worn-out theme?—but towards the Lord. He was facing me, going up the stairs backwards. I found him strong, with a strong sense of joy: I had thought he was defeated. He was staring at me and was sweating huge drops. One drop ran down his forehead and was static a moment as if surprised to be there, like a young chick on coming out of the shell and remaining immobile faced with the world, dumbfounded—I wonder if at that moment they don't feel like returning to their embryonic state. Then suddenly the drop falls. The bushiness of the eyebrows or of the beard where it nestles is dry and shining. Black, above all.

"Roche insisted on knowing where I was going. He was calm and talked in a detached way. His tone and calm manner are something unusual. I told him I was returning to the fold."

"There was nothing else to say."

"Did you..."

"...send him out to scout? Yes, I did."

"Tchitcho?"

"Your friend François as well."

"What's going on?"

He turns the switch for the light in the patio. I had expected to see the mattresses still strewn about, plus plates of *kesra* yellow in the center, and spots of children's urine dried and redried in the sun, wool in that place can only be felt or esparto grass from esparto dust.

There they are, four mattresses piled up, and on them, sagely, side by side and with eyes lowered and looking very hot, were seated—better to say they were perched—my uncle and Kenza.

"What has been going on here?"

"You are back with us. That is the essential thing, and our telephone call apprised us of your passing the examination. You made our cheeks blush with pride."

He seemed to be laughing, but he looks distracted, melancholy, tired out. I swear this man is laughing.

"Come in."

"I'm going to. Roche, Tchitcho, Kessel, I acknowledge. You were preparing for my return, but what about the beggar and the bearded man?"

There was the sound of a slap. It was my uncle's hand on Kenza's cheek. Perhaps she was on the point of coming out of her lethargy. In any case, an ex-mosquito.

"Their function was to distract you, and it was predictable that when you saw them, they would appear to you for what they were. You could have had the idea to walk by our door, and heaven knows with what impatience we have been awaiting you. Come in."

The doors were high ones, heavy and slow moving. They opened onto a perspective of lights and a play of colors. The polished nickel of a kettle shines and gives off little puffs of steam, tremble on a brazier of copper as red as daylight. Not a single bulb of the three chandeliers is lit, and I remembered how they had shone three nights before. A yellow butterfly with black spots flutters from one to the other. Is it the selfsame butterfly? I had accused the other one of being cheeky, because of its wings like sails, I should explain. I swear to you that there's something dramatic going on here.

But where? I ask myself feverishly. I don't like to suffer inconsiderately.

"Sit down."

The customary line of shoes stretches out on the doorstep. The air is heavy and hydrated. In the center of the room, on the carpet, almost at the Lord's feet there lies an object wrapped up in a sheet. It has been wrapped hastily, with two crossed knots, and that's all. Something has bled, bled a great deal, bled some ten or twelve hours earlier. The pools of blood have dried, and the lights make them stand out in a bright red that is almost intolerable to the sight. Probably a side of meat, some haunch of wild boar or perhaps of venison...

"A loaf of bread of tender wheat," cries the beggar, "half a pound of tea, or a leg of lamb."

Panting, I sit down. A shoulder of mutton to celebrate what? My passing? My return? My repentance? I am frightened by this meticulous stage setting. A large blue fly makes some spots on the wall, digesting. Is it blood that it's digesting? The weights of the clock at the end of their chain seems to shudder, and the pendulum moves briskly. I hear a slap. No doubt another ex-mosquito.

The trapeze is somnolent, with eyes swollen and red. Those eyes have been crying. Violently. Tac...tac...tac-tac...tac...tac...tac-tac...The pendulum is more than brisk: hallucinating. One might say a mechanical trollop placed in living flesh that, right-left, moves back and forth, torturing, torturing.

"I don't know why," I said, speaking to give myself relief, "I don't know why I came back. To rebel and then to have to face the fact that you're completely incapable of making your rebellion effective is what you'd call the act of a sad sack. I'm a poor jerk, don't you think?"

"We do not think so," said the Lord. "Because a poor jerk is not all talk, and you, if you have come home, you are not yet all talk. But never mind about that: let's just say you're a poor jerk."

That's all. His lips were sealed again. They were to open for another irony—or, as I intuit, to find another term to belittle me. The sense of drama, bounded, localized, has grown more intense. The drama is there behind those frigid lips. How cruel the pendulum, inhuman the trapeze, this tranquility, this kettle, these lights, this fly, this blood—and those two breathing beyond the door with its gilded nailheads and who don't even bother to wipe away their sweat. Just let it fall?

Something began to make a rapping noise a few seconds ago. At first it was light to the touch, as if on cloth, then it swelled into a real drumming. Was it rain, I asked myself?

"Rain," said the Lord.

And indeed it was rain, an immense cataract, incalculable, that flashed with fourteen strokes of lightning and twelve claps of thunder. I very carefully counted them. The thunder cheered me and the lightning flashes galvanized me. I would have liked to be a part of that torrent.

"You took refuge in the shade provided by your dromedaries, and birds like aerolites fell from the zenith, dehydrated. Your harvests were burned, your rivers dried up as did the udders of your ewes.

"Now, impious people, a supposition. There are no harvests, no rivers, and no ewes. The sun is broiling hot, and the King of the Universe is eternal.

"Now, from this sterility it pleases Him to bring forth abundance, like a torrential rain. Remember the Deluge ..."

Then suddenly a click.

More reddish hairs in the Lord's beard than white. The wings of the butterfly are no longer yellow with black spots, but black with yellow spots. A bulb in the chandelier in the center has gone out, I don't know when or how. It went out? So what?

Knots and lumps and coils came up in my throat. Viscous and slimy. I let them rise. There is an end to everything, I said to myself. I felt the last flux, then said, "Mother, where is my mother?"

In a quavering voice. You're a poor jerk, Driss.

He turned toward me. He looked at me attentively. Was it also fear? Why fear? He saw my eyes, my tears, my trembling. He took it in and sighed.

He lifted his finger and gradually lowered it. I could have done it better with a pipe, its bowl nestled in the palm of my hand and its shaft taking aim.

The finger stopped, pointing to the blood-covered sheet.

"She's here," he said.

# 5. ELEMENTS OF SYNTHESIS

*Rise Up and Walk.*

THE AUCUBA, the *aucuba japonica*, the Japanese laurel. Someday I'll make objects talk.

The aucuba. I had explained my mother's desire to be buried by that laurel.

"It's possible," said Boudra the gravedigger.

Just as one wrestles with Destiny, he wrestled for an instant with the shrub. Then, as one takes hold of the aforementioned Destiny, he grabbed hold of the aucuba, ho!, and pulled it out by the roots.

Boudra lifted it up with his two arms, very high, like a gymnast lifting up a barbell, right up to his dust-colored eyes. Then he giggled! He threw it over on top of Hamid's tomb that was already covered with brush, right over the top of that head of mine so heavy with lethargy, right over the living and the dead, far, very far, toward the blood-red horizon where the sun was sniggering.

The enormous Diesel made a racket, the straps hummed, and the pump poured out a great spray of bubbling water.

"Forty-two meters deep," said the Lord. "Recently, I had a surveyor come. He assured me that two kilometers from here there is water just level with the ground. Two and two make four: the water is briny, and the surveyor we're talking about pocketed ten thousand francs."

He bent over his hoe and dug a trench in the red earthen barrier.

Water poured out tumultuously, filled the furrows, and was soaked up in a sprinkling of powder and steam as if to say, I'll drown everything and transform everything into mud and sludge . . . full of spite.

"Five minutes per channel," said my father. "It's not really enough, because the roots of the tomato plants are barely moistened, but what can I do? The well would go dry. Of course, it really did rain the other day, surely some spraying!"

He had renounced his usual ceremonial use of "we" when he spoke. He was wearing overalls and a cap, and was standing with bare feet in the water. His profile was clearly delineated, powerful, facing toward a perspective of tomato plants as far as one could see, with their stakes of reed still with their twigs, and whistling in the breeze as far as you could hear. Here and there a head would emerge and disappear. Some farm worker of the seventy-four farm workers who picked the tomatoes, transplanted the young plants, weeded them, picked off their leaves, reweeded, and tied them up with palm and raffia. What was behind me? To my right? To my left? Tomato plants as far as you could see, as far as sound carries. Only a border of cactus added a meandering local charm. Plus the overhead of blue that constituted the sky. On the whole, nothing that was not very restful, nothing that was not very rewarding, so why whine at this particular moment, Valéry? A whole week had already gone by since my mother's suicide.

"No one who plants Barbary fig trees," said the Lord, "needs to care for them more than once a year just to strip them of fruit. They grow by themselves. They have no need of water, and when it rains, my heavens! . . . You know our national glory, humiliations, not a single innovation, no desire for progress. When I acquired this farm four years ago, there were some Barbary fig trees, to be sure, and undergrowth, rocks, ground strewn with gravel, such a mess you'd have thought it was a garbage dump. Look at that water. It costs me dearly, the drilling, the motor, the installation of the motor, the accessories, the cisterns, the equipment . . . I calculate it costs me ten francs a liter. That may sound ridiculous to you, my son. All the more so when you consider that a tomato sells today for one franc the kilo and not a cent more. Those partisans of the growth of fig trees don't see beyond. I'm going to explain it to you: five kilos that I get per plant, and I happen to own sixty hectares of land."

I emitted a whistle of appreciation. I was consciously playing my role. I was crouched in a wheelbarrow that had transported some horse manure and that smelled of cow dung. The morning sun propelled a cloud before it that it tinged with copper.

"It was these sixty hectares that saved me from ruin."

Suddenly he drove the handle of his hoe into the sludge halfway up the handle. His features had hardened. The Great Pardon, I said to myself.

"Ali!" he called.

Ali pulled out the tool and closed off the channel full of water. He was accustomed to it, accustomed to not being accustomed. He was born under the sun that tanned him, cooked him, and left him dazed—just as it will dry out his bones a few years or a few days from now.

The Lord had placed himself between the shafts of the wheelbarrow and strode ahead. The steel-bound wheel took no notice of anything, whether wisps of straw that it flattened out or greenfly or lizard, quickly deceased! He moved with a vehemence that was all the greater because it was unexpected. Also unexpectedly was his unloading me all of a sudden into a thicket of brambles. He picked me up, and his eyes were full of tears and his lips twisted by spasms. Get in! There was a Jeep half hidden in the bushes. He detached the plow from it, a good tractor, he said, and I got in. It backfired as it sped around the curves of the path, irascible also, and powerful. We drove as far as the stubble-covered shed, on go the brakes, on goes the handbrake, and out we get! That motor, a Japy, worked wonderfully well, as well as the Diesel up there, up there with what joy, and here what desolation! One day it began to bark, like a dog injured to the death, for lack of oil? There was some still in it. Lack of gas? I flooded it. Three mechanics, including Camel the handyman ... auscultated, dismantled, reassembled, and now it works, it didn't work. I kept at it, however, and put it in the Jeep and drove it to a repair

shop, and blow on that jet and clean that cylinder head, confabula-
tions of orders and counterorders, until that *taleb* from Aït Ouazza,
the sorcerer, going back to tradition pissed on it. What do you think
of that, Hajji? I gave out a *whew!* He pissed on it. Extreme unction.
The result? Here it is that motor, its driving belts back in place, thinking so what, that one day or the other it will wake up, explode its fuel
and grind up its existence . . . But not really. I am kidding. A bulky
mass lay there, sprawled over a cask. He picked it up in such a way
that I could tell that it was quite heavy. He struck it. I tried to hold
back his arm, but he sent me sprawling with his foot, all the way to
the fig tree from which someone had taken all but two figs, one of
them rotting and the other hardly formed but dried out, and he struck
steel on steel. Somewhere there was a bird—or a canary—that I could
still hear, the strokes of the hammer had not frightened it. Between
two blows there was hardly a respite due to the resonances, unusable,
therefore useless, therefore I'll reduce you to scrap, I'll reduce you to
powder. No doubt about it, as I stayed for a long time under the fig
tree. He picked me up, I had no choice but to play my role, the Jeep
drove off at full speed, if you have not taken into account the contrast,
just look at this Diesel, faithful, sure, honest, I give it its due, and no
going around and around, no pretense, no complications, no excuses.
Ali! Ali ran to clean up the shed and to bury the powder. Hocine!
Hocine located Ali's hoe and took up the irrigation interrupted by
Ali. Get in! He was not crying anymore. He grasped the wheel in his
hands (I was wrong; his hands are of steel) cutting through the mass
of heat from one part of the car to the other, with a breakaway, a
plume of sharp air that was almost cold. A nascent color of burnt
bread laughed in the sun. She was seated on her heels, rocking back
and forth on her rump, a stone's throw from the bungalow, and she
was laughing at full gallop. She was lifting up the wheat by handfuls;
the chaff fell refined and heavy on her hair. The Jeep's tires screeched,
and the Lord called her by name: Aïcha! It may have been the intona-
tion that seized her, or she may have comprehended at that moment
that she was going to laugh her fill of laughter, to sieve as much grain
with her hands as she would like, or none at all if she so pleased, far,

very far from those thousands of stone's throws from the bungalow. She was still jiggling the grain, and she was still sitting on her heels, rocking on her rump—but she had simply strangled her laughter. A white cock with a flame-colored tail was picking at some garbage and ashes. Did he understand also? The sun projected its shadow, and the shadow barely moved. It had no instinct to move away, it did not emit a sound when the Lord shot forth his hand and closed it on the rooster's head, then gravely twisted it in a frenetic whirl. She was the color of burnt bread. Aïcha. Everything about her at that moment was burnt bread, her eyes, the skin of her neck, and the palms of her hands, and the printed calico dress, and her hair covered with chaff— the sun on her and inside her, and her fear but perhaps it was something other than fear and no doubt she had no idea about it herself, nothing, didn't know or want to. And I knew nothing either, but that must have been fear. Then he went over to her and lifted her arm. The dress ripped under the armpit at the armhole so that the whiteness of her skin burst through. So white that the sun, the chaff, the dress of printed calico, when it burst through suddenly evaporated and, as the arm fell back down, I could no longer see anything of the color of burnt bread. That is the way it was: he stiff and leaning forward, forming with the horizon almost at a 45° angle, feet bare and muddy with mud that had dried so that they were the color of earth, so that nothing could distinguish them from the earth where they seemed to be rooted, and I said to myself that they did not belong to her, that they must be excrescences cropping out of the soil to which someone ought to have attached a scarecrow dressed in overalls and with a cap on that the wind would project forward. I also was stiff, watching him and trying to imagine myself behind my own silhouette as if I were a passerby who had paused there, behind me, and on whom I probably would have had the same effect as another scarecrow despite my well-shod feet and vertical stance. And so we watched Aïcha get to her feet and walk away, straight in front of us with the white cock dead under her arm, although right before her there was nothing but a vast stretch green with tomato plants into which she went until nothing but her head could be seen, oscillating for moments with the same rocking she had done leaning on her rump. Then we both began to run, causing the doors of the bungalow to slam as we went through, hurriedly climbing the steps and then, leaning out the bay window of the living room, we could still follow her.

"I loved her," he said.

But before he had spoken, I had understood. Just as Aïcha had understood, had run off with the cock with the twisted neck under her arm, without phrases or emphasis from phraseology, simply and with a natural sense of tragedy. For those who can, act, and those who are conscious of their impotence, write.

I had taken hold of his hand and had it crushed against my lips. I suddenly felt him close to me, susceptible of suffering, and in that suffering, more sincere, more fulfilled, more human. Aïcha was far away, a part of the horizon that she had gone to join, there where she might be either laughing or crying, but whatever the case, every step she took would liberate her further from herself, two or three horizons, she would go on walking until evening. Then she would stop in some little village that would receive her, would cleanse the cock and have it roasted. The rising sun would see her on her way again —with one or two rapes on the way, so what?—until she got to her own native village, the one that she had left, but should not have left and where she would return with what? Her breasts were still as hard as ever, her belly as complete, oh misery!

"Souk Larbaa," said the Lord. "I had gone there one July day to buy a mare I think, or some fenugreek seed. Aïcha was soaping her bare breasts under a tent, a white tent surmounted with a horseshoe, her breasts looked whiter to me than the tent and whiter than the soapsuds. They thrust at me like two bursts of laughter, thrust at me from behind, toward the ochre-ember colored sea, toward the setting sun. God permitted me to love her, Driss."

I was still holding his hand tightly pressed to my lips.

"Two bastard children you said the other day: that is correct. They are somewhere off there with the livestock on my lands. I'll show them to you tonight. They come back in at night, with the livestock . . . one four and the other two. You know, Driss, she was deformed with both pregnancies, even her face and her hands. I filled her in such a way that it seemed to punish her—I must sound sadistic to you, but don't think so: I am old, she is sixteen. She agreed to go to bed with me, and I loved her. Do you understand?—but as soon as she gave birth, she was young and strong again, and a torment to me. I think sin must have that very shape. What would you like to drink, my son? And take a cigar!"

He had pulled away from my grip and had opened a cupboard, full of dignity, but also with bitterness.

"Don't stand on ceremony. Go ahead ... Do I limit myself in any way, or have I ever? You really ought to hate me, don't you think? But then I provided my concubine with a rooster, provisions, a white rooster, resignation, and we both saw her leave, so that your hatred would have one less element in it and so that I might find some merit in your eyes. Let us talk, my son."

As he talked on, he seemed to soften. His gestures, the least in-flexion in his voice had long been like an open book to me. Now he had renounced any falsehood.

Normally he would have filled his glass so that the act would cut down the sentence (slowness, precipitation, assurance, trembling of the hands). No, he filled it like any other Shluh would have done it, because it had to be filled, because he was thirsty—then had put it down in the place he had taken it from. And that series of gestures was not to be disdained: he was not cheating.

A little while earlier, he had made the wheel of the wheelbarrow groan, the carburetor of the Jeep snort, sent the Japy flying, if he had wrung the neck of the rooster and sent Aïcha away, that was comedy, or better still, more human, the constitution of materials, whether parting from annihilation for the conquest of a position and, above all, for the reconnaissance of that position, the way those revolution-aries do who begin by putting everything to the sword and torch. Inside myself I was smiling, trying to compartmentalize myself. In the role that I had chosen for myself. Passive, humble, repentant.

But perhaps it was not wholly a role.

I think he began to bend a bit when we were standing together at the window. I didn't look at either his beard or his hands or his eyes. I followed Aïcha who swallowed up the green stretch of tomatoes. But no doubt his hands had softened just as his eyes had become empty and his beard crumpled like a bouquet that is withering. A sorcerer's apprentice, I said to myself, and in that way I began to feel love for him.

"There is no more hatred," I said to him. "I should add that there never really was any. I was lying. I tell you simply that there is no hatred anymore."

"Let's simplify things even more: drink your drink, light up your cigar, get settled into that easy chair, and listen to me. Don't analyze. Later on you can criticize at your leisure. The time has come to put things into perspective. Your brother is dead, my wife is dead, and the other day you passed judgment on me, you passed judgment on the whole lot of us. Passionately. Now I think you've calmed down. Together we are going to pick up the pieces, I, what is left of what I have created—my throne, you might be tempted to say—you, what is left of your family. Afterwards, you can act as you wish. If I had you come here, it was not without a purpose: we are free to yell and to fight each other, and your brothers have no need to know about our affairs, as they are wholly our doings, yours and mine. We are going to examine them with care in order to consolidate them as I hope to do, and as we only have words to deal with, and as with words . . . well, all right! I know: I may seem to be acting in bad faith. Let's use the word crafty, never mind: the table on which I place this bottle of port that we just took a drink from is in front of you. The bottle you could hit me in the face with, the table (it's of marble and wrought iron) with which to beat my face to a pulp. Light your cigar, my son."

He held out the flame of his lighter to me. He examined me good-naturedly, and in the background of his eyes there was a certain spot of bitterness. The bitterness of weariness. He was weary.

We were weary. Compilation of spells, I think we were enormously weary, as weary as the serf who sweats on his caïd's land. The caïd has just gone by. "So?" "So," says the serf, "damn it all! I'd rather be a caïd than to have to sweat the way I do."

We were weary.

We had been almost since the day that he had detected I don't know what kind of promise in me, what kind of premise that he had counted on: Good for service, the heir presumptive. He sent me to a French school, and from that time on there was not a moment that either of us let up, he from wanting to control me, or I, from rebelling. He, from supervising, from quibbling, from testing us and trying to anticipate us, from giving us advice and warnings, modifying the measurements from one instant to the other in view of the next second to come. Even at night there was no truce, just a revision, a revalorizing, a regrouping of forces—so ferocious both of us, sometimes, that I was surprised to find myself inside his skin, just as he must have lived inside of mine.

Now it was different.

Now, he reminded me, there were two people dead, two poor neutrals who had not even intervened. They had simply been present, and so they died. Now I was able to explain my rebellion if as a consequence I had been able to maintain it around me like a sash, and then I had returned. And we were face to face there, at Aïn Diab, his domain where, it is true, we had sixty hectares of land on which to battle and shout, quite free—or to conclude a pact (to bury the past? Who had said that, a novelist?). At Aïn Diab, a bit truer (just make the comparisons: a business man, a chemist, a bluffer, in brief, a *seated* man), there were: precisely sixty hectares of land. In earlier times it had been covered with loose stones and undergrowth. Praise be to Hajji Fatmi Ferdi! There were now sixty hectares of tomato plants. Wells, and well equipment, seventy-four workers, activity, productivity, life, and this resounding detail: five kilos of tomatoes per plant, my son—paraphernalia, scenery, strength. Being on this land, how could he be other than calm? To such an extent that I wondered if finally he really had weakened.

Or perhaps: a kind of play-acting, adroit sincerity. The extreme adroitness (I am your son, Fatmi) consisted of taking off the mask—and I, accustomed to the *actor*, I could only be surprised, agreeably or otherwise, but still surprised, and consequently rattled and already inclined towards indulgence. You added: the bottle on the table, the bottle to hit me … more and more adroit.

I might even say: mask or no mask, what difference does it make? Precisely that Aïcha, either before or after pregnancy (I go a step further: during) as tormenting as ever.

I would swallow the affront, however. He was faking: I would swallow it. Cards out on the table? Please reread the Koran. Why the Koran? Chaix the guide, if you prefer. Nothing is less identical than two identities. It's convenient to think so, and nothing makes us more limp than continuity. Continuing to exchange words with this man with the black beard. Knowing darn well that it would not be the last, but swearing to me that no matter what, it would be the last. Oh come on now!, and I spit in my hands.

"Oh come on now!" I said.

"Those breasts," he enunciated, and then said no more.

I missed the big clock. It would have been out of place in that room with its dark furniture, its bar, and its comfort. Not in the pejorative sense, but rather out of place in a complementary sense—those nauseating conversations of saintly ladies who cease to be ladies as soon as they hear a bit of gossip; those boorish peasants from Doukkala that my father used to invite for business reasons, and who farted loudly in the middle of the meal and then holding their buttocks with one hand asked where in the world that "hole for shitting could be found"—but who would recite the proper Koranic formula as they did so, very upright people, very honorable …

"What breasts?"

"White … and firm, I beg you to believe me. Sometimes as I caressed them, I pressed my fingers into them, heavenly days! So firm that they repulsed the fingers like the triggering of a spring … but what's the matter with you?"

I acknowledge: hot. In the proper and exclusive meaning of the term. Nevertheless, I am going to expand its sense. Take for example the English teacher who gave me private lessons. One day he said to me: I can't understand it. The human race gets uglier and uglier. A little while ago I saw a man with a head like a hog's, yes, my friend.

Yesterday, it was a horse's head, I can't understand it...Look here (he opened up his wallet), just look at this photo. My father. There at least was a man, a human being. Just look at that nobility, the regularity of the features, that majesty...I exclaimed: Oh, yes, of course! He was so pleased. A real fish's head.

"Hot."

"Isn't it? (He lit up another cigar.) On the one hand. On the other, you have had the opportunity to see, and don't tell me you haven't, to glimpse, the breasts of your mother and my wife, the Lord have mercy... Sit still and let me talk. Otherwise we have a conversation, straight out, or you get the hell out of here right now, and if you don't do it fast, my seventy-four workers will chase you off the last inch of my land. Still thirsty?"

"Yes, but something strong."

"Kermann?"

"Kermann."

"Or cognac?"

"No, Kermann."

He serves me. Then as he puts back the bottle, he sees that he is barefoot, and muddy. He looks around the room for an instant, picks up a huge vase in which a corpulent plant vegetates, throws it out the window, stops up the hole in the bottom with the help of a candle, fills it from the spigot at the bar and sits down again in his chair, his feet in the water. He knew the value of patience; I drank my drink straight down.

"No matter what," he began again, "that chapter is not over. During my journey to Mecca, I was away for three years. Three days for the pilgrimage, two months of journey, and the rest of the time in Damascus and Cairo. Not in the fleshpots, my son, but in the company of two women, one in Damascus and the other in Cairo, and they had breasts as suggestive as Aïcha's. Still hot?"

"Still."

"Well, we're right in the month of August (he began to smile). I know the recipe for a very refreshing cocktail, unless you. ."

He points to the vase. I move my chair closer to it and put my feet in. I had not taken off my shoes. If the water cleanses the feet, the water will unshoe me. It's a question of patience. I have never since been as completely in control of my nerves.

"Retain, weigh, and reweigh: you can judge later on. All of that so that you can judge with full possession of all the facts and all the details of all the facts."

First the water reached my feet. Now it's to my socks. I gently move my toes, but still miss the clock—I feel hotter and hotter.

Someone coming on us in that situation, with our feet together in a Kabyle jar, both of us smiling smiles the color of congratulations, and conversing pleasantly, would have come to ludicrous conclusions—ignorant in matters of the ludicrous or acting like a lout, but was not the ludicrous—and I was attentive, serious, on the lookout—precisely in this idea that I was capable of forming of someone who might have surprised us?

"One of the elements of my personal story," continued the Lord. "A story that never interested you, and why should it? My behavior toward your late mother and my former wife were as follows: authority, hard-heartedness, and disdain. And so you concluded: that man is detestable. I am going to be destructive, so listen carefully. Did you ever ask yourself why? Yes, why I treated her like livestock. You are not the only person to be born with your pride, your needs, and your ideal. I also had four brothers and sisters to feed because our parents died when I was fifteen. No money, no help, no diplomas. Just those brothers and sisters and my two arms. I fed them, and I fed myself. I was a bricklayer, a collector of cigarette butts, a sweeper, a broker, a donkey keeper, a coal and wine dealer and *tutti quanti*. There was nothing else to do. My ideal? At the age of thirty, with the situation in hand, I disinterred my ideal, like some lost child rediscovered, like some strange past, and I set out for Mecca on pilgrimage. In the meanwhile, the last descendant of an illustrious family, a family of geographers, theologians, thinkers, dreamers, poets, poor, your late mother, may God take her soul, had been put in my bed . . . You know our traditions. Those primarily concerned know nothing of the contract drawn up by the respective families, an escutcheon to be regilded, or, in my case to be gilded. At that time, I was a carpenter. And one morning in winter, at the stroke of the fourth hour, I possessed… oh yes! May God take her soul."

His smile had broadened to show his rosy gums, cracked and wrinkled, and some premolars, and an abundant and thick saliva. He tapped me on the cheek with his thumb in a gesture full of tenderness. The water was gurgling about in my shoes.

"They say that matrimonial unions begin with banalities in Europe and civilized countries. Here in our country, they begin with the end. Mine…"

A few centimeters from my own smile—we were of the same height and being seated in twin armchairs, sitting straight, we were at the same level—his smile did not become any smaller. To have lessened it would have implied a consequence, would have supposed an intermediary state, a new aspect. I say: without liaison, there was an immense pity, lips together, corners of the mouth shaggy. Play-acting? No: control.

"…at the end, of course. But understand this: a clear and succinct end, like a period. No antecedents, no follow-up. A scrawny girl… and so submissive…"

"You have no right…you egotistically ignored her. I know that she…"

"What do you think? That I had a quick dip and then turned my back on her and left her defeated? Child!"

He tapped me on the cheek again, child!

"And the children? The seven children? You, the late Hamid and the others, why? Routine, bestiality? You are insulting me…But rather—you think you're facing things, the most obvious things, which is to say those that hit you in the eyes—but rather: look deeply. She was specifically made for healthy and multiple fecundity."

Three fingers. God permitting, one day I would say: fingers need silence.

Those that he stuck out—the index and thumb bent down, forming a circle, that circle that points out to tourists the little rascals in the port area: over here, mine fraand, I know one of those *fatmas*…

eyes like a gazelle's mine fraand—looked like three bayonets. Suddenly and fully stuck out, right to the purpose, ah! you thought you were going to take a shortcut!

Moving his lips, he said, "Three simple verities, I understand," he went on. "Just remember that Moroccans born before the Protectorate were not ignorant louts. I even knew some who knew perfectly well how to read. And to write. And to count. In French. You no doubt wanted to point out to me ... or so I thought. Pardon me. Because you might well have pointed out to me, you with your high-school diploma, those truths ... How? or so I thought. Pardon me."

He stopped moving them. I add: they had lost their bayonet-like character. I was fixated.

"First: taking certain precautions with my wife, certainly praiseworthy, but I am not civilized. I would say to you: art for art's sake. You have to give those poor spermatozoons their chance—you would understand me perfectly well. I think you are athirst for absolutes. Now I ask you, what would your mother have thought of precautions?"

He bent his middle finger and went on.

"Second: widowhood, pure and simple abstention. Intellect padlocked and flesh taken into consideration,—remember this: the Prophet was a man, and damned well so!—there was flesh at home ... to be satisfied, and my own. I'll put the question another way: what would your mother have thought?"

The smile had barely left his lips, or had it reappeared? Very amiable.

"To be satisfied, yes. I left it in abeyance. Did I really satisfy her? You are asking that question. You should ask yourself: and if the thing she most wanted in the world, if precisely it were that deficiency, then what?"

He rebent the middle finger. No sequel this time. Payment made.

"Comma and surcharges. For the moment let us admit everything. In a certain sense I dispose of my assessment. Let us be logical. She was as she was, not my ideal and the devil take customs! But, as she was, your mother was one of my terrestrial contingencies. She prepared my meals, tucked in my bed, kept my clothes clean, was obedient, submissive, honest (fidelity is not even to be considered). And her defects! Because defects are also to be cherished, my son, and the man who marries, if such a thing is possible, a creature uniquely endowed with good qualities, or still uniquely for those qualities, purchases his own portrait. Defects, your mother had the normal dosage, was garrulous, a crybaby, and so on. But, above all, she was obedient, submissive, and honest, that yes! Fidelity does not enter into that either. Consequently, one of my contingencies. Now that she is dead, I admit to you I miss her. Not for keeping up the house, anybody can easily replace her in that . . . but that energy suddenly become useless, unused . . . Don't think about the hold habit has over us. Think of those railways that once were bustling with trains and that now are silent, deserted, where grass grows with time. They remind me of psychological complexes: they need trains."

The little finger was now rigid and menacing, as menacing as a stump and as rigid as the stump of a cadaver.

"Consequently, repudiation. Permitted and blessed by the Law. I never even considered such a thing. Perhaps because to put it into action, or simply to have thought about it, would have been the equivalent of *accepting* the idea of an error, a basic error—build me a house and come tell me later on that you forgot to put in the foundation, eh! I look for a lodging and, as such, that house will be as it is. Tend your boat! Your mother was twenty-four years old, and I'm being liberal. I know: that stupid accident, prematurely taken from us . . . I insist: she had already been dead for years. At the very most, let us consider the problem of a while ago. I said: perhaps because of that. Perhaps also for reasons that I have just brought up. There was still all the rest, also permitted, also blessed by the Law."

The auricular bent again. For an instant there was a fist beneath my nose, a fist with salient tendons, so salient that they were white with violet intervals. Then that fist opened up, a long, hard hand that hit my femur, a fine little smack, an invitation to general celebration, so laugh then!

"What about the four traditional wives permitted? I like peace. Moreover, I'm capable of handling one, not four. As for what is comfortably called 'the use of one's time,' I repeat to you: the devil take customs! You know the proverb, one way of inverting the problem: 'the plate that a beggar could empty, four will surely be able to empty.' Things being so, would you be astonished to learn that over and above all I am a modern man?"

He pinched my knee. Twice. My knee allowed itself to be pinched. Twice. I took two brief glances at the exterior world. I had annihilated it, and it put me back to rights. The water in the jar was strictly immobile—as immobile as that triangle of blue that cut through the open window. The heat? It could be felt even in that water that surrounded my feet, but perhaps it was the adaptation...

"She also made her life," I said.

"Of course!"

He arose, waiting for me to take my feet out of the jar, and went toward the bar. I heard the spigot whistle and the sink belch. I looked down at my shoes. They were the same ones that I had picked up at the Mosque of Qarawiyyin by way of compensation for the babouches I lost... Not that they had become heavy or, as they trickled brownish water on the white carpet, ridiculous—but because they looked new to me, newer than they had undoubtedly ever been. Now who can tell me what association of ideas made me think of Joseph Kessel, the sedentary, as I looked at that pair of boots? I took them off, took off the spongy socks, the cold water seized—they made me ashamed: very dirty—my feet for the moment.

"Of course," repeated the Lord.

He stuck his feet in the water—they did not make me ashamed, nor did they seem to make him ashamed—that got muddier and muddier—but that is how it was. He spoke, acted metrically, and sure of his metrics. He knew there would be no loss of saliva or of time. He had changed the tepid water for cool water, that's all. Accepting the pause. He did not put the hand back on my knee, but isn't that in the nature of things? I waited for him to do it, but said instead: "I was also waiting for the question!"

"Another cigar?"

"No."

The method of the perfect liar, a liar one ounce per ton. No, I didn't want to smoke. Nor to consent to having my life weighed per word. Words! ... as he went on uttering them, my life was becoming more and more narrow, more and more "bridled."

"Concubinage existed. I won't restate the arguments I spoke of earlier. I'll just point out to you that coitus is coitus, and I understand by coitus the hygienic and reproductive act. One of the attributes of your mother, God rest her soul! Nevertheless..."

"Have a cigar all the same."

"A cigar."

Childish. I don't deny it. But suddenly I needed air. I was beginning to doubt myself.

"One!"

He lights it for me and holds it out to me. He does not smile. If he had smiled, he would have lost his seriousness, the seriousness with which he treats my childishness, and he sticks to it.

"Concubinage has a character of identity, of course. I am a partisan of it. I was a partisan of it. In Damascus as I was in Cairo, as I was here. Entities that made an entity of me myself, gave me dimension and love that was lacking in the union that was blessed by the Law. Love that your mother never could arouse in me, God take her soul! In what way was she wronged? Didn't she have the lion's share? She was neither turned away nor diminished in her dignity as a Muslim wife, not forsaken, not cheated. I could not love her. I did love others. What could be more defining than a period."

I quietly pursue my inner ramblings. It is all registering, however, and I register above all—astonished by this sally, but not overly so. The stair landing will not be long in being rebuilt. A good little war, said Roche, that will wake you up. From which I inferred: and right after that the Arab will go back to sleep. The landing will be rebuilt. I smoke, holding as much smoke in my lungs for a long time as I can, then I blow it out in little jets.

"I judge it to be useless to talk to you about the ones in Damascus and Cairo."

"On the contrary."

"Pardon me?"

"On the contrary."

I blow a wreath of smoke into his face. A dense wreath that stagnates just as quickly and do not penetrate the black beard and the eyes. The previous wreaths stagnate farther on or end up by dissolving in the air. I am keeping a real violence for you a little later on, hajji. Not of words, but an act, in such a way that you will judge: pure and simple violence. As you say, an entity toward which you want to lead me—and toward which I go docilely. It will only be a game, a bluff, one likely to "possess" you. Later on, when I've finished my cigar. Meanwhile, it is so blissful to take deep drags on it—and to listen to you.

"Useful. *All* of the elements are useful to me *now*. Or perhaps the aftertaste."

"Pardon me?"

"In Damascus and Cairo?"

"Exact."

Perhaps. And I don't really care. The important thing is to have quibbled. The proper dosage to place me in the stream of things. My game of chess. Give up my queen. Put it into checkmate. I have carefully studied my role. From the beginning. Since the burial of my mother. My fear is: it's a question of a very fine chess player.

"On to aftertastes then. You may laugh. I'm vanquished and I admit to *you* that I am! Laugh! So that later on I can give you this blow with the fist: aftertastes that held on to me, that had the power to keep me away for *three years*."

He had not shouted that. He was still calm, almost happy. I would have said that he was out of the discussion for the moment. Something in me escapes him and displeases him. He searches. I know his cerebral faculties: he searches hurriedly, clearing away, sharp.

"And I loved two times, aftertastes, perfectly. The second blow of the fist. Listen to me and don't act like a Zouave."

"In your place I wouldn't have come back."

"A classical case. The priest takes confession and grants absolution. For sins that he only knows through books. With all the mastery of those who have book knowledge, using words for whose etymologies, sense, nuances, and relationships he has no feeling of value. About the term *aftertastes*, for example, you used."

"I still would have stayed there."

"Is that so?"

"Is that so?"

He is clearing away and is still searching. I give him some more bait. That ant . . .

"Absolutely. Then why did you come back? You thundered so loudly the other night, if I leave I'll never come back, you were thundering."

A red ant, one of those that have a sugary juice once they're squashed and when you suck them, had climbed up the bottle of port and then began to run.

"I was placed in different situations . . ."

"By any chance, do you know the ones I was in? Or would you permit me at least to exist? If the chief, the caid, fornicates, the tribe does not fornicate—a strange way of looking at things. Otherwise, you interrupt me, trick me, and put me off to gain time. How about ending this conversation?"

"No."

He supposed that. I *may* have need for a respite—while he *certainly* has need of one. He knows that for some moments now I have escaped his cerebral field. How, and with what in view? He's a capable chess player. I say "no." With him one has to be subtle, nothing but subtle, more subtle than he. Islam. People live here that way, from subtleties—and you can't escape otherwise, except by mental suicide.

I blow on the end of my cigar, apply it to the ant, that then climbs over the cork of the bottle.

"I won't interrupt you anymore."

He meditates on my gesture. He can qualify it any way he wants.

By God's grace! That detail took hold of him, like my trick of a while ago. I am satisfied.

"That would be wiser. I told you that I had laid aside my rancor. Let me divest myself of it. Weigh it later, or go your own way, that doesn't interest you. As far as I know, we are not enemies. You hate me—or think you hate me—and as far as I'm concerned, you are my child. No, we are not enemies, and even less so, strangers, a father and son that a misunderstanding has separated, that we are settling intellectually, like two men. If we were children—was I ever a child? and I won't talk with a child if that is what you still are—we will stammer a-ba-da-boum-boua . . . stop whimpering together for a good moment, then laugh together. If we were dogs, we would go outside, and we'd settle this misunderstanding, a bone, by the use of our teeth."

There is emotion and the quality of emotion. Some emotions, even sincere ones, barely touch us. Others, even when we know they are only theatrical expressions, skewer us. I have wondered why. "The role of dream, our reality so pressurized . . ." Roche had said to me, and then sent me off for more information in the French masters of playacting. I recommend Gide to you, a great simple man. Raymond Roche *dixit*.

Once he had finished his harangue, the Lord was very gentle. Crocodile or swan, I don't care—very gentle. Do you go to a beggar to ask for alms in coins of ten centimes or of one franc? Very gentle. Almost the gentleness of my mother. I felt my jaw bones stand out. A cow bellowed, but where? It sounded like the echo of a horn. The beard up close, the smile, the feet in the water, this setting, this heat, this shanty. The gentleness with which she had run her house was submissive, obedient, and honest. And her delicacy, to the degree of self-effacement, and *her love*—but those things aren't even considered, not at all, he would express with a faint difference.

"Let's start up again. A testimony of extreme fatigue, and of admiration for your casuistry."

I fished around in my pocket and pulled out the denture. That cigar . . . A Jew among my friends once had me read the imprecations of Astaroth. I recite one of them to myself—my mother invoked all sorts of saints—while I relighted the cigar.

"And I am revealing myself because you are cheating."

"Pardon me?"

"You are cheating."

He chews on his denture. He chews on it awkwardly, with delight: he had lost the habit. He rediscovers the alkaline taste of the metal and licks it with light touches, his tongue like a pointed tester, then charged with suspicion—and I would gladly listen to the horse whinny and the wife groan at the return of the master, of the spouse.

His eye is flaming, ferocious. I blow on the lighter. I'm used to cigarettes and to cigars put out that are relit. There is always a way to make a load of bread out of crumbs.

"You are cheating. I thought so from the beginning. You gave up your 'we', your majestic ways, you offered me liquors, you confided in me, you talked with me about the present situation. You are cheating. You traced a circle and enclosed me in it—and I let myself be enclosed. A little spicy discussion of several anecdotes, of powerful reasonings that you would wind up with my breakdown—oh fathead that wanted to play with hardheads!—and your apotheosis: the mastery with which you redressed the matter of the tea. And I did not leave the circle."

For a moment I concentrated on crushing my cigar, heavily—so that I'd make pancake of him—on the ant. I thought it was dead, but it ran across the table. Or was it another ant? It was red, however.

"So I cheat," he affirmed.

"And so do I."

His cheeks swell up. Left, right—he's like a pendulum!—he's still poking the dentures with his tongue. It's a way like any other to indicate that he has been patient for that long, just that long. Inside me, Astaroth completes her liturgy.

"And, between the two of us cheaters, from you to me and vice-versa, the discussion could still be a free one. Like that whore five feet tall that Camel kept working at, Camel's first prostitute. She had taken off her clothes, opened herself up, and Camel had pulled out his organ like a piece of artillery from between his coattails (he had kept the coat on because it was cold, but had taken off his cap). The girl watched impassively. My brother touched her navel with the end of his shaft, and she said nothing, gave a push, and she still said nothing. But where she lost all control of herself was when Camel desperately tried blissfully, fiercely, to force the navel. His first prostitute, I repeat. Finally he consented to move a bit lower."

A series of rapid gestures. Putting my hand under my armpit, placing my elbow on the table, setting the safety-catch—the steel, the blue steel of the Luger in my hand shone brightly.

"I tell you that I was cheating. Like this. With this. And I think— the newspapers this morning apprised me of it—that that pallid rascal, Kilo, molding away in some section of the Tadla, staged an armed holdup. Six months prison. I had shown my mother the way, been an example to that mother reduced to minced flesh and bones, to that mother who threw herself from the terrace just as I had emptied the sacks of the storeroom out the window that night. The sacks of wheat hardly made a sound when they hit the ground . . . minced flesh and bones. I'm thinking of Hamid. Meningitis, you declared. If you say so. Two years more and he would have learned the declensions of Latin verbs and who knows what else? Once a piece of chocolate was consumed, he counted on me to offer him some more, he wanted some so badly, he said to me: Christmas, tell me about Christmas—and I would talk to him about Christmas, Christmas eve, the snow, the tree, the bells, the Christmas masses, the gaiety, the laughter, the lights . . . Texts learned by heart so that I could tell him about those things. He would clap his hands, do you remember those hands? Like a sparrow's claws—his cheeks rosy: will you take me there? will you really? and I swore to him I would someday or other. I made a calculation: in two years' time. I'm also thinking about the laurel tree in the cemetery. The gravedigger pulled it out with his two arms and tossed it aside like an unhappy past. With his gravedigger's salary, meager salary, ascendency of reality, had he gone back to get it that night? An aucuba of that dimension is good for three days fuel. And I think about myself. You put a curse on me, I took to the door, and once through it my dry gullet, my empty gut, Berrada, Lucien, the others, my mediocrity, my complexes, the closed horizon, the horizon you had closed, and your gold denture all sneered at me—and I learned that that generation that was being educated was a generation of rotten apples, that at best one might get some cider out of them, a bitter cider, the first generation to be Occidentalized, that dreamed of reforms, of purifications, of earthshaking events.

But no! You don't understand anything. You could be a carpenter, on an old-age pension, old people now would want that, wouldn't they? Palatial residences of more clear and modern lines, and so I returned. Conscious of the lost years, conscious of the badly-timed rebellion and at least . . . I'm going to tell you: pure shit, just like the shit one shits in one's pants and then gets rid of, pants and all, and how! But they say a dog that gets screwed screws in turn, and no one can say that those nineteen years of loss, that idea of loss, would resign me to digest them. So turn the page, dog. Your denture helped me to earn a bit of money. Camel bought this Luger, Abd El Krim cleaned it, Madini loaded it, Nagib fastened it under my armpit, and Jaad gave me a recommendation: aim at the heart."

I took aim at the heart and pulled the trigger. Six times, one after the other, quickly and rejoiced as the cow bellowed once more, where was it? with an accent of triumph.

"Filled with blanks," I went on. "That is how I cheated."

His feet had touched mine in the water with barely a start. He looked at me, his eyes reduced to two slits, shiny and black. I could distinguish no sign of cornea. I mentally gave my thanks to the Astaroths and to the friend who had made me read them.

"There is one bullet left, a real one, that I was holding back . . . for me . . . for you, on equal terms. The future belongs to the Eternal One. See how I am: I am handing you the revolver."

He took it and placed it on the table, equidistant from his hand and mine. Three insects circled above us, one fly, two flies.

"I was determined to use it, however. My tactic was to listen to you, to concede, and then to fire six bullets, have a good laugh, oh that blessed Driss of ours! and then fire the seventh bullet. I was full of strange ideas—one of them was for one of us to take the rap. You: for two deaths, the antecedents and the rest. The world has evolved, and you have lasted too long; or me: come on! All of that is inflated and dramatized. There's not enough there to make a sheik fart, and the couch-grass in this garden has to be rooted out."

Two insects, two mosquitoes, flutter over us. The fly has departed.

It had found no carrion, but it had made a big mistake: there were two pieces of carrion here.

"That was my plan. You must wonder why I revealed it to you. The conventional thing to have done would have been to light up a good cigar, to have settled into my armchair, and sticking out my lower lip like this, I have plenty of time, then tell you: try to figure it out, daddy dear."

Two mosquitoes have stopped circling around. They have gone to join the fly. They had stayed a little longer than the fly, no doubt for the purpose of finding out what kind of carrion we were. Then they left too. We were carrion only in the figurative sense.

"Let us say rather that I was weary, worn out, not up to the struggle, even: not seeing the necessity for this struggle—and generous. I only want a plate of beans and peace of heart. Peace for those who are covered with red earth and peace for bruised hearts. Revenge for my two dead? Time has consolidated them, the time that I should not have let go by. My nerves are carrying another influx, new cells that have replaced the old ones that have already lived their existence."

Two pieces of carrion that suffer and play at chess, and as chess players have placed themselves between two parentheses. History conceals villages that have been swallowed up and races of people that are extinct. Don't comb those dogs' hair. They didn't ask to be combed. If we do so, it is simply because these combs had to have a place in our utilizations, are interested only in their conservation (greetings, Newton!). They want to live, to continue to live—and it is Islam, the true: neither time nor space are necessary, and everything else is superfluous that is not either nourishment, sleep, fornication, escape, and above all escape. Traditions? Neither I nor my father are illustrious Orientalists, nor has the Orient been what has made them such, illustrious. We clinched things, carefully and indispensably, then they rubbed their hands: they have their traditions, they seemed not to give a damn, now we can go around with them, distinguished, and with no mixing possible: and your traditions? Firmly in place.

And so three insects have gone to find some real carrion.

"For a return match, you stop cheating as well. No more intellect, no more theatre; empty your bag of tricks, all of it. I'm no longer a child, you told me. Then treat me like an adult. Are you afraid to?"

He wasn't afraid to. He got to this feet and treated me like an adult.

He got up, threw the jar out of the window, closed himself in the bathroom, came out close-shaved (he made a sign to his chin, what do you think of that? nothing has really changed, thank you), emptied out the contents of his bar, all of the aperitifs and liquors . . . into the sink. He wiped my feet, took me by the arms and put me into his bed, a camp bed, slaughtered a baby lamb and roasted it, cut me off a shoulder that he forced me to swallow, and followed it up with a pint of whey. He talked without stopping, he talked until evening.

Evening fell, coloring the windowpanes with ochre, sienna, and brick red, with halos of copper yellow and streaks of bright yellow.

"The world has changed. The first person that loves a man is himself. But if he has children, his dearest wish is for those children to be better than he in every way."

It was an evening charged with electricity, although the sky had been uniformly blue all day long, but what does that mean? A storm is coming, and even if it doesn't break over our heads, it will break elsewhere.

"The first person you lie to, when you lie, is to yourself. And for you to lie is to trap yourself. And for you to trap yourself, you must give little value to yourself in your own eyes."

Elsewhere, where *the others* are. Those who have too many cloudy skies, skies that piss, too much springtime, too much liberty, too many individual rights, too much respect for the human soul. Sometimes as an excess, a thousand excuses, they send us a storm, but their springtime, their liberty, their individual rights, their respect for the human soul, preserve. Are they right? They are right.

"Of course you rebelled. Just consider this: the man in the street, the boot-black, the porter, the riffraff have not rebelled in living memory, even though they are born poor, live in misery, and die like dogs. And heaven knows veterinarians are there for dogs. The population that I have here on my land, thirty francs per day is the going rate, and when the harvest is abundant, the right to glean rotten tomatoes. The populations of the cities and towns are more than vagabonds, vagrants that have no set ways, ferreted out by the police, a police made up of ex-vagrants, the most ferocious in the world. Sometimes they make them R.T.M.s, servants-service-service-comrade-afterwards—or else, putting them between four palisades in an open area, they show them to the tourists, that exists, that causes enjoyment. And then there are the people dispossessed of their lands. If I was in their place, I'd count the prints of my footsteps, they've been pushed back from mountain to mountain down in the Atlas region, turned from men into wild beasts, until they've even lost the character of wild beasts. I've seen them. Do you know what they call them? The savages, the dissidents. But peace be with them too and on the novelist, who would make a book out of their story, would hang the hanged. And what about you, the scion of the race of Lords?"

Ochre, sienna, and brick red, the streaks have dissolved and no longer color the windows except for what you might call broad brushstrokes of paint. Evening will soon die. Die? It will be born again tomorrow. Will be born. You have to believe in something. The thirst for belief that goes unsatisfied.

"Me, I'm the biggest rebel, lucid, practical, you know how? Rebellion is a crossroads where you loosen the cables, facile, passionate, let go; or, much more clever, stay in place and fight. I stayed in place, precisely that day that I disinterred my ideal, and I made use, powerfully, of all the theocracies that Islam confers on the head of a family, who in addition is a *fassi* and hajji, and who has a sense for business."

The windowpanes had turned black.

"Don't tell me you are superior to us in any way because of your schooling. Voltaire, Henri Poincaré, General Malet and Jules Isaac, and all the books you have read and the coursework of your programs have all been translated many times into all languages. I've read them all, learned them all, but in Arabic. Mea culpa!"

Blacker than the night. The night could not be blacker, that I know, that I accept as I accept everything. Not black—even though the wind has risen, a wind blowing from the ocean. I open the window and close it right away. It does not smell of ocean, anything but ocean, of tomatoes, of urine, of wet earth, of dung and livestock and oil, of centuries and secular miseries—and that peculiar odor, sui generis, that my father's clothes have always had, the breath of my father, his skull, his armpits, his hands.

"Legend has appropriated the case (pathological? let us reduce matters to simple verities: curiosity) of that young man named Taha. Taha had gone to school and was almost ready to graduate. One night he got dead drunk, one of those monumental drunks that our poet Abou Nouass used to tie on, by quantity, a small case of vodka. When he woke up, he didn't know a word of French."

Then the storm broke. There was no lightning against the windows. Beyond the windows the night remained quiet, even my nerves were quiet—that is no doubt why I knew that the storm had broken, but I did not see it break. You might say that it had never broken.

"Just so. Before the Protectorate. For all time. More or less since Omar and the Caliphs—and those who talk of reform might as well go whitewash Negroes. Then there was you, you the poison. And how do I know if the French Residency wanted its cultural message to reach our sons in the form of poison. If it is intentional, it has been a rape of the spirit. In any case, from the day you entered the French school, you have been precisely that, poison. You saw social injustice everywhere and, you saw, in a same person, from one moment to another, temporal injustices: who asked you to see them? And who the devil taught you that those things were injustices? You wanted to comfort the embittered—a knight errant in the age of the black market—you brandished the oppressed like a flag, you sowed rebellion among your brothers and you emptied *my* provisions and *my* storeroom to some jackals who just as quickly went back to their good old begging. A sack of barley or of oats enough to unsettle them? Not on your life! The poison was injected by you into the extreme resignation of your mother. The idea of revolting would never have entered her mind. You crammed her full of it. She died because of it."

A night-light had been lighted in the room, a soft blue of the same color that all the French aristocracy wore in the time of Francis the

First and the poets of the Pléiade—but then the century was full of orgies, was it not a constraint? That night-light, take off the shade and change the bulb: one hundred fifteen volts, five amperes, a night-light of soft blue has been lit.

"One morning your mother got down on her knees. She said her prayers in the name of Allah, of her husband, and of the saint of her native Fez. Prayed for her sins and for her weaknesses. She asked me to pardon you, and as for herself, she blessed you to the end of your days and to the very last of your descendants, if in fact God gave you such. She kissed my hands and my feet. I allowed her to do so. I had determined things for many years, and she had determined things for herself, once and for all. The instant afterwards, I heard an uproar at my door. I think she died instantly, ten meters' fall, and Allah is now bringing her to account: five thousand years of Gehenna because she committed suicide. I leave Him to be the only judge. I have neither to weep for her nor to approve of her act. She is no longer under my tutelage. My task was simply to point out to you that you were the cause of her death."

The light of the lamp had become even more tenuous, I guess through my eyelids, as I had closed my eyes.

"You are also the cause of my son's hatred of me. Before that they didn't even know what hatred was or the instinct for hatred. Now they hate me deeply. They consent to stay on in my house because they eat the bread I give them and drink the tea I pour them. Sometimes they empty out my pockets. You have to pay to get into the bordello, and these gentlemen get drunk, and their vices are expensive ones. Some day when I'm quite old and senile, I will no longer provide them with bread or tea, and they'll throw me the hell out. Oh, they don't say a word, don't explain their hatred. They are patient, taciturn, and determined. You taught them the way."

There was nothing left of the lamp to make out. I had fallen asleep.

"You whom *I loved*, even though the others *were my children*. One night, just remember the twenty-fourth evening of Ramadan, misery! I wanted to teach you a lesson. I wanted to stir your emotions with something spectacular, to call up that emotion, the only thing still left that is truly you. I had planted a stake at the boundary of the path. I had hung a sign on it saying: 'For whatever it is worth, attain this goal first.' And you attained it, in order to pull up the stake and brandish it over my head. You attained the goal through necessity, and once it was attained, you did not understand why you had gone such a long distance. As you went along, you had seen many ravines and much rubbish—you should not have noticed them. And you yourself consented to walk such a long time. What you forgot was that once at your goal, you should have looked ahead of yourself and seen the immense field of possibilities before you."

I know now that sight is the weakest of the senses. My eyes were glued shut with sleep, but I still could hear quite clearly.

"I wanted to teach you a lesson. I was ruined. I explained that to you, knowing, first of all, what your reaction would be, and it was exactly what I had expected. To struggle, to master the crisis? Of course I could do that. You can do anything when you are surrounded by love and comprehension, when you are surrounded by a woman worthy of the name of wife and by children who make you blush with pride. But surrounded by hatred? By hatred and suspicion. Even more than that: by silence? A silence so mysterious, so viscous, that sometimes, sitting on my prayer rug and preparing an infusion of tea, I wondered on what barrel of powder I had seated myself and if it was not logical, instead of filling the teapot to the brim, to only pour in a small amount of boiling water, just enough to fill a single glass, my own."

The ear is a particularly profitable organ. People talk about deafness. I can assure you that the deaf can hear.

"I'm going to tell you something: you are not the only one. I don't know a young man of your generation that isn't like you. In Strasbourg Street, the millionaires' neighborhood where I have my tea store, is filled with lamentations. The young people are insolent, twisted by their complexes, and proud of their complexes. They're willy-nilly thieves and cynical. If they go inside a mosque, it is to pray to Allah in a loud voice to make them orphans as soon as possible. It's a youth that brags about being nationalistic, the only elements in the population who are persuaded that Ataturk is their guide from beyond the grave. Still they complain: the French Residency should turn to them instead of to us, the *chibanis*, the old folk."

He spread a coverlet over my body, although I had no darned need for it. He spread it out, and I realized that I needed it all the same. It had suddenly turned cold. What he ought to have done, above all, was stuff cotton balls in my ears.

"The lesson I learned was a terrible one. Let's not talk about it anymore. I sowed the seeds for green peas one day, and I harvested field mice. Let's not talk about it anymore. God judiciously punished me in my son and in my wife, and in your revolt—for having dared to build a future in the future. Listen to me: I was ruined. The Twelve were ruined. We knew how to parry the blow, and we parried. Each one of us got together all his liquid assets, borrowed what we could, and mortgaged our properties and belongings. We were able to buy up all the tea there was for sale at a wretched price (one hundred thirty francs per kilo) on the black market. We then resold it, with the benediction of the French Residency, all legally, at the legal price of three hundred seventy francs. A fine little affair...To go on: the immediate benefits invested in the purchase of waste ground at the entrance to Casablanca at five sous the square meter was a windfall. I made a calculation. The Americans have landed. In the postwar period, that means businessmen, cities coming up out of the ground, airports being designed. In a few years if I'm patient, my lands will sell at five thousand francs the square meter. That's what's expected of a hajji in the twentieth century—and how a hajji rebels and utilizes."

The coverlet was of raw wool. He tucked me in, pulled it over my feet, they stuck out, he covered them, smoothed out the bumps and the hollows. He was preparing to close accounts with my destiny.

"Treat you like a man? Very good. That evening of the twenty-fourth of Ramadan, it was already done. Sleep. Already done: the American tea was rounded up, the scale of prices was fixed, the agreement with the Residency had been obtained—and it was a need that was shabbily human, the shock following the triumph that very evening that it was necessary to teach you a lesson. Sleep, my son.

Now you are a man. It's true that I treated you like a child, but understand. I had no need of you in my business affairs, but from now on I shall. My epoch, your epoch, the patrimony that is transmitted from father to son like a formula for a good old wine, like a torch, but also, successions of epochs on which one improves. My epoch: shaping to Allah's will, speculating in the name of Mohammed, buying, selling without pity, without scruples, for money. And only, and here I touch the veritable wound, only the Moroccan capitalists are taken into consideration and resist. You don't negotiate with utopians, but with oil. Sebti, the Sebti Brothers of whom you must have heard, are not Nationalists but simple millionaires. They don't give a damn for politics, for Islam, or for France. They alone, the three of them, do more for the national good than the whole lot of Nationalists. They are feared and respected. Why? Because they have the means, good to the last drop, to buy up the whole of Morocco. Your epoch: it will be a question of consolidation, of pettifoggery and chicanery. That was the reason I had you sent to school. You will be able to maintain your patrimony, in areas in which I have no experience. Sleep."

He caressed my temples, put out the lamp, and got up.

"One more detail. An important one. Why you of all my children to be my choice, to be the one I have directed with patience and care and to whom I have bequeathed my burden. Precocity would you think, promise . . . Not so. I'm going to be brutally frank: it's time for you to be a man, and by that I mean a hard man, fully armed and above all with no weaknesses for himself. Why you? One day I closed my eyes and pointed my finger. By chance the finger pointed to you. There it is. Now go to sleep."

The door closed. I opened the window wide, and there, leaning out down to the groin, I began to laugh into the night, laugh strongly and without holding back, one burst giving way to another, at full gallop the way Aïcha must have laughed, set free, at 3° or 4° of the horizon, as I suppose the dead must laugh. Hamid and my mother side by side in their red earth, set free also; and everything took on an intensity. The wind was soughing and lashing, the reeds whistled and grated, a blackbird called to another blackbird, clouds circled rapidly high above, and in the distance the ocean coughed like an old man.

I closed the window again.

I had come into my own.


An aged Negro sprawled under the portal of the *mechouar*. He held out his hand, charity if you please, the Prince of Believers will return it to you, Kch! Kch! said my father. He seemed to be chasing away a cloud of flies, the Prince of Believers did not tell you to beg. We stepped over him. "Ex-human," explained my father, "ex-believer, ex-Senegalese of the Black Guard of His Majesty the Sultan Mohammed the Fifth." The sun was torrid, and clouds of dust arose.

A potbellied man was seated under an umbrella combing his beard. Some lice fell out of it onto an official paper. The beard delineated a semicircle as we went by. That notable person dressed in a jellaba and with the serious air about him was to be expected, but what of this roumi, this "Christian dressed in European clothes with his hands stuck in his pockets?" A monk, explained my father, you've seen thirty of them in the cemetery, and here they're counted by the hundreds. Just one of the kinds of parasites that vegetate somehow in the palace of His Majesty the Sultan Mohammed the Fifth. The sun was torrid, and clouds of dust arose.

Half hidden in a pile of cushions at the end of a corridor, a young *fassi* stopped us to question us. Your papers? And yours, said my father. We went on. He has a certificate of studies at the most, he explained to me, and one day he installed himself in the middle of those cushions, translator, interpreter, kind help, nobody had requested his services, no one said anything to him, but now he gets big bribes. The corridor was dark and almost cool.

A sentinel pointed his machine-gun at us. Where are you going? To see the Sultan, said my father. Do you have a pass? Yes. He stuck an old copy of a bill under his nose, and the man bent almost to the ground. You who talk about reforms, my father said to me, take note. Between you and your prince, how many intermediaries there are to cut down! Fountains appeared in the midst of beds of flowers and well-kept lawns. The sun and the dust reappeared.

A thin man dressed in white and carrying some files under his arm and puffing on a pipe came striding toward us. My dear Ferdi ... "What, my dear Ferdi? Thank you. He is fine. Pardon?" He knows the way, thank you. What else? Who I'm going to see? That doesn't concern you. The pipe gave off a puff of smoke. An orderly, my father explained, a part of the establishment, and bilingual. He likes to make people think he's a power behind the throne, and happy the man who believes his own illusions, he's come to believe it himself.

In a dark room with a low ceiling there were four men on a straw matting playing cards who took care not to honor us with a look. We stopped at the entrance. Hello! Anybody here, called my father. "What's going on?" "Where is Fatimi's office?" "Don't know." "Then what in the hell are you doing here?" "You can see for yourself. We're playing cards ... and first of all, what's that tone of voice ..." "The tone of voice proper for use with four secretaries transformed into poker players. Nobody comes around to check you out? I'll put some order into things, you can be sure of that. Fatimi's office?" "Corridor to the left, follow it and then turn left to door number three." We went off in that direction. Jack of spades ... Ace ...

Fatimi said, "His Majesty is out hunting."

"I don't believe it," retorted my father. "I got my information from the freshest source, from General Noguès ..."

"What did you say?"

"I had breakfast with him this morning," he lied coolly.

The palace servants, the *mokhaznis*, took off their babouches and groveling, stayed immobile face to the floor.

"Come closer, come closer," said His Majesty the Sultan Moham-med the Fifth.

Just between us, he isn't an eagle: the massive and brute silhouette of a Joseph Kessel that I evoked as I was prostrating myself.

"Arise. Sit down. Speak."

No, he isn't an eagle, and no matter to me. He was seated behind a little desk whose legs had been sawed off, and with his lively eyes with their delicate lids behind blue glasses, Mohammed the Fifth examined us. He smiled, and two dimples appeared in his cheeks. His barber had just shaved him, and he smelled of rose water. He had a lisp to his pronunciation, and he spoke very softly. He does not like idle stories, but all of that is without importance.

"Majesty," said my father, "your time is precious, and I will be brief, but the few moments that your Majesty kindly accords us will suffice to illumine all the rest of our existence."

"Speak."

Yes, all of that is without importance. I say to myself that an artist on stage is either applauded or hissed. The essential thing is not to suscitate a complete indifference. The following: a packed house, *silent*.

"My son here ..."

I can recall one winter morning—was it decidedly winter?—when I was six years old. I had mixed in with a crowd of people acclaiming the sultan—he was then just called Sidi Mohammed ben Youssef. He was going to the mosque, delicate and dressed in white on a chestnut horse with a long tail that twitched. I recall the cries, the thick crowd, the black guard, the fragments of the Koran, the sweat and the fervor. Mischievously I pulled the tail of the horse. Was it a standard that loomed up beside my insignificance? I wasn't even afraid, despite the shadow of another horseman, his saber drawn and standing in his stirrups.

"I am sending him to Paris ... sacrifices ... a career ... if Allah and your Majesty, however ..."

They give permission. They don't really care anyway, either one or the other. For the latter, another post surmounted by a signboard, faith has no need of a genie. The writ suffices. He said: "Listen to him, follow him, don't mutter. He has spiritual and temporal powers that are not to be understood, not to be judged, but to be believed. That is all that is asked of you. Amen!"—these venerable parchments of the Lord, in the Lord's room and which hid a respectable bar.

For my part, I had my own post, my own signboard, and if I even thought of my prince, it was under the following vision: the horse's tail I pulled and the Senegalese of the Black Guard standing in his stirrups.

"Yes, my son," the Sultan said, "our country awaits you. Our university students are the weapons of tomorrow..."

He did nothing that I know of, didn't say anything either good or bad that would merit enthusiasm. He was happy just to hold up his sign. The devout expected something, but nothing happened. They made no protestation. Of no importance.

Of the three of us the one who will really sell sand to the Tuaregs in the desert, who could be malevolent, a tyrant, hard, the man to love or to cut down, that depends, but it's something that lasts a lifetime, is my father. You, your Majesty? The signboard. And I entertained myself a while ago evoking a full house, silent.

Yes, Majesty, it is not your blessing on me that he came to get. There is of course the offering, a sort of holocaust, for I am a kind of Abraham, a tattooed servant of Islam, or to translate: Orient, and Oriental parable.

The fundamental problem?

That boy, Satan and damnation, almost went over the enemy's camp. We taught him a lesson. Two people dead, that's true, but we made several millions in profit from the hugbub of the American tea... and on the waste ground. Now he is docile, reflective, armed for combat. We were sending him to Paris. He will return from there, increase tenfold the estate we will bequeath to him, and will become one to the leaders of the governing class. Come what may, whether our country becomes a colony, or a republic, or your head falls, of no importance: Driss will not suffer.

What is the reason for this audience then? You are far from comprehending, Majesty. He has traced out a plan, has executed it, is *winding it up*. The audience will stimulate my imagination, heads; and tails, he has triumphed in everything, above all over me. He has the need to come, a totally Oriental significance, to the possessor of supreme powers.

"In the name of the ninety-nine names of Allah, in the name of shepherd and keepers of the tribe of the Koreïch and of the Crescent..."

Then comes the absolution that I listen to prostrate.

"Go, my son, go my subject."

We both get to our feet and back out of the room. The sun is high in the sky. It is torrid, and the dust rises.

A German Junker 52 has been hurriedly transformed into a commercial plane. Air France has no space, and the ships are all full. The Junker is ready to depart.

Camel has stuffed my valise with liquor.

"It's cold in France," he explained.

He tied up my billfold and stuck it into the inner pocket of my jacket. Then he closed it with a safety-pin.

"There are gangsters in France," he explained to me.

"Remember this," said the Lord to me. "France is the whorehouse of the world, and the water closet of that whorehouse is Paris. We're sending you to Paris with full confidence."

He can do so. I have superlatively taken control of him. He will never know a thing.

His final recommendations are nothing more than a buzzing sound. I don't hear them because I don't want to and because the airplane whirrs on the runway.

Once I am belted into my seat, I shed no tears. The last words I heard were: "Our well-beloved son." The plane shudders, vibrates, moves forward on the runway, picks up speed and takes off.

I unsnap my seatbelt. I am going to the toilet. I see Casablanca slipping away and growing smaller. Now it's my turn to exalt.

Not an ounce of my past escapes me. It parades in front of me. Quite simply, I gambled and I won.

I the indigent had revolted, the revolt of an indigent, and *when one is indigent, one does not revolt*. Despite being indigent, shabby, something worthless a penniless student would have cast aside, face to face with the feudalism that even the French Residency could not shake—and face to face with indifference. Or I could have ended up by going back to the Julius-Caesar-marionettes-the-rebels-of-the-gullet-on-the-lips, and going no further. Or becoming a vagrant? Or bring down the curtain, living a quiet little life in a foreign country, in turn becoming indifferent. I don't think so. I am a Moroccan, and in a way, Morocco belongs to me.

You have to know how to be patient and logical. I'll rebel tomorrow perhaps, that's all. What about my father? I threw him off the track, that's all. I could have killed him. I had handed him the Luger. He deduced from that something quite different from empty promises. Yes, indeed! Sacrifice my queen, and checkmate.

He says that he gives my brothers their bread and pours their tea. By being docile and repentant, I was able to get him to send me to France. First, count it on your fingers. Then he subsidizes me, will lead me to a degree and to a position. I will return, will gratefully accept the fortune reserved for me that he holds out in his open hand. Then, but only then, will I revolt, suitably and with certainty.

Think about the colonials, the feudal lords, the petty Frenchmen who sing a kind of round before my house: the Arab is a fly, or the Roches who see Morocco as one vast Gomorrah, or the Kessels who take it to be a land of fire. He did not flunk me. The Lord paid him a fine couscous, and precisely I am on my way to Paris. And in heavens name there must be some people there to whom I can say a few words and who will listen to me.

Loosen the cables, and why not? Virtually, Lord, mark down a period. You are right in saying that in France I will become accustomed to hardship. I will imbibe in the stock piles of ideas about social reforms, labor unions, family allowances, strikes, and terrorism. Anything whatsoever rather than to digest the same old resignation that is served up to me in emulation of one another. I have lived my life like an alchemist. No doubt I have a few years ahead of me, twenty or thirty that I will lead like a chemist.

But here and now as I speak at random, take the following as a sample first. Look here. I am pissing. I am pissing in the hope that every drop of my urine will fall on the heads of the people I know so well, who know me so well, those people who disgust me.

As for you, Lord, I do not say goodbye. I say: see you soon!

*Villejuif, December 1952–August 1953*

# OTHER NEW YORK REVIEW CLASSICS

*For a complete list of titles, visit www.nyrb.com or write to:*
*Catalog Requests, NYRB, 435 Hudson Street, New York, NY 10014*

* *Also available as an electronic book.*